QUANTUM ENTANGLEMENT

NOVEL TWO OF THE GENTLE DOMINANT SERIES

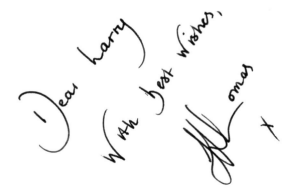

ALSO BY J.L. THOMAS

The Gentle Dominant

Poetic Rapture

J. L. Thomas

QUANTUM ENTANGLEMENT

Chimera

A CIP catalogue record for this title is
available from the British Library.

ISBN 978 1 903136 61 4

*Chimera is an imprint of
Pegasus Elliot MacKenzie Publishers Ltd.
www.pegasuspublishers.com*

First Published in 2018

**Chimera
Sheraton House Castle Park
Cambridge England**

Printed & Bound in Great Britain

For: Darius

You, without knowing, have forever been imprinted within my thoughts, and therefore you will reside forever entwined within my soul.

PROLOGUE

August 2016

De La Margherita Restaurant

Le Saxophonist

As the open shirted, dark haired man standing on the tiny sawdust encrusted podium at the back of this bijou eatery Connor and I are situated in loudly claps his hands together, we instantaneously halt our conversation and turn our attention towards him. Now having rapidly gained our and the other diners' awareness's, he then firmly taps his highly polished saxophone and slowly, as the chitter chatter of the audience ceases into a low, rumbling murmur, he then causes the majority of us to leap in our seats when he booms, "I need a couple of star-crossed lovers to dance and while they do, they will fall deeper in love while listening to my enchanting music. Who would like do me the honour? Who would be willing enough to complement my song with a brave display of swaying, and expressive body language?"

As murmurs rapidly turn into a hushed silence, no one takes up his offer, and as he asks again, he points over in the direction of Connor and me.

I cower, and Connor, well he grins broadly, and whispers, "Shall we?"

"Shall we what?"

"Take him up on his offer of a dance?"

"No..."

"Why?"

"I don't want to dance."

"I do."

"Well I don't." I firmly say hoping that is the end of the debate.

I turn my look away from Connor to the saxophonist. He is now gentlemanly bowing to us and as he then suggests, "What about the beautiful bella who appears to be hiding over in the corner with her handsome blond Adonis?"

Conversation reverberates through the garlicky infused air, and I feel as if the entire persons in the room are staring right at us. Still focusing upon the musician, as he graciously sweeps his hand through the air, with such professionalism he coerces the *audience* into turning towards him while enquiring, "Do you all agree that the fiery red-headed bella and her freckled Adonis sitting in the quiet corner over there should perform a dance for us?"

Light laughter is soon followed by a roar of 'Yes, they should,' which in turn is succeeded by the chinks of wine goblets meeting and the sound of cutlery scraping against crockery.

"Oh, damn it, Connor," I whisper. "This is so very embarrassing. We're... we're..." I hesitate and shyly add, "We're not even a couple."

Sticking out his bottom lip, he mimics an extremely sad face, quietly says that he wished that we were back together and replies, "These dear people don't know that we are not boyfriend and girlfriend, do they? So come on, let's have a dance. Let's show everyone some of our once upon a time hot and very sexy, dance moves!"

Taking a large sip of San Pellegrino water, I swallow and sigh, "No, I guess they don't know that we are not together, so... so..."

"So? Ellie, do you feel brave enough? Do you want to show everyone what you're made of? Do you want to get up and shake that tight, sexy booty of yours at them?"

I giggle at his choices of words and he rises from his seat, grins and offers me his hand.

"Come on my fiery red-headed single Bella! Your freckled Adonis, your *King-of-the-apple-orchard* needs you in his arms right at this very moment!"

"No," I whisper. "I can't... I won't. It's a stupid idea! I'm... I'm..."

"You're what?"

"I'm too shy... I'll feel embarrassed if I dance with you."

"Why?"

"I don't know... I just..."

Before I can finish my sentence, he flicks his blond fringe to one side and interrupts.

"Oh, don't be such a boring killjoy, Ellie; it's just a bit of harmless fun! And come on, be honest to yourself, when did you last have any innocent and charming fun? All you've done for the last six months since *he,* that bastard, girlfriend cheating and controlling film star so called boyfriend of yours fucked you off is..." I cringe inside at his references to Darius demeanour and he finishes, "is work, work, work, and you

11

know the saying, all work and no play makes Bella a very dull beauty!"

True. Since I left Darius, I am becoming, I have become a withered rose.

I frown, and only to uncrease my brow when he winks at me and adds, "No strings attached, my apple queen. I promise you that your king won't even attempt to kiss you... his queen."

Shame...

I smile at his sweet words and by the way a pleading look has spread across his face, and his green irises are sparkling, I give in to his request and to be truthful, quite frankly, I've become rather tired of worrying and fretting over Darius, so I guess this is the right moment to bury our once upon a time love-story, rise up and to start living again. I accept Connor's hand, and he helps me to my feet. Drawing me into him, he takes my left hand in his while placing the palm of his right hand flush to the curve at the lower of my spine, I settle my hand upon his right shoulder.

He feels so good...Too good. His fragrance is positively divine and I am gravitating back to him.

As the saxophonist starts to play and the notes of the sexy tones fill the Chianti infiltrated air I feel an all too familiar charge shift between us.

"Hey, baby?" he purrs with such an alluring tone. "Did you feel something strange surround us a moment ago?"

While we sway and the onlookers, in between their mouthfuls of food and over-generous sips of wine, briefly glance at us, I want to tell Connor that I did indeed feel what he felt but something's preventing me from disclosing, so I just inch a little closer into him and keep my lips sealed – *for now.* The music rises and falls, and within the secret romance of the instrument's notes, I feel so emotional, so relieved that

I have finally decided to put Darius behind me, that I try to stave off bursting out into a flurry of *relieved* tears. Connor senses my imminent wavering and holds me a little firmer, and I lose myself even further when he whispers over and over into my ear that he... he... still... he still loves me.

I still feel deeply for him too.

I am now so lost within translation, so vulnerable in affairs of the heart, when a familiar voice splits between us and asks, "May I break this dance?"

... I feel as if all of the air has been just be vacuumed out of my lungs.

My knees buckle and Connor, sensing that I am now unnerved by this intrusion to our dance scenario, grips me tight around the waist and steadies me. While we stare into each other's eyes, searching for answers, we are then again politely questioned by the mystery man if he may stop us dancing together. And as he does the gentle tones of his question settle upon my soul and second by second, as the powerful, alluring fragrance of his manliness overpowers Connor's scent and envelopes me, it slowly dawns upon me who this man may actually be. I instantly release from Connor's hold, and gingerly turn my head. Rolling my eyes to the right, as I see the owner of said voice standing tall before me, I don't know whether to flee or stay put. The reason for my confusion is there he is... After all this time... Here he is.

Darius.

On seeing him for the first time in six months, I feel as if I have been punched hard in the gut and the pain of that sharp, short blow has been multiplied and intensified in its agony. His lips are set into a firm, thin line and his eyes; well I've never seen them appear so lacklustre. His jaw line is camouflaged by a well-groomed beard and that silky dark mass of manly facial hair only serves to strip back another layer of my now once protective defence. How I want to feel him nuzzling into the crook of my neck, while telling me that he loves me...That he's always loved me. Trying very hard to squash the latter and any further thoughts of him that are threatening to manifest from the rear of my mind, I sidle up to Connor and I tremble as he slips his hand into mine. Squeezing my shaking palm tight, he leans to me and whispers to me that everything is going to be fine. Next, with such authority in his voice, he stands up to Darius and protectively says, "No, you can't cut in and have this dance, Carter. Ellie wants nothing more to do with you ever again."

I don't?

Darius then surprises me by not uttering a word in response. I'm stunned as I watch him flick his stare from Connor to me and then back again. Repeating his actions twice more, he then finally halts and transfixes upon Connor.

I wilt.

Darius half-smiles...

I die inside a little bit more...

His smile widens a little...

I half-smile in return.

Moments slow down and I open my mouth to speak, but as I do, his expression quickly changes, and I shiver as I see him tilt his head to one side and glare at Connor hard... too hard. I have to look away from Darius because I can't bear to look at the man I loved any longer, for if I do, I know I will take a step forward, fling myself into his arms and melt into his white t-shirted, taut chest, leaving Connor in a pickle of a mess, and, since he was my first love, since he is my best friend – and could once again be my possible future love, that type of behaviour towards him would never do at all. Staring at the floor, I focus upon Darius's Converse trainers, and while I try to mentally unravel the knots on his laces, I hear Connor politely ask Darius to do the right thing by me and please would he leave and never bother me again. Moments pass so agonisingly slowly. Darius still remains silent. And I remain mute. The air is now charged with a twisted, buckled, form of invisible strangulated electricity and I for one am seriously considering exiting the building alone. As I confirm to myself that that is exactly what I should do, what I will do, said Converse trainers shuffle, turn and vanish from my vision. I raise my lashes to see Darius, his back towards me. His shoulders have sagged. His hands he has stuffed into his jean pockets and he is ambling out of the door like a man dishevelled and defeated. I look to Connor.

"He's gone," I can't help but soulfully mutter. "He's really gone, Connor?"

"I'm sorry, Ellie... Well, I'm not apologetic in the least, but yes, he's gone and good riddance to him!"

My heart breaking and wishing that Connor would be a little gentler where Darius is concerned, I reply, "I... I..." I sniff. "I wanted to... to..."

"You wanted to do what, Ellie?"

"Nothing..." I reply. "Just nothing, Connor, forget it. I don't feel too good... I want to go home."

"Why?" He grabs out for me. "Why, don't you feel well?"

I step back, give him a sympathetic smile and half lie that I think I may have a migraine coming on.

He ruffles his messy blond hair, frowns as if he knows I am fibbing and replies, "Okay, sweetie... how about we leave your car here, share a cab? I want to take you home. I want to make sure that you are alright after... after... him..."

"I'll be fine." I again half lie. "Truly I will."

He sighs with defeat, steps towards me and I falter as he cups my face in his hands and leans close. I angle my face up towards him and I twist inside when he kisses me upon my forehead.

Right now at this very minute if he had kissed me on my lips instead of my forehead I know for sure that I would've given in to him and fallen back in love with him for the second time in my life – would I?

I blink away the salty emotions that are glazing over my eyes and whisper, "Thank you."

"You will call me if you need anything tonight?"

"I promise I will."

After settling the bill, and giving him a *brotherly* hug good night, I promised him that I will meet up with him for lunch tomorrow. He then with some reluctance let me go, and I with a whirl of torrid emotions surging through my soul, headed towards my car.

As the chilliness of the mid-evening began to set in, I wrapped my knitted cardigan around me. Fumbling into the left hand pocket I located my set of keys. Extracting them, I selected the key to my precious battered old Mini and inserted said key into the lock.

As I turned it I froze for out of the thin air a voice pleaded,

"Please, please just give me one chance to explain about everything past, Helena. Just one small chance and I promise you that after I've said what I have to say I will never bother you again and I will leave you in peace."

I spun on my heel to see Darius standing tall before me. Under the illumination of the streetlights he looked positively stunning. His dark hair was its usual crop of an unruly mess – maybe a tad longer that normal and the smooth facial hair that creates his beard shimmered under the artificial lighting that was allowing me to see him clearer.

With my heart vividly thumping in my chest, I took a deep breath, gathered my thoughts and declared, "If you talk to me anymore, Darius, I might just crumble right before your very eyes." He slowly batted his lashes, looked flummoxed, and I, with definition continued. "You might see me come undone; you might see me unravel before your very eyes. Is that what you want to see? Me, belittled before you once again?"

Stuffing his hands into his jean pockets, he woefully shook his head from side to side, affirmed to me a deep no and replied, "I want to see none of those things you mention. The only thing I... I...wish... I... wish for is that we... we..."

With hope, with curiosity in my voice, I asked, "What do you wish for then? What exactly do you want from me?"

He took a few steps towards me and I retreated back against my car, all the while anticipating feeling the hedonistic sensation of his lips settling upon mine. On reaching me he outstretched his arms and pressed his palms flush either side of my head, giving a stroke on both of my cheeks. By that touch of his alone, I was now left wanting. Releasing himself from me, he rested his hands upon the roof of my car, leant into me, and pressed his forehead to mine.

"I want you back," he declared with softness in his tone.

Before I could respond, telling him, lying to myself that I don't want ever him back in my life, he took a liberty, and his warm lips were once again upon mine. I curled my arms around neck and rested there for I didn't want to let him go. I couldn't resist against him any more for I had within an instant become so lost within the sweet infusions of his mouth that I felt myself being drawn back towards him. While this most passionate and loving of kisses began rekindling the love we had... still have for each other, I tried with all my might to tell myself that I must not under any circumstances fall head over heels in love with him again... That I must not allow myself to love him – *truth be told, I know that I never stopped loving him* – I was then left stunned when he broke away, gazed deep into my eyes, and with such sincerity in his voice, finally told me what I'd been aching to hear over the lonely months without him. "I love you, Helena."

My mind now in a total vortex, needing to hear him say those three little words to me again, I told him that I didn't quite hear what he said. Furrowing his brow, seeming a little confused to me, he dipped his lashes and repeated to the floor.

"I love you."

"Pardon?" I asked, needing to hear him to look at me and say that he loved me again.

He raised his lashes, and as his gaze met mine, he replied with such delicacy in his voice, "I love you, Helena. I love you now."

"Do you love me just now because you can't have me or have you always loved me?"

Focusing intently me, he spoke. "I have loved you before I was even created."

"How much do you love me?" I questioned, wanting more conviction from his admittance. "Just how much?"

"My love for you is... is... will always be immeasurable."

"If you loved me back then, like you claim that you do right now then why, oh why, oh why did you take me to your... your... that room... that place where you once took... took her?"

"None of it was planned," he sighed with heaviness.

"Honestly?"

"Honestly it wasn't arranged in my mind. Remember we were in that ridiculous heated argument?"

"Yes, I do."

The following is the past argument that six months ago passed between Darius and I. It occurred after my surprise meeting with my first love, Connor.

As Darius pressed his foot flat to the accelerator and the Porsche fired into motion, I was propelled flush against the back of the passenger seat. Slightly startled at the impact of my body slamming against the grey, sumptuous leather, I regained my composure and glanced over at him. I saw that his hands were gripping the steering wheel so firmly that under that pressurizing hold of his, his knuckles whitened. My vision travelled to his facial profile. He appeared to be clenching his teeth together and I guessed my assumption must be correct for I noticed a muscle spasming continually under the stubbly, midnight shadow that was highlighting his strong jawbone. We continued motoring in a strained silence only to halt when we approached a set of red traffic lights. His fingers were drumming on the wheel in such an irritating fashion that I decided I was going to ask him to stop doing that irritating annoyance.

As I went to speak his voice snapped through the snug confined space of the car and he spat at me, "Did he fuck you?"

The lights changed to amber and he repetitively growled under his breath, "He did, didn't he? The seedy little fucker! If he has, I'll murder the bastard with my bare hands if he touched a single centimetre of your body!"

Not wishing to speak with him, I stared out of the window wishing that I could reverse time and be with Connor in the apple orchard the moments before we lost our innocence.

Amber had now given way to green and with Darius' question still unanswered, we accelerated off again. A matter of moments passed and I was taken by surprise when he eased off the gas, indicated left and the car careered in said direction. As the tyres wailed a deafening screech, the motor swerved into a well lit underground car park, and it began to slow down. With my vision now focused straight ahead, I saw a parking space coming into view. The vehicle was rolled into it, the engine switched off and the handbrake applied. With us now stationary, he unbuckled both our belts and then, in such a blunt tone, ordered me to get out of the car.

Feeling utterly phased by this situation, I opened the door, if for anything to be away from him. Before my feet could even touch the tarmac, I looked up and saw him standing before me. In a split second, my forearm was grasped and I was hauled like a heavy sack of spuds out of the motor. Slamming the door shut behind me, he shoved me up against the car and his grip on me tightened. With my left shoulder now beginning to ache, I cried out, "What the fuck are you doing, Darius? Let go of me, you're hurting me!"

He quickly released me and while his brooding stare bored through to my very soul, he sneered, "Hush that filthy mouth of yours, Helena! I've warned you before about swearing at me!"

I groaned out and he snaked his hand around the back of my neck. His touch was bordering on electrifying. Entangling his fingers in my tresses, he lightly tugged at my locks and in a slightly calmer tone, asked me again if Connor had touched me. I'm was so exhausted by this whole day, this scenario here that I didn't even think about what may transpire from my answer and a *yes* fell from my lips.

His spine immediately stiffened and I was released from his hold in such a way that one would've thought that I was a tarantula who had just stung her prey with a deadly, black poison. He gingerly stepped back from me and ran his fingers through his silken dark curls. A look of stark shock was plastered across his handsome face and I couldn't hold his attention any longer so I averted my gaze from him and directed it to the floor beneath my feet. A few moments passed and he jolted me back to into this insane reality with a one worded question. "When?"

Still looking at the floor, I stammered, "When what?"

"When did you let that bleach-blond bastard fuck you?"

I raised my lashes, met his icy stare and defended. "He's not a bastard. His parents are married."

With his fists now knotted at his sides, he rasped, "Very droll indeed Helena... Now enough of the technicalities and tell me when did he fuck you?"

Desperately wanting to quash this scenario, I quickly answered, "When... I... I... was..."

His voice now straining, he demanded, "When exactly, Helena? Was it this afternoon, soon after we'd had our little tête-à-tête in Selfridges? Where did you do it? Was it in some urine stinking alleyway with your back flush up against the cold brick wall? You like being wall banged? Or was it on a single bed at some cheap knock off hotel?"

With the tears now forming in the back of my eyes, I tried so hard to hold back a sob for I just couldn't believe that he would even think that I would let another man touch me. After all, I had told him I love him previously, even if it was by a mere text message. While my tears freely fell, he crushed my soul even further, by leaning into me, tipping his finger under my chin and angling my face upwards. Glaring at me, he wiped away a lone salty globule of emotion from my cheek, placed the pad of his finger to my lower lip and rested it there.

"Crocodile tears, Helena?" he harshly grated. "Is my queen acting a little drama all of her very own?"

No... No... No... These are my truest heartfelt emotions, Darius. If only you knew.

With his touch alone, my heart splintered and it fragmented even more when he quipped the following, "Well, since you won't answer my question, try digesting these ones. Are you actually a closet, nymphomaniac whore? Couldn't my cock satisfy you for just a few hours at least? Did you get some kick out of being fucked by one man followed by another in the same day?"

My head was in a total spin at the dire vulgarity of his words, and I slumped against the car and without any forewarning, my legs buckled. I was now kneeling at his feet, and as my tears abated, I found myself answering to his navy blue, shiny Oxfords.

"I am not a nymphomaniac whore as you so cruelly put it!" Gasping for air, I hiccupped and soulfully sobbed, "I... I am a one-woman man." I drew in another much needed blast of air and with a hint of sarcasm wavering in my voice, I answered, "Yes, your perfect manhood does satisfy me and I can assure you this, Darius, it... You always will leave me replete."

As his feet shuffled before me, I then swallowed and honestly declared my final reply. "Connor was the man, to whom I lost my virginity when I was sixteen years old. So yes, I did have sexual relations with him but not today because that was the one and only time we ever... we ever," I sob, "we ever made love. It was coarse, rushed and… and…"

Finishing my sentence incorrectly for me, he added, "Foolish?"

"No... How can you say such hurtful a thing? You were a virgin once."

I heard him mumble, 'Oh fuck it,' under his breath followed by him cursing to himself that he is an idiot.

Right now, yes you are Darius!

His voice gentler, I heard him say, "It's all right, Helena."
Is it?

But I didn't look up to him, I just continued. "It... It wasn't a mindless joining of bodies and souls... It… it... was…"

I took the deepest of breaths that I possibly could and as the word… *Love* left my soul his Oxfords disappeared from my view. I couldn't choke any more words so I took a secret look upwards to see him stooping down to meet me. Without passing any further judgment on me, he then scooped me up in his arms and my body went limp. On hearing the lock of the car turn, he cradled and carried me like I was some sort of precious cargo in the direction of what, through my fogged-out tears, I assumed to be the lift that leads to somewhere only he knew. And now with hindsight I know that that suite we resurrected our love for each other in was indeed a room that I came to name as... *The fuck pad!*

Pushing the aforementioned argument to the back of my mind, I turned my attention back to Darius.

"Well, Helena," he continued, "it was pure coincidence that we passed the car park of... of the hotel. I desperately needed to cool my temper down or we may have had an accident.

"Okay, fair enough, I understand."

I sort of understand.

"But..." I resume. "But why did you feel that you had to take me into *that* room and bed me in a bed that you seduced *her* in?"

"Helena, you had me crazed. You were at my feet on the cold stone floor answering my stupid jealous questions while crying and all I could think about was taking you to bed, keeping you safe and making you mine and apologising to you in only a way that I know how to."

"Couldn't you have thought about just taking me back to your condo?"

"With hindsight, yes, that's what I should've done. I'm sorry."

"And what about, "I bravely say. "What about Alice?"

That was the moment when he recoiled from me and his face turned to an ashen shade of grey.

Quickly regaining his composure, he answered, "Under no circumstances will I talk about her here out in the open but if you would do me the honour and consider coming back to the condo with me, I'll promise you that I will explain everything that occurred within my past – with her – and also anything present that you wish to know. How does that sound?"

"It sounds okay... sort of."

"Are you sure, Helena? You do sound a little hesitant to me?"

I am feeling uncertain, but I need conclusive answers before I can move on...

"You'll answer truthfully every single question I have to ask?"

On giving me the curtest of nods, he then completely bewildered me when he offered me his hand and said one very powerful word to me and that definitive word was – *Come.*

I went.

The Revelation

Perched on the edge of the kitchen stool, as I watch Darius slide out a bottle of wine from the fridge rack, I can't help but stare at his t-shirt cladded back. My vision travels over the top of his broad muscular shoulders, down past the centre alignment of his spine, and I now find myself shamelessly imagining what it would once again be like to be pinned beneath him while he claims both my body and soul. I am broken from my inappropriate thoughts when he turns around to face me, holds up the chilled bottle and asks, "Would you like a glass of this rather delicious fresh, fruity rosé wine before we start our rather important and insightful questioning and answering session?"

Mesmerised by him with that gorgeous, silken beard of his, I can't utter a word in response, so I nod as to signal yes because not only does that particular bottle that he is holding contain my most favourite of wines, but right now I could most certainly do with a glass or two of it to spear me with the Dutch courage that I need to listen to what he has to say. Seating himself opposite me, he glances at me. I am hooked upon him for his steely-blue irises seem to have lit up with the enticing, hypnotic sparkle that I have so missed. He looks away from me and pours us both a generous measure of the pale pinkish coloured liquid. We mirror each other by simultaneously take the first of tastes. Again, reflecting each other's motions we place our glasses down onto the marble work surface and I stare at the label on the bottle.

Domaine Otto Romassan Rose Bandol

Looking over at him, I smile. "That's my most favourite of French wine, Darius."

Arching an eyebrow, he smiles back. "I know."

"How do you know?" I exclaim. "I've most certainly never told you?"

"There are lots of... Lots of, how shall I say... There are many, many bits and pieces that I have come to know about you over late. In fact, Helena," he takes another sample of his drink, "I've made it my mission in my life to know every single little detail about you."

Oh have you now? How bamboozling!

Next, for some strange reason I then blurt out, "I've always wanted to visit France."

Picking up his drink, he places the rim of the glass to his nose, inhales the bouquet that houses a combination of peach, lemon, cinnamon and vanilla aromas, and without taking his vision off me, he says amusingly, "You've never been to France?"

"No... I've never been." I sigh, take taste and as the liquid falls against my lips and the coolness tingles on my tongue, I relish in the flavour of its fresh summer fruitiness.

"Well, I guess that I shall have to rectify that by taking you there one day and making slow, sweet love to you in the fragrant lavender fields of Provence."

Circling the rim of my glass, I stare into the goblet imagining such a scenario and mutter, "That would've been nice."

"Would've?" he exclaims, aghast.

I look at him.

His face is tainted with hurt.

"Why are you're talking in the past tense to me."

"I don't know."

"Why don't you know?"

"I'm sorry... I just said what I did... My words just came out the way that I was thinking."

He deeply sighs and asks, "You don't see a future for us ahead even though I told you less than an hour ago that I loved you?"

"I... I... Don't know, Darius. This, the past... It's all so very puzzling for me right now."

Taking my glass from me, he settles it down onto the counter. Placing his drink next to mine, he leans over the surface and takes both my hands in his. Upturning my palms, he strokes the pads of his fingers along my skin. "I know it's very confusing for you right now to trust me let alone even be here with me, but please, Helena, I implore you to come and sit with me on the sofa and let me explain about the fateful day when you left me and I broke apart."

He was hurting too?

Seated opposite each other, Darius strokes the soft, dark hair that graces his chin and asks, "Are you sitting comfortably, Helena?"

Sitting cross-legged and I tell him that I am and please could he now begin with his explanation. Without a hint of readable expression upon his face, he tells me that when he does divulge the truth, he would prefer it if I did not interrupt him during his speech, and he will answer any questions that I have when he has finished explaining everything that there is to know. *Okay* – He parts his lips, opens his mouth and I listen intently as the truth tumbles forth.

"Approximately two years before you fell into my world, I purchased what you crudely have referred to, as my fuck pad."

"Well it is what it is!" I can't help but quip. "It's a horrible, ghastly room where... where..."

He frowns and I snap my mouth shut. Taking another taste of his wine, he swallows, draws in a breath and continues.

"I have never been the type of man who finds it easy to scour the field for female company, so in order to satisfy my sexual needs, I... I... I used..."

I take a large gulp of wine and with my curiosity now peaked, I have to refrain from asking – you used what?

Running his fingers through his spiral of curls, he resumes, "...the services of an elite escort agency... An agency so discreet that they are only known by word of mouth."

Oh...

"On occasions I would select a lady and have her sent to up to me as and when I required. Sometimes I would finance for her to stay one for one night, sometimes two if... if..."

If what?

"But most definitely never three nights."

Why never three nights?

Two nights in the company of the same female I knew would enough to satisfy my needs. Three nights, however, would only serve to breed a certain type of intimacy that could entail ruses of a romantic nature and back then, I wasn't in it for love – just sex.

Just vanilla sex or kinkier?

"I know what you're thinking, Helena, and the answer is plain old fashioned Vanilla."

I shrug my shoulders pretending that none of what he is divulging to me is killing me inside, and he shakes his head from side to side.

I wonder if he knows that all this is painful for me to hear.

"So," he pauses and then asks, "are you ready to hear the next part of my story?"

No...Yes.

One day, six months or so into my *adventures* with the escort agency, I asked for them to pair me with a lady who was interested in one of my hobbies – photography. They did. Her name was..." he sighs, "was... Alice. Over time, she and I became what you would call, close. I broke my golden rule and became personally involved with her. She had a certain magnetic charm about her and I was powerless to resist whatever the force was. As we became *fond* of one another events took an uncanny twist and within the innocence of her surprise admittance that she was a submissive, I discovered that I began to display thoughts that pertained to aspects of dominant behaviour. I had never before entertained the fact that there was a mere *soupçon* of dominancy within me, but she had somehow discovered it within me and ignited the blue touch paper, and," he waves his hands in the air and I almost fall backwards when he declares, "voila! I, the gentle dominant was born."

I take a breath and bluntly quiz, "So... So... It's actually her fault that you are the way that you are?"

"And what do you mean by that, Helena?" He frowns.

"I... I... mean that she made you... she created you... she turned you into a dominant?"

"No." And with a strict seriousness in his voice, he, without hesitation, tells me this. "I believe that I have always had hidden dominant tendencies. It was fate that she had to be

the woman to unleash, unravel – whatever you wish to call it
– extract me from within my dark prison?"

"Do you like being a dominant?"

"What do you think, Helena?"

"I… I… think that you do. I think that it is a fundamental
part of your physical and mental makeup."

"Explain."

"Well, this is how I see you. You are a man who is
extremely disciplined in all manner of things...Yes?"

"Yes I am. Now may I continue?"

I nod. He resumes.

"I would see, Ali… *her*… on Friday evening through to
the Sunday ending our time together at six p.m. If I needed a
sexual release during the week, I would of course take to
pleasuring myself. As I became more and more sexually
replete with her weekend visits, the need for self gratification
during the week began to peter out. One Wednesday, after
days and days of rehearsing one short scene, a scene that
eluded me, it was finally in the can. I was so hyped, so driven
that I needed a release, and of course being the middle of the
week, she was out of bounds, or so I thought so. I drove to
my... my pad, indulged in a relaxing bath and then finally
settled down in bed. I then selected a pornographic movie, and
I viewed it with the full intent of … Well I think you can guess
what I mean, Helena."

I can!

"After satisfying myself, I took a cold shower – no need
to explain why. While I was under the jets of water,
unbeknown to me, Alice had let herself into the room. What
happened that night within the confines of my room, you do
not need to know, but all I can say is that the note you saw

from her to me was written upon that day. Two years before I met you at the premiere."

A hushed silence fills the room and as I process what he has just explained to me, I look away from him and shakily ask, "Where... where is she now?"

He takes another taste of his wine, raises his shoulders briefly and responds, "I do not know where she is and neither do I wish to."

"Oh I see. Can you tell me why you broke up with her?"

"Do you really need to know why we parted?"

"Yes, I do."

"We parted." He closes his eyes momentarily and as he opens them he breathes, "Because I couldn't give her what she wanted."

"What couldn't you give her?"

He looks at me and I shiver as he answers, "The whole package."

"I don't understand what you mean by that Darius?"

"Then let me spell it out for you. I didn't want to get married back then and I certainly didn't wish to father children."

"And now what do you wish for?"

Rising from his seat, he approaches me, and rests his hands firmly upon my shoulders. And whispers, "I wish for you to be mine."

"In what way do you want me to be yours? Do you want me to be your lover, your girlfriend, or your submissive?" I pause, he stills, and then as I hear him whisper the word, wife, his eyes mist over. He's now transfixed upon me, and telling me that he wants me to be his forever. I'm now weakening inside at the vision of this tall, dark, handsome man standing before me who wishes for me to be Mrs Carter and while the fresh scent of his persona once again penetrates and infuses my senses, I part my lips in anticipation for one of his heart melting kisses. He knowingly smiles. Maintaining eye contact with me, he slowly trails his hands down my arms and the combination of his magnetic aura coupled with the delicacy of his touch both cause me to feel light headed.

"I... I..." I mutter. I stutter, "I... I... Did... did... did... you just ask me... me... to... to.... mar... marry..."

I can't say the final words that I wish to express to him free from my soul and he senses this by affirming to me an understanding nod.

"Shhh, my darling Helena," falls from his bowed lips.

I immediately quiet.

"There is no need for any words to be exchanged right now," he softly whispers, and then adds, "none at all."

I couldn't agree more with him, for if I was able to offer my thoughts to him they would be projected as nothing more than a jumbled mess of undecipherable sentences. On reaching my trembling hands, he makes no hesitation in entwining his fingers with mine. As our skin meets, I find myself being drawn into his taut chest. Burying my head into him, he tenderly strokes my hair, and breathes, "Now that I've found you, Helena." His voice weakens and he murmurs, "I'm never going to let you stray from me again... Even," he hushes, "even if it means putting a ring on your finger."

He is asking me to marry him?

I look up at him and I'm totally confused at this whole scenario, so for the moment I choose to say nothing about his impromptu proposal. On spotting a lone tear trickling down his cheek, from my heart, I respond, "Now that you've located me, Darius, I don't... don't want to be apart from you ever... ever again."

"Am I forgiven then?" he asks with hope, with longing in his voice.

"Yes," I affirm. "I wholeheartedly pardon you for your past behaviour."

His torso heaves heavily with a sigh that is filled with a burst of relief and I respond by standing on my tiptoes, breaking my hands free from his, and flinging them around his neck. While I hold onto to him, never wishing to ever let go, he seals this moment in time by whispering to me a secret – *One that I have yet to unravel.*

Wonderland

Settling his naked, taut body over me, Darius's warm lips skim lightly over my throat – *I'm free-falling.* And while his mouth travels down the centre of my cleavage, and the heat of his breath warms my flesh, I arch my back and part my legs in anticipation of his body entering mine. My voice is light and wispy, and I breathe, "That feels so good, baby. I've missed your gentle touch so much."

He looks up at me, weakens me a spine tingling, slow bat of his lashes and then bows his head. His lips are now clamped around my erecting nipple and he, with such intensity draws upon it, coaxing it into a hardness that I have never experienced before. As a series of sensitive shivers radiate through my hips and collate at my now dampening centre, I moan out his name with such intensity.

Continuing the onslaught upon my breast, he asks, "You want me to stop, Helena, or do you want to experience some more of my sensual teasing?"

Angling my hips up towards him, I whimper out for more.

He fleetingly glances at me and with his forearm now pressing into the silk covered mattress; he suckles away upon my flesh, sliding his hand between my thighs and I burn inside when he says, "You're mine, Helena. Don't ever forget that."

With my inner core aching for his touch, "Yes," I hiss between my clenched teeth. "I'm yours, Darius. I won't forget."

He's now released me from his hold, shuffled up and we are face to face. Gripping a fistful of my hair in his hand, he caresses my tresses, dips his head and while his beard tickles my face, he seals his mouth over mine. His tongue is hot and delectably moist and as it darts around mine, a series of needy, wanting sounds rise from both our souls. Clasping my buttocks, his hips circling, with one powerful propulsion of his midriff, he is fully inside me and I, well I have instantly become lost within him. His voice is soft and syrupy, he drawls his words long and slow, and he has my undivided attention when he warns, "Be prepared, Helena, for this is not only going to be a long, slow sexual onslaught of skin upon skin, it is also going to be the deepest, the hardest you have ever felt me inside you."

He was correct in his assumption, for he is grinding into me so forcefully that my nails are trailing down the sides of his back and I am 'hanging' onto him for dear life.

Rocking me hard, in between each on one of his upward thrusts, he pants, "Where are you, my precious? Tell me where you are."

With my orgasm threatening, I shudder and wail, "I am right with you."

"Good. Now dig deeper into me," he demands. "When we come in unison, I want to feel you leaving your mark on me."

On the final thrust of his cock inside me, as he cried out my name in a way that I have never heard before, I did indeed leave my imprint upon his beautiful body. As we shuddered, shook and slid against each other there was no need for any more words because intimacy and the power of touch had once again prevailed.

On waking, much to my disappointment, I find that I am alone in *our* bed. While I adjust to the new day, my new life, I must admit, I am feeling slightly heady and a little delicate between my legs. *Thank you, Darius!* On catching a whiff of the aroma of coffee brewing, I relax back into the sumptuous cushions that surround me. With the aromatic scent of the dark beans alerting me to the fact that I have located Darius, – *He's in the elaborate kitchen on the lower level of the condo* – I smile at the thought of him preparing breakfast for two. While I reminisce at the sensual and erotic thoughts of our recent love-making, I smile with a divine pure happiness. I am now so engrossed in reliving the moment when we both declared our love for each other, that I can just about make out the ascending sound of a phone buzzing within the room. As the volume increases it raps ferociously against the surface of his bedside table, demanding to be noticed. I groan out and mentally insert my private thoughts into an imaginary box. Tying said box up with a make believe red ribbon, I secure both the ends into a bow and lay said box down to rest, *well for now.* Turning onto my side, I grasp his pillow and scrunch it up to my nose. Inhaling the scent of his manliness that has been left impregnated deep within the cotton fibres, I hold onto the breath for as long as I can; arousing at his fragrance, as moments pass by, I am soon left with no choice but to let that most precious of breaths escape. *His phone continues interrupting!* As I do, air whooshes out from my lungs, and Darius enters my mind. On the thought of him, I press my thighs together. *Ow!* Very tender indeed!

Outstretching my arm, I locate the irritating, intrusive phone, slide it off the table top and flop onto my back. With his pillow now resting upon my bare chest and his phone now firmly in my grasp, I linger it above my face. Blinking a couple of times, as the screen comes into focus and the caller's title flashes back at me, my all too brief perfect moment implodes and I am propelled into a state of a blind-panicking trauma. Feeling like I am alone, in a dinghy that has been bobbing about on the roughest of seas for days, my stomach begins to violently churn and my hands tremor. The reason for my display of fear and the uncomfortable sensation of nausea is that the five letters on the screen staring back me, taunting me with its now silence has a name and that name is:

Alice.

This is no wonderland that I have been left suspended in. It is in fact pure torture.

Once again, I felt that the only choice I had left was to leave Darius... but this time my departure, I am sure would be non returnable.

Chapter One

Three months later...

Monday, 2 November 2016

7.36 a.m.

Just another quiet, unassuming Monday... Or so I thought so.

Taking a sip of my freshly, pod brewed coffee, I place my favourite scrabble designed mug down onto the breakfast bar, and look blankly at the small pile of this morning's mail. Two brown envelopes which indicate to me that they are requests for utility payments. The three white ones, I assume are just the usual bumph of spam mail. I shove the unopened letters to one side – I'll attend to those a while later. For some peculiar reason something makes me glance up, and as I look to across this small kitchenette of my studio flat, my vision falls upon the small photograph – *A memory that I can't bring myself to eradicate* – that is secured by a heart shaped magnet on the door of the fridge. The photo is of Darius and I sharing... a tender kiss, and as I stare at the picture, I can't stop myself from secretly wishing that I was, for one last time feeling his warm, soft lips brushing along mine – I am also secretly pining for him in another manner, for today is his twenty-ninth birthday, and that if all had been well between us, we could've been celebrating his special day together. I wonder how he will mark this day of his? Maybe with his film star chums? Maybe with her, Alice? Or maybe he's chosen to spend it on his own? Probably not solitary I conclude – I just couldn't envisage that.

A part of me will always continue to miss him, miss us dreadfully, but how could I go back to him after she, Alice, had made her presence known to us both on that fateful day when Darius and I had only moments ago rekindled our love for each other? I sigh with heavy sadness, and look back to the mail. Still choosing to ignore the task of opening them, instead, I turn to picking up this morning's newspaper and having a perusal. As my vision settles upon the headline strewn across the top of the front page, the words jump out at me, each individual letter yanking at my heartstrings and then finishing their powerful onslaught by stabbing me straight through my already broken heart. I now feel anxiously sick to the inner core for the words have just informed me that Darius, the man I am still in hopelessly love with, while filming on location in Italy, has been involved in a serious motorbike accident. As I continue reading through the blur that has now misted over my eyes, the print brings around to my attention that he is at present in ICU and that his condition is life-threatening. He's going to die? Horror engulfs me. Reciting his phone number off by heart, I glance at the time on my phone, 7.36 a.m. I shakily dial. The number is unavailable, and as my mind spirals into a total whirl of confusion and misery, and I try to work out what to do next, my landline gives an urgent ring. I rush over to the coffee table, almost tripping over and grab the receiver – Darius?

"Yes?" I answer, my voice all a tremble... "Who... who is this?"

"Helena, it's me, Xavier..."

Xavier – Darius's brother... Thank goodness...

"I am really sorry to call you so early, but I have to tell you some... some... dreadful news. You may need to sit down before I explain what has happened."

Darius is dead? He's gone?

A strained, eerie pause elongates.

"Helena?"

I'm breathing for you Darius...

"Helena, are you still there?"

"I am..."

"Are you all right?"

"No, for I know what you're going to tell me," I cry. "I've just seen this morning's newspaper. Please tell me you're not calling to say he's... he's... he's not... not... not... "

"Helena... Helena..." I lose myself while he gently coerces. "Just try to take a few, slowing breaths, and focus..."

I do and then can't stop myself from bursting into a flurry of uncontrollable sobs. "Has he gone...? Has he left us all? Has he left me? I need to tell him that I still love him!"

"Sweetheart, sweetheart, my dearest angel, he's still with us, but dare I say it, only just barely."

Almost breathless, I say, "He's hanging on by a thread, so to speak?"

"Yes, my angel, I'm afraid that he is."

"I need him," I wail again. "I've always needed him... I just didn't realise how much I did until this god awful moment arrived."

"I know my darling girl... And trust me when I tell you this, he's needed you too."

Out of the blue, I say, "Then if he needed me then why didn't he ever attempt to call me?"

I hear Xavier sigh deeply down the phone, and I wilt inside when he replies, "He toyed over and over with calling you, he most certainly did, but he, after much soul searching, came to the conclusion that it was far better to write to you to speak to you when everything between you both was still so dreadfully raw."

Yes, I know. My cache of unopened letters.

"Oh." I simper. "Did he truly think that?"

"He did. Tell me, did you ever receive his letters? Did you open them if you did?"

"I did receive them but... but... I couldn't bring myself to open them... I should've, shouldn't I? I should have at least given him the common courtesy to read them..." I sob again. "I am a stupid, stupid blind fool."

"It's all right, Helena... You are not a fool... You were just heartbroken as much as he was... There is no need to torture yourself like this... The time will come when you might feel like seeing what Darius has written... Maybe not now but maybe one day in the future, so please, Helena, I just suggest you keep the letters, don't discard them. The written words of love letters are so very precious and so very powerful."

"Yes, I believe that they are... I promise I will keep them..." I reply while knowing full well that after this conversation had ended, I will be holding the pile of seventeen unopened letters that are tied up with a violet silk ribbon in my shaking hands with the intention of reading each and every single one in its order of postage date.

"I can't make sense of anything at present, Xavier." And I just launch... "I am sure that I can feel him thinking about me right this very second. I am positive that I can hear him calling out for me to come to him."

"Hush, hush, Helena..." he soothes. "Everything will work out fine... Now try to calm down a little and listen to me."

"Okay," I weakly mumble. "I'm listening."

"Go pack a bag... Bring the letters with you." He then gently says, "You, Angelica and I are booked on the next flight from Heathrow to Italy..."

My best friend, Angelica, Xavier's girlfriend is coming too? Thank goodness... Right now I need so much moral support.

"We should be with Darius in a few hours time."

Please hang in there, Darius... I'm coming for you. We're all coming for you.

"We're going to him? We're going to Darius?" I sniffle, wiping my snotty nose onto the sleeve of my pyjama top. "We're actually going... I'm going to see him?"

"Yes, we all are. A taxi will be with you within the hour. Angelica and I will already be inside waiting for you. So go, dry your eyes, and pack. We will see you promptly."

"Oh thank you," I weep with devout gratitude... "Thank you, Thank you, thank you, Xavier."

"Hurry now..."

"Bye, Xavier."

"Bye, Helena."

After ending the call, I rush into my bedroom, and open my bedside drawer. Extracting the letters from Darius, I sit back on my unmade bed, and with my fingers trembling, I carefully unravel the ribbon. Staring intently at the top letter on the pile, the first one I received, something makes me place the envelope to my nose. As I deeply inhale the scent of the perfume – his cologne – that is impregnated within the folded pages that are safely secured within the host, my tears rain forth, for the aroma that has infused my senses has activated the most beautiful memory of him that will reside within my mind forever. Right now I can visualise the untainted images of the man that I love –the man that who at present is in the throes of dying and I am not where I should be – by his side. Without a single conscious thought left in my mind, I rise, search out some clothes, not caring whether they are suitable, and roughly stuff them into my holdall. Next, I automatically shower quickly, dress into yesterday's clothes of jeans and a t-shirt, and half heartedly apply the briefest of make-up. Not that my chosen shade of blusher or lipstick will make any difference to the pale, unbecoming look that has already enveloped me. Slinging my luggage bag over my shoulder, I bend down, pick up the letters from Darius and slide them into my tote bag, along with my passport and my purse. Now ready to fly to him, and with a dreadful, aching, searing burning in my heart I whisper out to Darius that I am coming for him... I wonder if actually heard me?

I heard you, Helena.

Two-forty-five p.m.
Leonardo Da Vinci airport – Italy

As the wheels of the private jet that Xavier had chartered for the saddest journey I have ever had to embark upon, as they screech along the tarmac, I carefully fold letter number one in half and place it back into the envelope. Even though I received it a few months ago, this is first time I was able to bring myself to read what was written between the scented pages. I have never, ever in my entire life read anything so emotional, so honest and so beautiful scribed in ink by another. By Darius's words, by his delicate admittance of his love for

44

me, I am not only left breathless, but I feel as if I have been left suspended in love with him for eternity – but without him.

I just silently pray to God – And say, if you, The Supreme Being actually do exist – please could you do me an enormous favour and keep Darius's heart beating? Please don't let him die. Also please could you tell him that I, Xavier and Angelica are just a few hours away from his hospital bedside? And finally can you tell him that I love him?

I always have, and I always will.

Amen.

Chapter Two

Monday 21 November 2016

Amalfi Coast – Italy

"It hurts to breathe, Helena, because every breath I am trying desperately to take proves that I could never exist without you."

6.30 a.m.

Standing among the winding olive groves, I look out to the Tyrrhenian Sea. Placing my motorbike helmet over my head, I pull it down while pushing my protective glasses up over the bridge of my nose. While I watch the sun slowly reach the peak of her early rise, as she subtly casts her soft glimmer over the azure blue water that stretches out for numerous miles before me, I greet this new day with the most heartfelt of smiles. Today is my twenty-ninth birthday. I am so very lucky to be alive, and not just systematically breathing in oxygen. Flipping open the lid to the small, red leather box that is nesting in the palm of my hand, I sigh heavily on seeing the heart shaped, diamond solitaire ring, glinting back at me. With Helena imprinted firmly in every single daily thought that has invaded my mind since the day I last saw her three months ago

– I hope she has read my letters then she will know exactly how I feel, what I will always feel for her. I snap the lid shut, stuff the box into the pocket of my leather biker trousers while pledging myself this promise: Now that the shoot for my latest movie is at last in the can, and tonight as my private jet departs from the Aeroporto di Salerno Costa D'Amalfi, en route to Leonardo Da Vinci airport, I will, when I touchdown at Heathrow Airport, London, make my Helena my first and only call. I have concocted so many great plans for us both, for our future together, and I can't wait to share each and every single one of them with her. She is the only woman I would ever take a blind risk for. She is my soul mate and that after time our time spent apart, I couldn't be surer that she is the woman for me.

Securing the clasp of my headgear underneath my chin, I swing my left leg over the weathered leather seat of my Harley Davidson, and curl my fingers around the handlebars. Gripping on tight, I prepare myself to take the final invigorating, super speedy ride down the coastline of this beautiful Amalfi coastline. Next, I turn the key in the ignition, and on hearing the engine of this beauty of a machine that I am seated upon roar like a magnificent lion who is king of his pack, a triumphant smile spreads across my face. Finally, I take a deep breath, whisper out Helena's name – *I'm coming for you, Helena. We are destined to be together* – and as I take another draw of fresh morning air, I turn the throttle to its fullest pelt.

I briefly saw it you know... I momentarily saw the ogre of a heavy goods vehicle on the wrong side of the road advancing precariously towards me. As it swayed and swerved uncontrollably, I tried to slow down, and steer out of its growling path but I couldn't for my body had become stricken with a death defying, blind panicking fear... All I could think of at that particular moment in time was Helena and the last time that we had made love. We'd made up after the dreadful misunderstanding about, dare I mention her, Alice, and while we were in the after throes of our lovemaking for the shortest of moments, Helena and I were blissfully happy. Replete one could say, until I disappeared off and went for a shower. As I bathed, unbeknown to me, my phone became active, and that it was discovered by Helena... When I returned from showering, much to my horror, I found that she had left... left me... forever? And the reason why she fled was that the caller happened to be my ex submissive... that conniving bitch, Alice. She had risen like a phoenix from beneath the charred ashes, and as she did my world with Helena had imploded. After all this time, after giving the situation much careful thought, I'm sure that Alice had carefully planned to destroy my relationship with Helena with just one unanswered call. Well I won't let Alice win... I will not let her ruin or quash my love for the woman that I will always hold a bright, burning candle for, my Helena.

It's getting darker for some reason, and all I can visualize through the dusk that is surrounding me is this exact image of Helena – With my naked body, I have her pinned beneath me. Her chocolate-caramel coloured irises are alight with an infinite love for me, for us... I've taken her to the precipice of erotica with my words, with my body and my soul, and watching her finally let go is pure breathtakingly beautiful. Her climax is ripping, raging through her svelte, sweat soaked body... and I am left... well I am left more than just being physically and mentally drenched within her love... I am in fact left wanting, needing, craving for so much more of her.

As the latter scenario flashed all to briefly through my thoughts, much to my disappointment, as it began to fray and fade around the edges, my hearing heightened, and all I could translate were the bone-chilling sounds of splitting metal crumpling all around me – bringing me back to this fateful reality. As I became constricted, I cried out Helena's name in desperate vain, and as an overwhelming blinding flash followed, I believe that I saw death extending its decaying hand to me, beckoning me forth with his bony, gnarled fingers. Within a split second as something jagged seared through my jacket, I felt the unknown object pierce the flesh that lies over where my heart is situated. Bile rose rapidly into my throat, and I was descended into the eeriest of darkness. Through the pain, the shock, and after making out the cloudless sky above me, I became aware that I was now lying flat on my back upon the dusty, knobbly road beneath me. My mouth was now filling with the taint of what I can only decipher as warm, life giving fluid. My natural instinct was to tilt my head to one side – thankfully I managed to do just that, spewing out blood that was almost on its way to choking me towards a certain death. As the pain jarred down my spine, my lungs heaved hard for fresh oxygen, and I began to gag furiously. While the entire contents of my stomach revolted, and I vomited, washing away the blood that was repeatedly filling my mouth, I began to ebb away, and as wave after wave of excruciating pains splintered throughout my entire body, the last thing I remember was the sound of sirens approaching way, way in the distance. I was now suspended in the bleakest of times... was there any way back for me? Did I have any chance of averting my imminent death? After all it wasn't my fault that I am laying here all messed up and writhing in the throes of dying...Without Helena. It just isn't.

Eight-thirty-five a.m.

From out of nowhere, my subconscious whispers, *"You do know that you're not quite dead yet, Darius don't you?"*

"I'm not," I sigh with exhaustion. "So if I'm not dead then what do you call this? A moment of divine grace... perhaps?'

'Not really..." my subconscious replies. *"It's about your heart... It has one beat left before the sinoatrial node... the pacemaker cuts out... I'm afraid my dear chap; you've just about run out of charge."*

"What do you mean, 'I've just about run out of charge'?"

"Shhh, Darius.... Don't fret.... You'll see what I mean in just a second...."

One second later...

With the metallic taste of blood still fouling my mouth, I try to purse my cheeks, and form some saliva with the intent of washing the awful tang away but I can't for there is something alien invading my throat. Forcing my tender eyelids to open, and as they slightly part, I can just about make out some vague shapes surrounding me. This experience is all very alien to me, and I'm feeling extremely frightened. Where are you, Helena? I need you by my side.

"Stats, Sister?" I hear a male's, muffled voice from faraway ask.

A female's voice responds. "There doesn't appear to be anything remotely life giving left to work upon, Dr Franco."

I'm failing...

I'm freefalling...

I'm fading...

Flatline.

Time of my death - 8.36 a.m.

One minute later...

8.37 a.m.

'Love gives light even in the darkest of tunnels.'

Through the cache of doctors and nurses surrounding me, I can
see the continuous straight line that is displaying on the heart
monitor indicating my cardiac failure. I want to cry out to them
that there is still life within my soul... Please, please, don't give
up on me, I silently beg... I'm still here... trapped in this
bloody, tangled, bone shattered shell of a body... Please don't
leave me hanging here... alone.

Now line is static and with the numbers rapidly
descending upon the screen, it has become apparent to me that
I actually no longer have any choice in embracing this
wonderful adventure one calls life, so with much sadness in
my heart, I now know that I am leaving my world, my Helena
behind. With this penultimate, saddened thought of mine, I
make the conscious decision to let go, and as I drift away,
suspended in eternity forever, I imagine to myself that Helena
is with me. As my mind regretfully begins its failure, this is
what, through my dreamlike haze I envisaged:

Helena is looking down upon me, and I am drinking in
every facet of her beauty for the final time. While I muster my
last ounce of energy, I blink slowly twice as if to say to her a
temporary goodbye – I'll see her one day on the other side –
Which I am sure of.

She places her mouth to mine, and lingers for a while. Her
eyes are dewy with salty emotions, and as she breathes against
my lips, "Will you watch me closely from beyond, Darius?"

I want to tell her that I will, and that I want her to live
every second, every minute and every hour of her life to the
dizziest of heights, so that when we do finally align again as
one, we will have so much to discuss. But alas my thoughts,
my wishes, my dreams for our future together, and my hopes

for a long and fruitful life with her become lost in my own translation, and as I gravitate towards an enveloping orb of white, calming light, I, with much sorrow begin my metamorphosis and join hands with my oldest of friends, *Mr Snuggles the bear.*

With his bare feet plodding over the soft green, grass, the seven-year-old, blue eyed boy stops, hold his six-year-old beloved teddy bear up to his face and asks, "Mr Snuggles? Where are we going?"

As quick as a flash, Mr Snuggles turns his head, looks to the boy, creases his furry brow, and replies, "I don't know where but I've just been informed by the Supreme Being that you and I are not allowed to pass any further down this route.

"Puzzled, the boy asks, "Why so?"

"Because the Supreme Being is not quite ready yet for our presence..."

Confused and a little scared the dark, curly haired boy urges, "Please ask him, Mr Snuggles. Please find out how long must we have to wait until we can continue travelling?"

Moments tick away and Mr Snuggles shivers through the brown, matted curly hair that he has been created from, and then woefully replies, "Supreme Being estimates approximately about seventy years?"

A gasp escapes the boy's lips and he exclaims, "That's an extremely long time to spend suspended here in negativity with you, isn't it?"

Scrunching up his scratched, round button nose, the teddy sighs, "Yes, I'm afraid that it is."

Managing a smile, the boy asks, "Well since we are going to be friends for decades to come, what you suggest we should we do now?"

Frowning, the teddy taps his paw on his temple and quietly says, "You would like to go back home, wouldn't you?"

"Yes, I wouldn't mind. I quite miss it there... And what about you, Mr Snuggles, would you like to go home too?"

"Yes I would, but only if you promise when we get home that you move me from sitting on your telescope, and place me on the top of your piano."

"Why do you wish for me to move you? I thought you liked looking at the night sky with me?"

"I do, but I've been perched there for so long looking upwards my neck aches, and I must admit that I really do fancy a change of view."

The boy then warmly smiles at Mr Snuggles and says, "Okay, because I cherish you, I'll move you to the piano, and then you can look out at the London skyline. It's pretty at night like the twinkling stars suspended above the chimney tops."

After thanking the boy, his best friend, the teddy's eyes glaze over and he muses, "Do you want to know something?"

"Yes, Mr Snuggles, I do."

"The Supreme Being has been listening to our conversation, and he's considering letting us return home but before he makes a non-reversible decision, he has three asks of you to which he requires clear, concise answers to all."

The boy's heart flips and with hope he leads, "Oh pray tell, Mr Snuggles; enlighten me as to his terms."

"One, when you grow up, and become a man, you have to be a very good husband to your wife. You have do all that weird grown up stuff like love her without condition, honour her soul, and cherish and obey every facet of her being."

"Well, I suppose that goes without saying, Mr Snuggles, but nevertheless, yes, I will do just that. What else must I do?"

"Two, you must to be a loving and doting father to your three children."

Hugging Mr Snuggles tightly, the boy marvels, "I'm going to have children?"

"Yes."

"How many little ones will my wife and I create?"

"Three. Two boys and a girl"

"Oh my, that's the best news ever, Mr Snuggles."

"It is rather isn't it? And your answer is?"

"Yes, I will be a loving and doting father... and what is the Supreme Being's number three ask?"

"When the time comes, you must be a caring and kind grandfather."

"Well, that goes without saying too."

Tut-tutting the boy, Mr Snuggles hushes, "You must answer the Supreme Being properly or we won't be able to go home."

With delight in his voice the boy replies, "I promise from the bottom of my broken heart that I will be a caring and kind grandfather."

"So?" Mr Snuggles continues. "Are you ready to return home?"

"Yes, I am."

"Good, then let's go because we've been here a little too long for my liking, Darius."

"Yes, we have, Mr Snuggles, we have, haven't we?"

So as I watch my seven-year-old self release Mr Snuggles from his tight grip, and lift him up in front of his face, I, Darius, at twenty-nine years old, with a mixed sense of reluctance and relief watch them slowly both fade away. Next on hearing the faint, dulcet moans of a woman's sobbing ceasing somewhere in the background, I realise that I (without Mr Snuggles who I will most definitely move to the piano when I get home) have arrived back to the present year. Seconds pass me by, and as the familiar scent of Helena's perfume surrounds me, my heart takes the first, fresh beat, and it doesn't fail, not even for a second over the next god-graced and precious seventy years. With excitement flooding through my veins I mentally call out for her...

"Helena, are you close by?"

"Almost Darius... It won't be long before I am right next to you... I promise."

"Oh... that's a relief... I want to tell you that I will love you for eternity and if there is anything beyond that, then in that most magical and mystical of places too."

"I love you too, Darius... Stay strong. I'm coming for you."

"I will try, but please hurry. Without you by my side I don't think I can breathe let alone return."

"I'm flying now."

"I'm running towards you now..."

From the distance I hear a loud blip followed by another, and then another...With a steady rhythm maintaining in my chest, I hear the briefest of conversations wisp over me...

"Dr Franco?"

"Yes, Sister Mary?"

"It's... This... him..." she gasps. "This is all a miracle."

"Why, Sister?"

"Because I believe I can feel the faintest of pulses...."

Time of my rebirth – 8.38 a.m.

Trying to inhale a breath of life-giving oxygen, as I go through what should be a natural organic motion, I gag strongly once because something alien has been situated in my trachea and it is breathing for me. My stomach coils extremely hard, and I feel my back shudder strongly against what I assume is the over-firm mattress beneath me. My knees powerfully flex upwards towards my pelvis, and I jolt. Grief that pain burns deep. I want to vomit so very badly. Now realising that I have been intubated, I grasp the pipe beneath my chin with the full intention of yanking it out of my parched mouth. On feeling the serrations moulded around this artificial lifeline that is invading my person, I give it a sharp tug, and as it refuses to dislodge, I wretch not twice more, but thrice. A female's voice pitifully wails through the air,

"Please God, if you're with us right now, help him! Help him someone! He's going to choke to death!"

'Helena is that you?'

'Yes....'

A masculine voice interrupts her, and urgently commands for the sister to sedate me.

"He's trying to retract the endotracheal tube, Sister. We must sedate him immediately."

'No, please, please don't send me off into a calming sleep for I really do need to locate Helena.'

Just a little infusion and I was left comfortably numb.

Thirteen months later...
Sant'Angelo Hospital – Italy
23 December 2017

On this eve, the one before Christmas Eve, I stood by Darius's side, and rested my hand upon the roundness of his left shoulder. Giving him a reassuring squeeze I then asked him if he was sure, after the last year and one month past, that he ready to see what the second (and hopefully final) heart operation had left imprinted upon his chest. Naturally, he paused, in indecision. After his hesitation had ebbed away, he nodded. Both of us stared straight ahead into the full length mirror, and as he shuddered, I whispered to his reflection, asking again if he was completely confident with his decision. He responded with a curt nod, and his long, lashes, he dipped. Coiling his fingers around the lapels of his hospital gown, his knuckles whitened, and it was then, as he drew open his clothing to reveal the aftermath of the sutured ravine that had once been stapled over the shaven flesh that coats his heart, I felt a deepening sadness surge through my veins. For what seemed like forever, we both fixated upon the site of past trauma, and we counted out each puncture mark that once aided in holding together the edges of the wound – One, two... pause... three, four, five... pause... six... On reaching the final seventh, we both shivered... lucky or unlucky number seven? His spine stiffened. Next, I came around to meet him. Rising onto my tippy-toes, I carefully draped my arms around his neck, toying with the rogue curl at the nape, and looked deep into his red, rimmed eyes. As our eyes simultaneously misted over, I found it within me to reassure us both with the following words, "Over time, the scar will fade, Darius."

He drew in the sharpest of breaths, and bowed his head so low that is was impossible for me to maintain eye contact with him. Our lips briefly swept along each other's, and I quietly murmured to him that I loved him, that I have always loved him.

"I love you too," he wistfully breathed in – between my partly spaced lips.

And while I pressed my mouth to his, he drew back a little, and he left me light-headed when he added, "I adore you so much, Helena, that you, without consciously realising it have become a tremendous, vital part of me. You are a part that I cannot, a piece that I don't wish to, ever exist without."

Still absent-mindedly twirling with the rogue curl at the nape of his neck, I looked deep into his eyes and affirmed, "I understand, my love. And I feel exactly the same too."

"You do?" He sagged with an enormous sense of relief. "You can never be without me either?"

Now sliding my hand around his midriff, being delicate so as not to pull him too close for fear of hurting him, I splayed my palm flush on his lower back and softly began to stroke him there. While he moaned my name into my mouth, followed by a light, teasing dip of his tongue, the memories of our last love-making session, before I left him, came flooding into my mind, and as his kiss intensified and multiplied in its hunger, he pressed his body into mine. He then winced as a shard of pain spliced through his left hip and he groaned, "I wish we could lie down in bed together and cuddle."

Breathing into his mouth, I, through this most jumbled of kisses told him that his cuddles quite often lead on to intense, heated sexual intercourse. Halting the kiss, he took a step back from me, creased a worried frown and then briefly smiled. With a slight teasing in his voice he asked, "Fancy a snuggle-cuddle with me then?"

Laughing at his words, I explained to him that considering it was nearly five-thirty p.m. and his consultant would soon be here to assess whether he could be discharged or not, a snuggle-cuddle would be out of the question. Pulling a sad little boy lost face, he pitifully replied, "Oh well, I guess I shall just have to wait until we are in-flight one day in the future to have my wicked way with you once again!"

"I've missed our bodies joining," I say with softness. "It's been so long since us... we... we made love."

His voice sounding sadder than mine, he breathes, "Too long, baby, and I missed us too."

"Anyway," I chirp, trying to lighten the mood. "In flight... What do you mean by that?"

He never got a chance to reply to my question because as the hour struck six we were interrupted by a soft knocking on the other side of the door.

His consultant had arrived.

Chapter Three

24 December 2017

Eleven-thirty a.m.

Leonardo da Vinci Airport – Rome

'The truth is that airports have seen more sincere kisses than the wedding halls, and the walls of hospitals have heard more prayers than the walls of a church.'
Author unknown

Stepping out of the hired car first, I don't look around at my surroundings; I just stand and wait for the moment when Darius has assembled himself together and has finally decided to step out of the vehicle. As he comes into view, I offer him first my hand and then I hesitate. Secondly, I take the walking cane from our driver and place it in front of what appears to be a very nervous Darius. With a heartbeat, the cane is forcefully swatted away from me and as it scuffles against the stone pavement, I startle.

"I don't need it, Helena!" he garbles, "I've already explained that you before we left the hospital that don't I want it!"

"I think you..."

Before I can finish my sentence, his voice marred with hopelessness, he pitifully declares, "And I don't ever want to see that old man's walking stick ever again... Do you of all people understand what I am saying, baby?"

I do make sense of what he is conveying to me, and I think about protesting that he should use it, but because of the desperation in his voice, I decide to let things unfold as he wishes. Again I extend him my hand to him. This time he takes it. Patting my red leather, gloved hand, he then places his black fedora woollen hat on his head while hiding behind a pair of dark sunglasses. I link arms with him and support him on our short walk into the airport. On entering we are swiftly guided towards the VIP departure lounge and are instructed to seat until it is time for us to board. While I watch him brooding at his unfortunate predicament, he takes small sip after sip of his tumbler of over-iced water, and I while I sit opposite him, I chose to remain quiet. *I'm quite exhausted by his past and current mood swings.*

Moments before we were about to be the last passengers to board the aircraft, with his voice sounding miserable, he tips the brim of his hat back so I can see his face. Removing his sunglasses so I can see his informative eyes, he then looks to me, and I sadden inside when I hear him so miserably grumble, "I wish...I truly wish that we didn't have to take this commercial flight back home."

"Why? I don't mind," I reply while trying to lighten his mood. "We'll be seated in first class. It could be a bit of fun...

A new experience. You never know you might gain something from it."

"Fun?" he says with horror. "I very much doubt it! And to learn something from being cooped up with others while flying high up in the air? I think not!"

Now exasperated with him to the point of thinking about asking to have a seat in economy class where I can ride home with normal human beings – people who don't have an enormous chip carved into their shoulder – people who just enjoy making simple conversation, I chastise him firmly! "That's so very snobbish of you to say so, Darius. I don't think I like this brash side of your personality. It really doesn't suit you in the slightest. If fact I don't like you very much at all at present."

He creases a bemused frown and pushes me by quizzing, "What doesn't suit me? And why don't you like me? I like you!"

"You don't suit you!"

"Explain?"

"No, I won't explain because right now you are acting like a miserable, stuck up beast!"

Cocking an eyebrow at me, he gives me a warning glare, but I'm not in the mood to submit to his over bombastic behaviour, so I coolly finish, "You, Darius Carter, think that you are better than everyone else... The way you are performing now leads me to believe that you are actually dead certain in your thoughts, and that we... us mere mortals, us lowly peasants, are beneath you!"

His face horrors, and he says, "I don't think that I am better than everyone else, and I most certainly don't think that I am of a higher authority in any way shape or form."

I bite the corner of my lip and wish I never retorted so harshly at him, and he in response, momentarily dips his lashes, which then rise to meet my eyes. "I'm so, so sorry," he says apologetically. "Truth be told, Helena, I would have much rather have chartered my own private jet to come and fetch us... At least we could... we would've been able to have our privacy together aboard her."

On hearing his words, my short temper quickly abates and I am stunned, "You have your own aeroplane?"

"Yes, I do," he replies in a matter of fact tone.

"So why didn't you charter it to bring us home then?"

"Because she, my plane, wasn't... well let me just say, she wasn't ready to fly over today."

"Mr Carter? Ms Payet?" A smartly dressed gentleman with the name badge, Fiorenzo, interrupts. "It's time for you to board the plane."

I look up and reply for both of us, "Thank you, Fiorenzo."

While he leads us through the tunnel walkway, and we exit onto the tarmac, a mere few steps away from the stairwell that leads up and into the aircraft, I remain confused at Darius's last answer. I am perplexed at his references to giving the craft, she, a feminine gender, so I for now, push the thought of him possessing his own jet to the back of my mind, and switch my focus upon the following; the gossip hungry paparazzi who are at present being firmly held at bay by Italian Airport security. As we move on forward, I place my hand upon Darius's left shoulder, and rest it there. Next, over the deafening shouts of the muck raking, untruth uncovering, hungry journalists, and the repetitive sounds of the clicking of shutters from the abundance of photographers who I may add are all needy for that first picture of Darius since his release from hospital, I gently urge him to take another step, a very careful step upwards.

I then jump of my skin when I hear over the babble of tongues, Darius snapping, "Stop fussing Helena! I can bloody well climb the stairs without you or anyone verbally guiding me! I'm not an invalid! Next, I imagine, when we get home, you'll be applying to the local borough council and ask them if they could provide me with a blue badge so that after Giorgio or you have ferried me about, you can then both park one of my fleet of cars in a disabled bay!"

Snob!

I still at his most ridiculous outburst, and as I do, he perplexes me even further, by grumpily finishing with unkindness, "It's bad enough having the fucking paps baying like whining, spoilt bastards directly behind us while they bask, while they revel in my misfortune, let alone you, and... and," he points to the glamorous stewardess who is standing motionless at the summit of the steps, wiggles his finger at her, and adds, "and her... Little-Miss-Pretty up there! I truly wish that you'd both stop... Just stop hovering around me like a pair of over-attentive, fuss-pot wet nurses who have nothing better to do with their time than pretend that they are being helpful to someone like me!"

I ache painfully inside his crushing words, and as poor Little-Miss-Pretty looks down from the top of the stairwell, she rolls her eyes to the heavens, and I look up to her. Shaking my head from side to side – were both on the same wavelength where bad-tempered Darius is concerned – I answer to his coat covered back. "There's no need to be curt with me, or rude about her, Darius. I'm... we're only trying to help you." – *It's all I've been doing for the past year or so... that everyone's being doing –remember?* "And the paps..." I add. "Well, just try ignoring them – they only want a fragment of this moment... Tomorrow all this will be yesterday's news."

"Bastards!" he mutters under his breath, and then proceeds to take, rather uncomfortably, another couple of steps... Next, he steadies against the handrail, and finally turns around. On seeing I am exhausted and ruffled by his recent short temper, his face crumples, and he quickly apologises.

"Oh fuck! Oh fuck it! I'm so, so sorry my baby, Helena. It's just a little difficult for me to be..."

With my patience fast failing, I ask in an irritable tone, "Be what? What is it difficult for you to be?"

"To be partially incapacitated in this way... for everyone to see."

"Well, at least you're alive!" I say with such conviction... "You could've died and then where would we..."

I can't finish my sentence for a sob is forming in the back of my throat and I am ground down by him and his strong emotions.

Loudly choking my sadness back, he apologises, "Oh blast it! I'm sorry, Helena. I've been so selfish with all my thoughts and with every single of my outbursts of words. I'm truly sorry."

I droop and nod in understanding.

"Come here?" he softly asks.

"Why?" I sniff.

"I want to hug you."

"No, not yet, Darius. Just carry on moving. We can hug later inside privately."

If I have any energy left

His face crumples and he obeys my instructions. Tentatively resuming his ascent, both of us reach the summit in turn. I stand next to him, place my hand in his; it fits perfectly in his. On entering the craft, I glance to the right, and set eyes upon our seated fellow passengers. Some are openly pointing at Darius and I, while others are angling their smart phones trying to snap the latest shot of Mr Darius Carter and his girlfriend. I am astounded when he reveals himself to everyone by removing his hat followed by his sunglasses. Offering them to the stewardess, she kindly takes them from him, and gives me a warm smile. Next, as he, with such professionalism breaks into the most beautiful smile imaginable, I am amazed as he gives his audience a slow, royal wave. As a rush of excited whispers ripple through the crowd, he turns to me, and I pray to God that he isn't going have another untimely flare-up. God was listening because Darius has, this instant taken my breath away by standing unaided while cradling my face in his hands and bestowing a long, lengthy lingering kiss upon my lips. When he does release me, as I see the dark, rogue curl that is corkscrewing over his forehead, I too can't help but smile. Next, he gives aforementioned spiral of black hair a light puff of air, blows it out of his vision, and grins.

"You weren't expecting that, were you?"

"No, I wasn't," I say with much relief. "Not at all."

Kissing me lighter this time, he whispers into my mouth, "I bet every one present enjoyed witnessing that kiss."

"Mmm... I can tell you, Darius, I enjoyed it much, much, more than they did!" I giggle.

"You did Miss Payet?" he amuses.

Surprised at him using my surname, I reply,

"Honestly, yes I did, Mr Carter."

"Would you like another kiss right this very moment?"

As I go to reply that yes I would like another one of his delicious kisses, the stewardess interrupts by handing Darius back his accessories and asking, "Mr Carter, sir?"

I can't help but titter again at hearing her add 'sir' onto the end of her sentence. If only she knew what that particular three lettered word not only entailed between Darius and I, but what sensual and erotic images it had just conjured up from the depths of my imagination.

"Would you and Miss Payet like to follow me please?"

Grasping my hand, he chuckles, "Come on Miss Payet, you and your sir had better follow this lovely lady, who I may add has been rather patient with me and my sullen mood, for I have a slight suspicion that we may be holding the flight up a tad."

"Yes, sir..." I quietly say while he squeezes my hand.

Slowly ambling along with him, we follow her up the final flight of stairs until we reach the first class compartment. Ushering us towards our seating area, she then trots off to attend to her duties. Sinking back into the ochre coloured, velveteen sumptuous seating, I turn to the man I love, and ask, "Are you ready to finally fly back home, Darius?"

He reciprocates looking dreamily at me. Again squeezing my hand, he answers, "I'm very, very ready, Helena."

Simultaneously we both draw a breath, close our eyelids, and without another word crossing between us, as the aircraft elevates from Leonardo da Vinci airport, we recline back into our seats, and relax into the two and a half hour journey that will take us back to England.

Heathrow Airport
1.48 p.m.

After leaving the comforting warmth of the private arrivals/departures airport lounge, Darius and I now find ourselves standing face to face outside upon the lightly snow dusted pavement. While the humming sounds of aircraft pass high above us, and the swirling, windy chills of this joyful season's offering stings upon our faces, I breathe in an icy breath of oxygen, and he does the same. On feeling this man of mine, who against all odds has cheated death, snaking his leather gloved hands under my woollen cloak, I shudder with a mixture of a great sense of relief that is combined with hefty wave after wave of nervy anticipation. He then takes the lead by coiling his arms around my waist, and slowly drawing me closer into him. While the all too familiar fresh scent of the top notes of his manly perfume envelope and invade my senses, I weaken at the knees at the heavenly fragrance of this divine being who has once again finally found us. He quickly senses that my strength may be dwindling, and as he does, I find myself supported firmer within his cosseting embrace. With a few ounces of my stamina still remaining, I rise onto my tiptoes, wrap my arms around his neck, and gaze lovingly up at him. He looks down upon me, and our eyes meet. While I survey him carefully, he blinks away the tiny snowflakes that are lingering upon his dark, curly lashes and I, well I can do nothing more but stand rooted to the icy floor beneath my snow boots, while drinking in his dark and handsome charming beauty. Seeing myself reflected within the delicate pools of his steely blue irises, I feel as if I am about to do one of two things; either faint in his muscular arms or lift off to an undiscovered level. Leaning into me, he presses his body into mine and nuzzles into my tresses. While the soft hairs of his beard tickle the side of my cheek, I become lost within his heavenly aura, and he weakens me even further when I feel his taut chest rise and fall as he breathes in deeply the bouquet of my being. We are now oblivious to the world that is hurriedly scurrying around us. We linger like this for some time. As our souls silently join together, these most precious of moments turn into present memories that are now thankfully in the making. On hearing the soothing tones of his velvety voice murmur, "You're so petite, my angel from above." I shiver. My shudder is not caused from the battering of nature's wintry elements, but it has been brought forth by the encompassing warmth of the love that is exuding from every pore of his being.

My lips now trembling, I murmur against his cheek, "Am I?"

"Yes, Helena, you are," he whispers. "You... You, feel so, so delicately fragile within my arms."

I am.

With his words filtering fast into my heart, dusting off all the cobwebs that have so painfully manage to weave their way around my heartstrings during his recovery, I now know that I am now not going to pass out. Back home here in England, and cosseted safe in his arms, a place I never, ever want to depart from, I bury my head into his firm chest, and consciously try not to press to hard upon where his scar lays. He wraps his coat around me as tight as he possibly can. While the December snowflakes cascade upon us and Mother Nature dusts us with her virginal beauty, the noise of the airport around us fades into a non-existence. Replete in his company, I quietly say one word to him and that word was –breakable.

"Never," he tenderly soothed. "You will never fragment as long as we are together."

"You promise me, Darius? You promise me that you will never let me shatter again?"

Stroking my hair, he took in the most heaving of sighs, and as he breathed out, he, with such devote honesty in his voice, affirmed to me, "I promise."

Stepping back from me, he outstretched his arm and offered me his leather gloved hand. I placed my hand in his, and he gave me a truly warming smile. "Walk with me?" he asked.

Well it was more of a slow hobble than a striding walk.

As I did, moments passed, and when I realised that we were not heading towards the car park to meet Giorgio, his friend, chauffeur and right-hand man, but we were actually walking back towards the airport entrance that we had recently exited. I enquired, "Why are we going back into the airport? Have you forgotten something?"

Continuing walking slowly, he softly said, "Quite possibly... "

Bemused, I questioned, "What? What is it that you've left behind?"

"Oh," he murmured, "you'll see soon enough."

He was right because when we re-entered the private lounge, he led me to the floor to ceiling glass window and stopped. Next, as he stood behind me, he placed his hands upon my shoulders and whispered into my ear, "Do you like what you see parked outside, Helena?"

On seeing the black nose of a pristine, white jet staring back at me, I curiously replied, "Yes, I do Darius. It's rather cute to say the least."

"Good." He breathed with a *soupçon* of relief. "So now we've established that you are happy with what you have just seen, would you like to fly away to somewhere secret with me in *Helena*?"

My tummy flipping on hearing his question, I turned around to face him and with a quizzical voice, I asked, "I... I don't understand. What do what you mean?"

Tipping his finger under my chin, he gave me a sympathetic look, tilted his head to one side and answered, "Well then, my precious, why don't you let me illuminate you as to what I mean?"

I did, and after he had done just that and I had become aware of just exactly what he meant, I was left stunned and amazed. The reason for my surprise was for the following two reasons. Firstly, he explained to me that he is the owner of this aircraft and secondly, I was left breathless when told me that he had named said aircraft after me – and added that I have and I will always be the love of his life.

There were so many emotions running through my soul – the relief of him surviving the motorbike accident, the named aircraft, and the uncharted future stretched out before me, as he swept his lips along mine, and murmured against my partly open mouth, "Are you ready to embark on a new adventure with me, Helena?"

My heart gathering speed, I barely managed to whisper against his lips, "I'm ready, Darius."

Pulling back from me he held me in his dreamy gaze and grinned. "Good," and then he added, "...because I have so much more to show you along the way."

I dissolved right into his arms – instantly forgave his displays of recent bad temper- And so, as he bestowed an extremely deep and passionate kiss upon me, it was then at that precise moment that I felt his soul reach out and touch mine and the first of our adventures together began.

Heathrow to Inverness...

As the male flight attendant, who dare I say is a dreadfully handsome specimen of the male species closes and secures the hatch door to the aircraft, he turns around to face Darius and I who are seated, strapped in and ready for takeoff. When I see this blonde Adonis beam a rather over the top smile at Darius, which is followed by a saucy, sassy wink at me, I smile as I watch him saunter off in the direction of the cabin crew's domaine. Darius then breaks into a lingering scowl, and when I hear him mumble under his breath that said flight attendant has just taken a liberty by batting his blond lashes at me and therefore his career might end promptly after we touchdown, I muse, 'Oh dear, sweet possessive and terribly jealous Darius of mine what am I going to do with you? How on earth am I going to be able to temper down the jealousy that burns to precariously within you?'

He's now grasping my hand firmly in his, and as he places my hand to his lips, he moves me by tenderly kissing each fingertip in turn while asking, "Are you absolutely ready to fly away with me, Helena?"

I look lovingly over at him and reply, "Yes, Darius, I'm very, very ready to leave with you."

As *Helena* angles away from terminal number one, she slowly taxis down the runway, and I glance over at the man who I love with my whole heart, and over time have come to cherish so unbelievably dearly. His head is reclined backwards and his mass of dark curls tumble loosely in split directions over his head. His body is outstretched to its fullest capacity. Watching his chest rise and fall through the white shirt that he is wearing, I focus upon the third handcrafted pearl button, and imagine slowly undoing said button followed by the fourth, fifth and the final sixth. His deep sigh breaks me from my rather how shall I say, inappropriate thoughts? – And when I see him squeeze his eyelids tightly shut, I then detect a slight tremble of his hand that has been entwined in mine for the best part of the last half-an-hour.

"Are you okay, baby?" I whisper. "Are you in any pain at all? If so I can fetch your meds."

He lightly presses my hand in acknowledgement that he has heard me but doesn't offer a single word. I take his silence as that he's quite possibly not tremendously fine – I wonder if it's the final impending flight that is unnerving him which would be unusual since he's never given me reason to think that he is a nervous flyer... or if not, then it must definitely be the injury to his hip that is causing him some discomfort. Resting back into my seat, I quieten. Moments pass and the aircraft eventually elevates from the tarmac beneath her wheels. For what seems like an eternity we steadily climb until finally we level off. Next, the sound of an alerting ping is followed by a brief voiceover from the pilot who informs us that we may now unbuckle our seatbelts. We simultaneously do just that. I watch with curious interest as Darius pushes himself up from his seat, straightens his back, and then flexes his arms up in the air while cricking his neck to the right then left and repeats. I can't help but simper inside when I see him engage in limping the short distance towards the mini bar while asking,

"Would you like a drink, Helena?"

I reply, "Yes, I would please, Darius."

Turning around to face me, he asks, "What would you like to drink? A glass of your favourite wine, Domaine Rose Otto or perhaps you would like a chilled glass of San Pellegrino water?"

Knowing full well that he isn't allowed alcohol with his medication, and even though I would dearly love a glass or two of wine right now to steady myself, I opt for the water.

"Water, please."

He pours us both a glass, and slowly ambles back to me. Offering me the crystal carved tumbler, I take it from him and sip slowly. Next, I am mesmerised as he bends down, and very carefully positions himself onto his knees in front of me. Pulling a grimace – he's most definitely in pain, he rapidly discards that aching look, beams into a smile, and looks directly at me. Holding me in his dreamy gaze, he asks,

"Do you actually realise how much I love you, Helena?"

"I do." I smile back at him. "And do you know how much I love you, Darius?"

While he attempts to rise to his feet, he grits his teeth and clumsily stumbles forward. Falling over me, he retracts and then steadies himself by placing either of his arms upon the seat rests. I melt inside when his face comes close to mine and he brushes his lips along mine. Murmuring to me that yes he does know how much I love him, he inspires me by simply explaining that our love for each other is immeasurable – Our love is timeless. On both of those accounts, I have to agree.

"Does *Helena* have a..." I go shy but continue, "a... a, you know... a sleeping area on board?"

He's looking exhausted and he needs to rest – and I need nothing more that to curl up around him and feel the warmth of his body against mine.

Suddenly he draws back from me. His backside hits the floor and as he shuffles on his bottom retreating from me, he stills and looks to the floor. I am horrified when I see his broad shoulders sag.

"Look at me, baby?"

He does and as I watch his face crumple into a state of blind panicking fear, a part of me dies inside for I have not seen that particular look upon his face since the moment he first saw the scar that was left over his heart. Shaking his head from side to side, he hitches a breath, and stares extremely hard at me.

Confused at his reactions, I gently ask, "What is it? What's the matter, baby? Have I upset you in any way?"

"I can't..." He abruptly halts. "I want to... I thought I could... But... but... I... I..."

Reaching out for him, I steady my hands upon his shoulders and sink to my knees so we are both at eye level.

"Hey, sweetheart," I soothe, "You can't what?"

He looks into his lap and knots his hands. His knuckles whiten and he swallows hard,

"If I tell you, promise you won't give up on me?"

Aghast, I respond, "Never, Darius... Surely by now you know that I would never, ever give up on you... On us, don't you?"

He nods and after he had with such sensitivity and such compassion divulged to me exactly what has been bothering him since the day he first opened his eyes after his motorbike accident, I enveloped my gentle dominant in my arms, and I welcomed him crying until he had nothing left to bleed out, nothing left to purge from the darkest depths of his delicate soul.

Chapter Four

Christmas Eve

After driving the short distance from Inverness airport to what Darius has described to me as a secret destination, we pass through a set of sensor activated, wrought iron gates. While the satellite navigation system informs us that we have almost reached our journey's end, Darius speaks. "We are almost there, Helena... feeling happy, excited?"

"I'm very happy indeed, Darius," I respond as I steer the Porsche Cayenne in the stated direction, and while the headlights powerfully shine their beams directly ahead, I warm inside as Darius pats my lap, and rests his hand upon my person.

"I think you are going to be pleasantly surprised when you see what I have in store for you..." he pauses, "for us."

"Why am I?" I ask with curiosity in my voice.

Squeezing my thigh, he replies, "Oh, you'll see in a short moment."

I can only smile with divine happiness, and as we reach the end of the road, so to speak I slow the vehicle down to a halt, apply the handbrake, and switch the engine off. While the windscreen wipers settle into their resting position, I look straight ahead, and as twirling flakes of Scottish snow decorate the view ahead, I am left stunned at was is revealed before me, before us – It's quite simply picture, postcard perfect. Surrounded by an abundance of snow covered pine trees, that are twinkling under the light of the silvery moon, is a well lit, 'A' framed shaped house. One could say that its design had been based upon a Scandinavian lodge, but this house is actually more luxurious in its size than one of a sweet, cozy log fired retreat.

"Oh my goodness," I gasp out, "it's absolutely beautiful."

His voice chirpy, he replies, "Yes it is, isn't it?"

"Agreed..."

Turning to face him, I then enquire, "And tell me, Darius, who owns such a beautiful place as this? Who are we renting it from? I bet it's from one of your film star chums, isn't it?"

After unbuckling both our seatbelts, he leans close to me, and I am left stunned when he whispers into my ear that we are not renting it for the holiday season, and that the creation standing before us actually belongs to us.

Placing my fingers to my lips, I startle and gasp, "What? You're teasing me, aren't you?"

His voice gentle, he replies, "No I am not. Why would I joke about something so important?"

"Truly you're not?"

"No," He sighs. "I'm definitely not."

My voice light and full of surprise, I reply, "Then this is... ours... It's... it's our first home together?"

Grinning broadly at me, he replies, "Well, at the moment it's just a new build, but I am hedging my bets that with your style, grace and personality we will soon turn it into a loving home filled with love and laughter, and many, many happy memories."

I'm so taken aback that I barely manage to whisper, "You had it built especially for us? You did all this from over in Italy without me knowing?"

"Yes, I did. I wanted you, when you saw it for the first time, I wanted it to take your breath away."

"Well it has..."

"I had it designed, and he adds in a hushed tone, "I had it tailored especially for us."

"What do you mean tailored?"

He gives me than knowing look of his and I quickly realise that he means that somewhere within the walls of this amazing looking house there will be a particular room – A room with no view, just a room where he and I can express our sexual fantasies within the limits of safe, sane and consensual sex. With so many emotions running through me, I fling my arms around his neck and shower his cheeks, his nose and his lips with a flurry of peppered kisses. While he tries unsuccessfully to wiggle out of my hold, I tell him that I love him so very much, and that I always will. He chuckles in a triumphant fashion, and peels my arms from around his neck. Holding both my hands in his, he gazes lovingly at me.

"I adore you, Helena."

"I know," I say with the uttermost truth.

Winking at me, he gleefully asks, "Want to go inside and do some exploring?"

"Do I ever!" I excitedly exclaim.

"Wonderful!" he says with the sparkle that I love so much returning to his eyes – the eyes that have been so very dull of late. "Then let's go inside and create a new adventure for I have so much more of me that I can't wait to share with you."

And with that latter statement of his warming my heart, we walked hand in hand the short distance towards the front door. On reaching our ultimate landing place as he turned, held my face in his hands and kissed me so deeply, so passionately, the first moment of the rest of our lives had just turned into a new and untainted chapter.

Inverness
Scotland
25 December 2017
Christmas morning, seven-thirty a.m.

Darius is still sleeping and I am currently alone and situated in the window seating bay of the lounge of our recently acquired new home, which I may add was the first of two surprises that Darius sprung upon me en route back from Heathrow last night ago – the other, I will divulge to you a little while later. I snuggle the tartan blanket around my shoulders, and press the pad of my finger flush to the icy cold window pane. While I trace the pathway that a singular, pristine white snowflake randomly decided to embark upon, as it slides down the glass, and the morning light that envelopes it catches a facet of the heart-shaped jewel that has so recently adorned my finger. I warmly smile to myself, while I recall, while I reminisce about Darius, who in the wee small hours of this morning asked me a life changing question.

In the wee, small hours of Christmas morning...

With us both sitting cross-legged, and facing each, and with a tartan blanket draped over our laps, I leant into Darius, and with each undoing of the pearl buttons on his shirt, I swept my fingers lightly along his chest. As I paused, lingering upon the pinking scar central to his heart, he shivered. The reason for him shaking suddenly was not only because of the lightness of my delicate touch, but it was also because of the following, frightening moment from the past that had just resurrected from the hidden depths of his memory.

He divulged to me the following:

You were standing by my side, and as you rested your hand upon my shoulder, you asked me if I was sure that I was ready to see what the operation had left imprinted behind upon my chest. I nodded, and as I stared straight ahead into the full length mirror, you again asked me if I was completely confident with my decision. Truth be told, I wasn't feeling in the slightest bit sure, but I would never, ever, ever let the woman I love and cherish know how scared I truly was. That just wouldn't do, would it, Helena? Grasping the lapels of my gown, I then, without hesitation, drew open my clothing to reveal the scar that had been left over the shaven flesh that coats over my heart. As I fixated upon it, mentally counting each pinking, puncture mark that was once holding together the edges of the wound – the injury that caused you to come back to me – my spine stiffened, and my stomach violently churned over. You then entwined your fingers with mine, and came around to meet me. Rising onto your bare tiptoes, you tentatively draped your arms around my neck, toying with the rogue curl at the nape of my neck. As you gazed deep into my eyes, yours misted over, and you assured me, 'Over time, the scar will fade, Darius.'

It will.

So still facing each other, I settle my lips upon Darius neck, and while I do, I am slowly brushing the shirt from around his shoulders. He trembles. As he draws in a breath of air, I raise my head to meet his gaze, and I bat my unmade lashes while tentatively pushing my body into his while seeking out his lips. He hitches a breath, dips his head low and sweeps his lips along mine. Rolling his shoulders, he frees himself from his shirt and with his cuffs still secured; he extends his arms to me and with his voice a quiver, like a forlorn child he asks, "Help me?"

I blinked, smiled and then obliged by taking his left hand in my right and slowly trailing my finger along the centre of his palm. When I reached his wrist, he watched in silence as I, with such gentleness released the wolf carved, onyx cufflink from its hand stitched buttonhole. I then repeated my actions with the right. With the nakedness of his torso now on display to me, I looked directly at him. He opened his mouth to speak and within one fluid motion I was kneeling behind him with the blanket trailing behind me. I wrapped my arms around him and with the delicacy of my touch; he let out a deep sigh. He feels so very comforting. I whispered into his ear, "Make love to me, Darius? I've missed us so, so terribly."

The gentleness in my voice alone was enough to bring back some self-assurance to him so as I told him that I was now going to undress, while I began to discard my clothes he stood up, and peeled out of his trousers, followed by his black, silk boxers. Both bare, we sat before each other. He placed his hands upon his upper thighs, and then bowed his head, momentarily fixating his stare between his legs. As he saw his manhood standing proud, he then emitted the hugest sigh of relief imaginable. The reason for his gasp was for the first time since his accident, he had finally succeeded in... Well let me just say, his physicality had finally returned! With his courage now fast retuning, he shuffled around to face me, and within moments we were entwined within the softness of the sheet sized, blanket and I was beneath him. Shakily supporting myself on my elbows, I breathed out his name, and admitted to him how much I loved him. I am sure I saw through the misty glaze in his eyes, his heart swell. With his confidence peaking and within the tender moments that followed we both found ourselves once again cosseted within the safety of each other's undying love.

Chapter Five

"The only thing I want to change about you, Helena, is that ringless finger on your left hand."

As our breathings began to labour and Darius, who was naked and pinned by my body beneath me, let out a sated sigh. I leant closer into him, pressed my mouth to his, and told him for the zillionth time within the last twenty-four hours how much I loved him. He without hesitation repeated to me the same. While his blue irises sparkled with a mesmerising, hypnotic look, and his cock still pulsated away inside me, he then surprised me by suggesting that he may be soon wishing for more of me – And considering this was the first time we had made love since his motorbike accident, I had to admit too, that I wanted much, much more of him. Shifting my body weight, I bore down over him and clenched him tight between my legs. On feeling my eagerness, he closed his eyes and groaned, "I think you've drained me, Helena. That was one very powerful, pent up climax that ripped through me."

Tentatively rocking over him, circling and enticing him with my hips I smiled, "I know, baby. I felt every drop of you flow into me."

On hearing my response, his eyebrows shot up and within a flash I was deftly flipped over onto my back. Looking up at him, I gave him a concerned look. He then pulled a grimace, and through the discomfort that I could see was clearly etched on his brow he was most certainly in pain. Hitching a breath he then asked, "You want more of me?"

"Of course I do." I gazed into his dreamy blue eyes. "Now I have the addictive taste for you once again, I'm craving for so much more of you."

"Me too..." He bats his lashes, and repeats, "Me too."

Next, I then placed my hand over his left hip, and ran my fingers lightly over the ravine of a scar that was now turning to a fading shade of pink. He shuddered at my touch. "But I can see," I whispered. "I can see that you are feeling slightly uncomfortable at present, so for now I think we should just lay here, wrap ourselves up in the blanket, and enjoy a warming snuggle-cuddle."

His gaze momentarily shifted away from me, and he muttered, "I'm not in any pain, Helena."

Sighing, and knowingly full well he was white lying to me, I shook my head and affirmed again that I could see he was experiencing soreness. He looked down upon me, frowned, brushed his lips along mine and mumbled, "I'm really fine, baby. My hip's not aching in the slightest."

Knowing full well it was hurting, I questioned, "Are you sure? You did wince quite hard a moment ago."

"Sure." He dismissively fibbed, and then tickled me to the core when his face lit up and he teased, "If I do decide to pleasure us both again my little femme fatale, there is one very important thing you must consider."

"Yes, sir," I laughed. "And pray tell what is it that you wish me not to forget?"

With one arm now pinned by the side of my head, he slid his hand under my buttocks, and I curled my legs around him. Giving me a gentle thrust of his hips, as another pain surged through his hip, he grimaced – he's most definitely in pain – he rattled off, "You must remember that I am recovering from a very unfortunate accident and you, as my private nurse must be at all times very, very attentive towards me."

"How can I be your nurse for I am not wearing a uniform?" I jested.

He stilled – a little too long for my liking and then had me in fits of girlish giggles when he suggested that he should buy me a nurse's outfit for he would quite like to see me strutting around the bedroom in a short white dress, stockings and high heels – Kinky! Next, he completely took me by surprise when he withdrew from me, and rested upon his haunches. He flinched. I rolled onto my side and watched him as he grabbed the tartan blanket from by my side and wrapped it around his midriff. Wagging his finger at me, he mischievously chortled, "No more of my impressive cock for you right now, Helena."

I then creased up with amusement when he with such a serious tone in his voice, stated, "I think you've had enough pleasure from this struggling invalid's body for the moment!"

Cheeky devil!

Rising up onto my knees, I tried to grasp the tail of his blanket with the full intent of whisking it away from him, but as he leapt up and with a slight hobble, he strutted as best as he could off in the direction of the Christmas tree. With his back towards me, I warmed as he knelt by the side of the pine, scented Norwegian fir, and started to flick with his thumb and forefinger a lone hanging gingerbread cookie that was dangling off a central branch. I wonder what he is thinking at present. So while I watched the spicy, festive biscuit swing back and forth, he turned around to face me. My view of said cookie was now blocked from my view. With his hands now behind his back, he beamed at me what I can only describe as the most divine, majestic smile I have ever encountered, and then asked, "Come over here, my sweetheart." He paused and continued, "I want... I want… I want..."

Intrigued, I quizzed, "You want what, Darius?"

"Just please come over, Helena. Please?" he implored.

"Why?"

"Come. Please?"

"Why?"

"Just come over and stop questioning me. Please?"

Reaching to the floor, I picked up his discarded crumpled shirt, slipped into it and wrapped it around me making haste over to him. On reaching him, I positioned myself onto my knees, mirroring his stance. He faltered a little to the right, and as he shifted his body weight onto his knee, his good side, I asked him again, "Are you sure you're all right? Your hip is giving you gyp again, isn't it? Do you want me go and fetch your medication?"

With a hint of irritation in his voice, he answered, "Please, Helena. No. I'm fine. No meds. It'll take more than a motorbike accident to cripple me and make me co-dependent on drugs."

Stroking his beautiful beard, I softy repeated for the final time, "Are you sure no meds, baby. It will take me moments to fetch them for you?"

His shoulders sagged and his voice a tad tainted with annoyance, he responded, "I'm positive."

"Well, if you're certain."

"I am."

"Okay, if you say so."

"I do."

"So tell me, Darius, why have you asked me over to you, and why are we sitting at the base of the tree?"

He beamed a glorious smile, and slipped his hand underneath his makeshift tartan sarong. As he fumbled around under his *camouflage skirt*, I rolled my eyes at him for his display of rude actions and he quipped, "Don't worry, Helena, I'm not playing with my cock." Still rummaging around, he then laughed quietly to himself. "And even though I would like to be stroking it right now into a magnificent peak of erectness, I do believe that caressing it is your... your..."

"Exactly my... Tell me?"

With the cheekiest smile imaginable plastered across his face, he blurted, "It's your job!"

Shaking my head from side to side, I tut-tutted him and scolded, "I don't see it as a job; I see it as more of a..."

Before I could finish my sentence, he's quieted me with his look. His arm he has outstretched, and his fist is curled up into a tight ball.

"What are you doing, Darius?"

He smiled...A smile that for some reason made me blush demurely. Upturning his hand, as he unravelled his fingers, what I saw nesting in the centre of his palm left me stunned. The cookie was not alone! Pinching the red ribbon that the cookie was attached to in his fingertips; he held the gingerbread man up in front of my face and as the flickering flames of the hearth fire reflected within this gorgeous man of mine's sparkling-blue irises, he so sweetly asked, "Do you like the gift Mr Gingerbread Man has brought for you?"

With my mouth agape and speech void, I nodded, for I liked the gift very much indeed! Unknotting the ribbon, I watched in awe as he slid the jewel from its host, leant into me and softy whispered, "Give me your left hand, baby."

Oh my, he's not... he's not... he's not going to ask me what I think he is, is he?

Offering him my trembling hand, he took it in his and warmly expressed, "There's no need for you to shake, Helena." he smiled. "I love you so very much you know."

I love you too, Darius.

While he looked adoringly at me, and I reflected his manner, I felt him slowly slip the ring over my finger, down past my knuckle and settle it at the base. Not daring to look down at my hand for fear all of this may be a dream, I was brought back into reality when he leant closer into me, and settled my hand over where his heart is situated. While it beat harder and faster than normal, I consciously ran the pad of my wedding finger down the central dip of his scar. He sucked in a large breath at my touch, and then in the most delicate of voices, when he spoke, the course of our destinies changed forever.

"Will you marry me, Helena?"

Firstly I glanced at my hand resting on his bare chest, and on seeing the heart shaped diamond solitaire gleaming back at me, a lump quickly rose in my throat. Silent moments passed and the only background sound to be heard was the ins and outs of his increasing breathing, coupled with sound of the fire crackling away in the hearth.

"Baby?" he squeaked, "Don't keep me hanging on any longer. Please give me your answer."

As his small, weak plea filtered through my being, I looked to him. Even though the room was warmed by the heat of the fire, his torso was showing signs of a judder. With a dewy, melty veil now casting in his eyes, as he blinked stark and the wetness that was coating his dark, long lashes glistened within the shadowy light of the room, I finally managed to find my voice. Next, I broke into a smile, rubbed the tip of my nose against his, and as I pressed my lips to his, I told him that, yes, I would love to marry him. His following reaction was so amazingly tender that it stripped me back to my very core.

On hearing my reply, he curled his arms around me and buried his head between my breasts. From deep within him rose a huge sob. He didn't try to hold it back. I didn't want him to contain his pent up emotions, so as his feelings left his body, it was followed by another and then, as a series of consecutive cries engulfed him, I held him in my arms for what seemed like hours. As time passed by and the moment arrived when he was drained of sentiments, his chest ceased heaving and I whispered, "Come. Let me take you to bed and we can consummate our engagement."

He nodded against me and I felt him smile against my tear-soaked chest. I rose first, reached out for him and helped him to his feet. Now both upright and facing each other, he cleared his throat and with his voice subdued, he sighed, "I wish I could carry you, my beautiful fiancée up to our bed."

I rose onto my tiptoes, draped my arms around his neck and affirmed that I wish my darling fiancée could do that too.

"I will get better," he soulfully murmured against my lips.

"I know you will. I have every faith that you will go from strength to strength." I gently kissed him back.

Next, he completely took me by surprise when I was swooped up into his arms.

"Darius, please put me down," I desperately begged. "You're going to do yourself another injury upon past injury."

Ignoring me, he began moving slowly, and carried me, albeit unsteadily towards the stairwell. While he held me firm in his embrace, he took one brave, broad step and then another, and another. Through the daggers of pain that I know were attacking right to the marrow of his hipbone, he eventually made it all the way to the top of the stairs before reluctantly having to give in. Carefully settling me onto my feet, he wobbled a tad and groaned,

"That's about as much as I can do, Helena."

Scolding him for even attempting to lift me into his arms in the first place, I exclaimed, "You shouldn't have even aimed to do that, Darius."

Nodding, he took my hand in his and pulled me into him. Snaking one hand around the back of my neck, he caressed the nape of my neck and I shivered when he called me the following; "Mrs Carter-to-be..."

"Yes, sir... What is it you wish to say?" I dreamily asked.

On hearing the word, sir, his eyes lit up with a mischievous sparkle and because of my choice of title for him, we never made it to the bedroom. Our engagement was not consummated between the silk sheets as one would've imagined but it was in fact celebrated right here on this very landing.

Chapter Six

"A *gentle* play, that during was safe, sane and before we
began it was deemed verbally consensual by us both."

'Six of the best'

Whisking the blanket from around his midriff, Darius tosses it
over the banister revealing his nakedness to me.

"T'dah!" he sings, and I laugh.

"You're completely bonkers, Mr Carter."

"I am?" he quizzes while tugging at his cock.

"Yes," I reply, while trying not to seem as if I am greedily
ogling his manhood as it rises to this special occasion of ours!

"Turn around my beautiful fiancée."

I turn, grasp onto the ornate railing directly in front of me.
Assuming a pose, I spread my legs, and while I stare at my
engagement ring, I take in a large breath.

"Are you ready for a gentle instruction into my special six
of the best, Helena?"

"I'm ready, Darius."

"What is your safe word?"

"Checkmate. Why?"

"I just need to be sure that you remember it... always."

"Why? Will I need to use it this time?"

"No, not this time for it has been quite a long time since I spanked you and we have to start soft."

"That sounds nice, a soft spanking!"

"It does?"

"Yes, it does."

"Would you prefer it if I smacked you hard until you had to use your safe word?"

"...Another time, perhaps?"

"Oh yes, Helena, there's no perhaps about it. There will be many other times after this that I can assure you of. Now be prepared because I am only going to give you a gentle teasing of my hand six times and I want you to enjoy every single one!"

"Why gentle and why six?"

"Just because..."

"If you say so..."

"I do."

And as the first light impact of his hand contacted against my left buttock, I take small jolt forward. As each following *slap* follows, he alternates from the left cheek and then to the right – also making sure that slight, arousing sensations that are warming through my skin are not positioned in any same place more than twice.

Two passes... That's barely a touch...

Three passes... Warming...

Four passes and tickles...

Five passes and I begin to wish he would make six a tad harder... Was that his plan? ...To make me crave his dominant touch?

Six passes and sadly ends.

"You are so bad making me tease you like this!" he chuckles into my ear.

"You're generally much more badly behaved more than I!" I rebuff.

Aligning his body over mine, he then slips a finger between my legs, and gently touches it against my damp folds. By hearing him sensually growling into my ear and just by his light touches alone, I have become perfectly, and suitably moist to receive him; I arouse even further. Without hesitation I then feel him rubbing the warm, sturdy crown of his cock between my dampening folds, and while I moan out at the eroticism of his actions, he in an authorative manner questions, "How much do you wish to feel me this time inside you, Helena?"

With my buttocks lightly warming, and my breathing heavy, in between several draws of air, I pant, "I want you so very, very much, sir."

Pressing his body into mine, he asks, "Why do you want me so much?"

"Because... Because... once again," I responded, "I find myself aching to the inner core for your firmer touch."

Continuing taunting me with his hardness, he then insists for me to call him by his title again, and this time please could I emphasise it with more conviction in my voice. I was then left perplexed when he added, "If you do, I may just give my entire being to you."

"Sir," I instantly answered, for the way he was mentally and physically enveloping me, I needed him right now to be inside me or I would climax without... without... his permission! His hand is now snaking around my throat and he is holding me with such tenderness while praising me. Feeling his lean muscular thighs quivering against me, as he took his pleasure, as he gave me pleasure in return, he ground into me hard, and I winced out at the deep penetration of his cock as he plunged fully into me.

"Ahh," I moaned, "Where have you been all my life!"

"I've been right here, baby," he sexily enchants. "I've always been right here waiting for you to come to me and make me whole."

I melt at his declaration and I am surprised when he gives me a sneaky seventh slap and asks, "You like?

"I love." I groaned as he bit into me, suckled hard and left his mark upon the thin flesh that coats the side of my neck.

"More?"

"Much more..."

"More of what?"

"Just more..."

"Do you wish for another slap or another love-bite?"

"Love-bite..."

A bite of love it was.

While he left a series of secret love notes buried on my shoulders, and my neck, he claimed me, he consumed me, and he filled me, not only my body with his, but on hearing his all consuming words of hard core erotica, I found myself visiting a place so dark that even I, a lover of creative words could not decipher its final venue. On the penultimate pummel of his hips against my body, his grip tightened a little around my neck, and as an airless breath escaped from my lungs, his body juddered, racked, and shook in a fashion that I have never felt before. With his cum, hot and abundant, I was flooded with spurt after spurt of his precious fluid, and my legs soon began to weaken and buckle. He sensed my imminent faltering, and moved his hand from my throat to my midriff. Holding me up, he whispered to me that I if I wished, I may now climax.

I do so very much need to let go over him.

And as I let my orgasm thrash through me, I pleaded out for him never to leave me ever again. Slumping over me, he heaved, "I will never let us separate. I promise."

Now gently aiding me to the floor, as we both crumpled into a tangled heap of a sex-drenched mess, he looked adoringly at me, and swept the damp hair that was sticking to my face to one side.

"You look one hell of a sight of a scary sigh of a mess, sweetheart. I think you need to be bathed."

I retorted, "If you think I look a mess, you should go and take a look in the mirror. You look positively horrific!"

Rolling his palm over his left hip, he moaned out at the touch, and quietly murmured to me, "I seriously think I may have just actually gone and over done it... I'm going to have to give in and take my meds, Helena."

At last.

So with that in mind, we shakily rose. He leant on me, draped his arm around my shoulder and I took the lead. With our bodies mentally and physically exhausted, we, like a pair of athletes who have just completed a marathon, headed in the direction of our bedroom.

We are now both enveloped within the soothing warmth of water of this lavish tub that graces our en suite. I lean over, take the two capsules and a tumbler of iced water from the side table, and shuffle up to Darius positioning myself between his legs. Offering the meds to him, I then wiggle the glass in front of his face. Smiling, he takes the pills and water from me.

"Go on... swallow," I request. "You know it's good for you!"

Raising his eyebrows, he amusingly chortles and breathes, "I'd much prefer it if I could watch you swallow as I…!"

Knowing full well what he is suggesting, I can't help but jest, "As you do exactly... what?"

Popping the two painkilling tablets onto his tongue, he takes glug of water, tosses his head back and I slide back to my end of the bath. Placing the empty vessel back onto the table, he relaxes, closes his eyelids while confirming to me exactly what I thought he meant by answering explicitly,

"I'd love to look down upon you while you're greedily fisting, while you are hungrily sucking away on my big, thick cock, and..." he growls with such seductiveness, " I quite honestly would be more than grateful to hear the moment when you..."

He stops end of sentence, opens his eyelids, and shoots me a dandy wink. I shake my head from side to side, and with confidence in my heart and voice, I respond, "Be careful what you wish for," I chastise, and then teasingly added – sir.

Jiggling his toes against mine, he jokes. "It's all right, sweetheart, I'll spare you that pleasure for now because quite frankly," he laughs, "I'm not really in the mood right now for a blow job!"

"Me neither." I mirror his laugh, "Anyway," I add. "Tell me, why on earth people refer to oral sex on a man as a blow job? Is it because there is a lot of huffing and puffing involved?"

He bellows out a booming laugh and floors me when he launches, "Blow jobs are slang term for fellatio, and the reason being is because in the act of performing oral sex, exhaling or blowing will ease the act of taking the penis deeper into the mouth while reducing choking or gagging reflexes!"

I quieten!

He's now placing his hands behind his head, and as he opens his other eye, he flexes his shoulders and with curiosity in his voice, he asks, "And why do you ask, Helena? Have you never performed fellatio before?"

My face reddens and I squeak with mixed words, "No, I've never done... sucked... erm... you... you... know... blown... erm... erm..."

Winking at me, he teases, "Ah, so you, you, my darling fiancée, are in fact an oral sex virgin... "

"I am."

"I must say," he grins, "that I'm very, very pleased to hear that."

I blush deeply, and ask why he's happy.

"Well, I'm pleased knowing that I will be your first... and," he then adds with firmness in his voice, "and that I will be your last."

Before he disappeared underneath the water, he stunned me by declaring, "I am so lucky to have a beautiful, blushing, cock-sucking virgin laying here in this bath with me. What an unbelievable honour!"

My cheeks heat again at the thought of the whole oral sex issue and as he pops up from beneath the water, I respond, "That's very forward of you to say, Darius. You've left me rather embarrassed by your forthright words!"

"I know..." he gleefully says. "I do so love making your skin blush! And not just that peachy arse of yours!"

Darius... You are insatiable!

Maybe you," he arches an eyebrow. "Maybe you would like to perform such an intimate act on me later, and revel in the unique flavour of my offering?"

Giggling at his words, I scoop up a handful of creamy, scented bubbles and blow them in his direction. He blows them mid air back, smiles and continues, "I can assure you once you've tasted me you will be amazed at the unique flavour of my thick, opaque fluid!"

Trying to look and sound nonchalant, I shrug, "Maybe..."

His hands now disappear beneath the water and as the water ripples around him, the purpling crown of his cock peeks at me through the surface of the bath bubbles.

"Mmmm." He arches his back, groans, breathing. "Just the mere thought of your virgin mouth sucking me and me hearing you gag as the first spurt of my fluid hits the back of your throat has got me so deeply aroused."

Oh gosh... The mere thought of performing oral sex on him is positively swaying me....

"We need plenty more bubbles, baby"

"Why?"

"Because..." he chortles, "I am going to relish in bubble-fucking my beautiful fiancée very, very shortly."

Now tittering away at his daft words, I try so hard to eradicate the thought of performing oral sex upon him. Realising that twenty minutes have passed and by now the medication should've hit the spot, I close my eyelids and dream. He sinks back down into the warm water, and lets out a replete sigh. Outstretching my hand, I press the button on the rim of the roll top bath and the jacuzzi whirrs into motion. While the bubbles increase in their volume and the delicate scent of white lily perfumes the air, I peek from underneath my lashes to see him spreading out his muscular arms out over the edge of the bath. His torso heaves strong, and the crown of his cock rises and hides within the motion of the swirling water. As the soft, spongy circumference of his purpling crown appears, I sadden as it quickly disappears under a wave of opalescent bubbles.

"Now you see it and now you don't!" he laughs with mischievousness.

I pull a miserable face, and he gives me that knowing sideways glance... That look is one that I have become so accustomed to of late. With the heavily perfumed bath oil coating and highlighting his biceps, accentuating his manly beauty, I feel a familiar tingle radiate in my hips and then collate at my centre. Pressing my thighs together, my toes move against his, and I go a little demure as I see him take a secret spy out from underneath the sexy, long eye lashes of his – I then arouse as he bats me a rather captivating wink! His voice curious, he sings, "Are you having delicious, filthy thoughts about me and my handsome cock, Helena? I do hope that you are."

I burn even further inside, and I reply, "Yes sir. I have to admit that I am having extremely erotic sexual thoughts about you at present."

"Would you care to advise me as to what they entail?"

"I'm... I'm..."

"You're what, my gorgeous, sex addict of a fiancée... Tell your sir exactly what you crave from him."

"I... I..."

"Get on with it, Helena," he coaxes. "My cock is getting very restless!"

Is there no end to this man's insatiable sexual appetite?

"Actually do you really want to know what I am thinking?"

"I do," he groans. "Inform me?"

"Well, I am actually remembering the time, back in your condo when you allowed me to first enter your personal room of pleasure."

His eyebrows shoot up and he amusingly enquires, "Are you now, my little femme-fatale? Mmm... why don't tell me all about your memory of that momentous moment."

"All right," I smile. Do you remember when I took a small step forth, and I saw the room laid out before me?"

"I do." He smirks, "You stood rooted to the spot. You looked like a freshly carved waxwork! A beautiful one, I may add."

"Yes, I suppose I must've looked rather rigid... And do you want to know the reason why I froze?"

He nods so I continue.

"It was not only the alluring fragrance infused within the air that was enticing me in, it was also the abundance of candlelight shadows that caused me to draw in a gasp of a breath. While I stood stiff, I amazed at the flickering silhouettes to and froing upon the bare walls, and something urged me to look upwards towards the ceiling."

With his face now lit up with, well, desire, he questioned, "And what did you think after you had finished looking upwards?"

"My curiosity was stimulated – heightened, and I was trying to decide what on earth those objects suspended from the intricate weave of the upper inside surface of the room were. I wondered if they were collections of *objet d'art*."

He creases a thoughtful frown at my answer, and I hide my ignorance by rapidly blurting, "I must admit, Darius, I felt a little unnerved, and a little awkward at not knowing what those material things may be, so I quickly averted my gaze to the floor beneath my feet.

Smiling he says, "But you know what they are now, and what they are for now, don't you?"

"Yes," I say. "And after you explained the following to me, I fully understood that they were wrist restraints."

Drumming his fingers on the rim of the bath, he asks, "And what else did I say?"

"You said that one of the acts that a dominant should never perform on his submissive is to suspend her from the ceiling by her wrists alone. The reason being it is impossible to do such an act to a person without causing strain, pain or injury to the submissive in play. Domination and submission is not, and I emphasize not about causing excessive hurt to the one you honour and cherish. There is so much more to domination and submission that meets the uneducated eye."

His face is now dead pan serious, and I can't help but mimic his voice and finish with… "Do you understand what I am informing you of, Helena?"

He rolls his eyes at my jest, sighs and then answers, "Well mimicked... And yes, I did say exactly that, Helena, and I must say you have an excellent memory… So tell me, what else did I say? Can you remember?"

"Yes, of course I can remember."

"Tell me then."

"I just nodded as to signal – yes, for there was not a single word I could find to express how I was feeling at that particular moment in time. Suddenly, you whirled me around and tipped your finger under my chin. While I gazed into your eyes, melting at your beauty, you focused intently upon me and thawed me to the inner core when you declared, "If I was so lucky to have you bound this way, your body would be supported beneath you either by a cushioned footstool, or if not that, then I will most definitely be cradling you within my arms."

"And what I have just described," I finish, "is what I wish for you to do to me, with me... soon."

His voice surprised, he is amazed, "You seriously want me to suspend you? You think you're ready for that step?"

"Yes," I quietly whisper, "I do."

"Why?" he perplexes. "Why do you feel the desire for me to perform this act upon you?"

"Because." I pause. "Because I'm extremely curious as to not only the outcome but what pleasure, if any it would bring to me during the... act."

"Is that the only reason, because you're eager to know and learn something new?"

"No, there are a few other reasons."

"Tell me with just one of them."

"I want to experience what is like to have no control over what you will be doing to me and my body."

"Ahh," he breathes, wistfully smiles and adds, "that is where you are wrong in your assumption."

"Wrong?"

"Yes... wrong."

"Explain why?"

"Helena, you will always have control over any situation that involves play."

"How could I possibly have the power to control if I am suspended, restrained as such, and you are cradling me?"

He shakes his head, frowns and replies, "You don't know? You haven't a single clue in that curious brainbox of yours?"

"No."

He sighs deeply and thus enlightens me... "Your safe word, Helena.... Your safe word is and always will be your highest form of control."

"Oh, yes, checkmate, I understand now..."

As my answer trailed away, he rose from the bath. While the water spewed over the rim of the Jacuzzi and spilled onto the floor, he grasped a robe from the heated towel rail, and fluffed it out to its full capacity. While he held it out for me, waiting for me to step into it, I too rose from beneath the warm bubbles, and asked, "Have the meds hit the spot, yet?"

"They've kicked in very nicely, thanks." And, as he chirped, "I think I'm good to go!" I stepped into my robe and he wrapped it around me.

While he shimmied into his gown, I asked, "Good to go where exactly?"

Chortling away to himself, he answered. "You'll see very soon."

"Oh."

"Do you know, Helena, I can't wait to entice, tease and pleasure you below decks!"

I am then informed that our personal room of pleasure is actually in the basement.

"... Really?"

"... Truly!"

"Why on earth is our playroom situated in the basement?

Turning to face me, he tips his fingers under my chin, tilts my face upwards and quietly whispers,

"Oh, my precious Helena, what am I to do with you?"

"Umm, I don't know?" I say, baffled.

Giving me a light perfunctory kiss upon my nose, he then answers, "The reason our room is designed in the basement is that when we play together, nobody would ever be able to hear your cries of dark pleasure when I do indeed bind you firm, suspend you from the ceiling and arouse, tease and finally penetrate your body..."

A startled oh escapes my lips and he creases a worried frown. Fleeting along mine, he murmurs, "By that sound you've just made, Helena, I don't believe that you are ready to embark on something a little harder than a ten mark spanking, are you?"

Not wanting to admit that I had suddenly become a little off balance by the thought of being suspended, I shrugged my shoulders and with a tone of I couldn't care less in my voice, I told him that it was now his call. I truly shouldn't have flippantly acted in that way because, he rose to my bait and this is what happened next on this Christmas night.

Interlude

'Unravel Me'

My breathing ragged, and with a blind state of euphoria encapsulating me, I pant, "Is... is... this how newly engaged couples celebrate, Darius?"

While he cradles me from behind, holding me in his grasp, he thrusts deeper into me, and as my wetness slicks over his cock, he moves his left hand from my quivering thigh. Still managing to support me with one arm, he coils his fingers around my neck, and slips a finger under the rim of the diamond encrusted choker he recently gifted me with. He pauses and as his entire body trembles powerfully against my sweat soaked back, he lowly purrs into my soul, "It's how I, your lover, your fiancée and your dominant, parties!"

Now so sexually charged and with every nerve ending I possess on fire, I outstretch my neck to the right. He lightly kisses me there, and on that soft touch of his, I moan for him to please let me climax.

"Soon, baby," he delicately whispers. You can orgasm with me very soon."

Chapter Seven

After having seen what I can only describe as *objets d'art* adorning the ceiling of our personal room of pleasure, feeling excited and breathless at what may transpire within the forthcoming scenario, I avert my gaze to a mirrored wall across the room, and my vision settles upon Darius's reflection. He looks positively carnal but so very delightful at the same time. Lolling his head upon my shoulder, he holds me firm around my waist, pushes his semi-naked torso into my back, and murmurs a rather erotic phrase into my ear. On deciphering what he actually means, with surprise in my voice, I catch my breath.

"You wish me to do what with you?"

His voice, alluring and enticingly low, responds, "I wish for you to let yourself go, loose all your inhibitions relating to sex, and for you to indulge in playing unashamedly with me, Helena. Can you let go?"

My head lightens into a whirl, as he sensually breathes, "I can't wait to see every part and piece of you unravel while I claim your body and soul for eternity."

I am quivered to the very core of my being.

"I... I... I'm not really..." I stutter and then continue to try to convey my thoughts. "I... I... I'm not..."

"You're not what, Helena?" he softly asks with a hint of disquiet in his tone.

"I don't know if... if... I could take this next step."

"Why?" he whispers to me from behind. "I promise you that if you are brave enough to take the leap, after you have experienced being suspended for the very first time, the places I have taken your body and soul to will be locations that you will crave to revisit time after time."

I look up to the ceiling, and as I whisper my safe word, checkmate, into the heavily ylang-ylang scented air, he takes two steps back from me and with his voice firm, he asks me to turn around, face him and kneel. And for some reason a wave of certainty washes over me and without any further hesitation, I slowly sink to my knees and look up at him. He smiles, down upon me, and I am immediately drawn into his aura. With the floor beneath me, I look up to Darius in a submissive fashion and he looks dominantly down upon me.

"Before we begin, Helena," he says, "I have this gut feeling that you are still not one hundred percent positive that you wish to enter into play."

"I am," I say with conviction. "I honestly am, sir."

"How sure are you?"

"Sure enough not to wish to leave this room until my curiosity has been sated."

"So you are telling me that you are only entering into this scenario just so your inquisitiveness can be satisfied?"

"No, not just my curiosity."

"Then what else are you hoping to gain from me suspending you?"

"I am hoping for... for..."

"For exactly what are you hoping?" He strokes the crown of my head. "Tell me."

"I am hoping not only to see how my body indulges and copes with an unknown sexual act, but I am hoping to please and pleasure you, sir."

He sighs loudly.

"I am now going to explain something to you that will either make you rise, walk out of the room and consider the lesson as an informative one, or it may make you remain in situ. Do you understand me, Helena?"

"Yes, sir, I understand."

"Are you fully ready to listen to me?"

"I'm ready."

"No interruptions?"

"Of course, sir... No interruptions."

After Darius had read the following rather informative and long winded manifest from his memory, while I looked up to him and *drank and digested* every word that fell from his lips and after he had finished his reciting, I chose to remain in situ.

"Helena, the common dictionary states that safe is to be secure from liability to harm, injury, danger or risk. In this context, Dominants and submissives see safe bondage and discipline, sadism and masochism (BDSM) as taking care of their partner so that no matter how intense the scene may be, no unwanted injury, transfer of danger or disease will occur. All precautions must be taken to minimise any potential dangers. This means doing research and being knowledgeable about the chosen kinky activities we desire to partake upon. In order to be safe, you must know the risks of BDSM and which activities add spice so to speak without causing permanent or lasting damage to the emotional, mental or physical sate of either me, the dominant (top) or you, the submissive (bottom)."

He takes a breather and continues, "Through the BDSM lens, dominants and submissives must act responsibly and exercise good judgement at all times. The ability to engage in an appropriate self control is a big part of the 'sane' portion of this philosophy. If you cannot control yourself, you should not, and I repeat, not enter into a situation where power exchange is a key respect. BDSM should not be used as a solution for serious psychological conditions or mental health concerns; playing with a partner where one person has some deep rooted concerns can trigger emotional releases that neither person is able to handle within the boundaries of the BDSM scene in play."

He pauses momentarily and then resumes into his final speech.

"Consensual – giving informed consent.

"The importance of it being consensual is paramount to keep within the BDSM ethics and ensure that this relationship of ours is a healthy one where both partners are supported by each other. If consent is not obtained by either of us prior to play, then it is not only damaging to our relationship but it can point to an abusive dynamic. It is important that consent is obtained prior every single session we choose to embark upon and most certainly never and not during or after play has ended and after care is about to be brought into the scene. This is particularly important because when endorphins are running hot from play, neither you nor I will be able to make sound decisions and by this, we will fail to think through the situation with sensibility. Do you understand all, and I mean everything that I have spoken about here, Helena?"

"Yes, I do."

"Sure?"

"I'm very sure."

"Do you wish to exit the room?"

"No, I don't."

"I shall ask you one more time. Do you wish to leave the room?"

"No," I reply with firmness, "I do not wish to leave the room."

"Then let us begin."

So on asking me to rise to my feet, I rose to meet him. Wanting to drape my arms around him and have a romantic interlude before my suspension, I remembered that I was now in submissive mode and the man standing tall in front of me was not at present just my glorious lover, he was in fact, my educator, my mentor, and more importantly so, he *is* my gentle dominant, so I adopted my submissive stance with pride and waited for his first requirement.

"Give me your hand."

I did. After he had aided me in stepping up onto the pouffe, he took his place behind me, and slowly peeled my robe from around me to reveal my semi-clad person. Seeing myself in the floor-to-ceiling mirror opposite, something dark, something so powerfully sexual and highly erotic surged through my veins. Am I becoming reminiscent of the hidden me? As he ran his fingers over my left hand, he lingered over my engagement ring, and he broke his dominancy by sensually whispering into my ear, "You look amazing, Mrs Carter-to-be."

I responded by jumping out of my submissive stance, and replying, "Thank you, Mr Carter, and so do you."

Nodding in agreement, and while his fingers move to my throat, he slowly pats them over the thin leather choker that is gracing my neck. Drumming away, a low grating sound rises from the back of this throat and I quiver inside at that manly sound of his. Trailing his fingers down my sides, he slides them over my hips only to pause when he reaches the lace-tops of my silk hold-up stockings. While aiding me in parting my legs, he caresses the insides of my thighs, and I moan with delight at his touch and lounge back into his bare chest. Again he turns from dominant into lover.

"You like, baby?" he whispers.

"I like." I change from submissive into lover, and softly breathe.

Nuzzling his face into the side of my neck, he nips the leather strap secured around my neck, and morphs back into a dominant by instructing, "Raise your arms, and place your wrists, pulse side, flush together."

While the fresh, floral top notes of his cologne combine with the scent of his freshly showered persona envelopes me, I close my eyes and do as he has asked. On feeling the *objet d'arte* make contact around my wrists, I shudder at the coldness of the man-made bracelet that is now chilling my now quickening pulse. Now restrained by him, with his tone equally cool as the cuff that is binding me, his voice so low, he asks, "Comfortable?"

"Erm, I about as comfortable as one can be when one is trussed up like a prize trophy!" I nark, and then as he sighs out loud, I quickly remember to address him as, 'sir'.

Next, I look dead pan ahead and stare into the mirror. Seeing him without a hint of decipherable expression upon his face, I hear him mutter under his breath, "Trophy... That's a very interesting choice of word, Helena. Why did you choose it?"

"I don't... don't know, sir. It just popped into my mind."

"Mmm… however, it manifested from that complex mind of yours, and I must say I like that word very much indeed."

I go to speak but as I open my mouth, his hand comes around to the front of my face and he slides his middle finger between my lips and drawls, "Suck."

I do just that, suck while imagining that his finger is in fact the girth of his pulsating cock. As I revel in my private, erotic thoughts, I whimper as he begins to stroke me between the legs.

"You like?"

"I like."

Taunting me with the lightness of his touch, my legs start to quiver, and my lashes close. With my neck outstretched, into my ear, he devilishly suggests, "You're imagining that my finger that is stroking your swelling nub is in fact the tip of my cock that is seeped with pre-cum, aren't you? You are aching to feel the warmth of my fluid flooding your tight, plush pussy, aren't you?" Withdrawing his middle finger from my mouth, he asks me to answer him promptly.

"Yes I am, sir."

"Perfect… Now, that's enough pleasuring for you for the moment. I want you to keep your silence unless asked."

I nod.

"Now focus upon the mirror because I want to you to see and to remember every single thing that I am going to do to, with you. Now, take a deep breath for we are about to commence."

"Lights!" he snaps.

What?

With my lungs now full to capacity of the scent of ylang-ylang that has been infusing the air, as I go to exhale, suddenly the room falls into blackness and it is, after several moments of me feeling disorientated, relit by one stark beam of light. As it warms me from above, my heart begins to gather speed. I drop forward and dip my head. While my chin rests on my décolletage, I feel him caressing my pony tail and I am taken by surprise when he jerks my head back and reminds me to keep looking dead ahead. While I do, and his grip lessens on my hair, I hear his voice, deep, snapping the word, 'play'. I begin to feel extremely confused at what is meant by the latter. Breaking silence, I ask, "Play what?"

Another tug on my hair occurs and he rumbles, "Hush, hush, hush, Helena... I didn't ask you a question, did I?"

No... No... sir, you didn't, but I want to converse with you.

Before he sank his teeth into my shoulder, leaving his love note imprinted deep within my flesh, and I yelped out, he grated into my ear, "What do you say now to your dominant, my precious?"

Taking a sharp intake of breath, I answer, "I'm sorry, sir, for speaking when not asked."

Another yank of my hair follows and he softly enquires, "Tell me exactly what you apologising for."

With the mark on my shoulder now burning in my flesh, I morph again, and I can't help but sarcastically quip, "That's not a question, Darius!"

With a final, forceful wrench of my ponytail, my head jolts to the left and he slaps me hard on the arse, while deeply growling, "You're pushing the limits here, Helena. Now answer me or I will take an unrestrained liberty with you."

"I'm sorry for speaking out of turn, sir," I say dripping with sarcasm.

A too long of a pregnant pause follows and I begin to wonder as to his response. When he finally speaks, I rise on my tiptoes and my arms begin to quiver.

"Very well, Helena. Forget again, and I will have to punish you accordingly."

Yes, sir, Thank you, sir! Three bags full sir!

"In answer to your question, Helena, 'play' is the voice recognition for the recording of this erotic lesson in your art of submission."

Oh how wonderful sir! I can't wait to watch it back!

I am now supported by him, and I feel him fumbling behind me. Realizing that he is unbuttoning his jeans, as I try to push my buttocks into him, wanting to feel him pulsating against me, he lets out a throaty chuckle, and lightly pushes me away from him. As I swing back and my body brushes against his, he cups me under my buttock, holding me firm. I am then cradled by him. Resting his left foot upon the pouffe for balance, within a blinding flash, he has driven his cock deep as deep into me, and I fill with joy at the surprise of his swift motion. While he begins teasing me, arousing me further by licking the curvature of my outstretched neck, I moan out at the sensation of his thick, veined cock that is powering into me in a series of sharp, short bursts.

"Darius..."

"Shhh..."

While he slithers his tongue over the choker that is claiming me around my neck and with such softness in his voice, he tells me, "You're so very beautiful, Helena."

Thank you

"Now keep your eyes forward and watch as we now evolve into a pair of wild, crazed sexual animals."

I break silence again and ask, "How wild, sir?"

"Shhh, Shhh, Shhh," he soothes, "Not another single word or I am afraid that I will have to release you from your restraints and regretfully leave us both wanting."

Yes sir.

"While I continue claiming you," he says, "in a moment you will feel something explosive internally and externally consume you."

I do indeed erupt when a sudden sting impacts on my centre. As the pain radiates through to my inner core, my eyelids drag and I am immediately stricken again alerting me to flick my lashes open.

"Keep those peepers open, precious or you will forfeit the game."

Now watching him grind his hips into me, his hair is damp and the concentration on his face is so prominent, so wolfish that his glaring eyes are all I can focus upon. I don't see me, I just see him wildly penetrating, claiming my body. As lash after lash of the thin leather crop proceeds, on the ninth strike of the bulb upon my swollen nub, I mentally prepare for saying my safe word. Through my misty peepers, I again survey the scenario in the mirror and as our concurrent climaxes rip through us, for me, as the room falls away, my arms and legs tremor, and I can do nothing more but slump back into his heaving, sweat-soaked chest. While a feeling of euphoria, a feeling of exhilaration surrounds me, he quickly frees me from my restraints and as my arms drop like two heavy lead weights to my sides, my knees buckle, and I sink forward, falling onto all fours onto the pouffe. He lovingly wraps his arms around me, holds me gentle but strong and we both slither onto the oak floor beneath. Now draped in his lap, my skin sticking to his, he bows his head to me, presses his forehead to mine and

I am stunned when he continually repeats over and over to me – "Thank you."

No - Thank you, sir!

As I take some time to regain some sort of normality, he separates from me, and moves away. I look up from the floor beneath me, to see that he is now across the room from me and is seated a leather batwing chair. His head is flung back, and his mass of dark curls is an alluring mess of a wild wanton, creativity! His body is outstretched to its fullest capacity. While I survey him under the second spotlight of this room, I quell to my core when I notice that his taut torso is drenched in minuscule beads of over exertive moisture. On seeing the warm, salty trails of liquid run down the centre of his chest, as it pools in the dip of his tummy-button, I feel something deep within me burn so torridly that I have to try so very hard to eradicate the images in my mind that depict me taking complete control of him. His breathing has returned to its base rhythm.

On seeing him shift position, as he leans forward, and rests his elbows upon his knees, my body shudders, and I keep him within my hold. While I watch him place his palms flush together, he nestles the crook of his chin in his hands, and I am too held within his unfaltering and magnetic gaze. With devout gentleness in his voice; he breaks the silence by softly informing me that I should come over to be with him. I quite simply rise from my position and head towards him. Every physical part and piece of me is aching from my recent suspension. (Including the reminding of 'who-I-belong-to-soreness' that is intermittently throbbing between my upper thighs.) So as I falter a little en route, he changes his position, and perches on the edge of his seat. I think he may be intending to stand up and meet me halfway. Is he going to aid me on my short journey over to him? No, for he chooses to remain seated. Now sitting proud, he pats his left knee, rubbing his palm over the rip in the left knee of his jeans, and I assume that that is the signal for where he wishes me to rest. Settling upon his lap, as I snuggle into his chest, he coils his arms around me and while I inhale the heavy, thick, post-sex scent of his person, I whisper to him my eternal thanks of gratitude. Tenderly stroking my hair, he breathes into my damp tresses, "You are grateful for exactly what, Helena?"

While a small squeak escapes from my soul, I murmur against his chest, "I am appreciative for you unravelling my deepest inhibitions... I am thankful for you firmly coercing my body and soul into embracing a whole new sensual level of... of... love, sir."

He sighs deeply with what I can only describe as a sense of replete calmness, and while he rises with me cradled in his arms, I dissolve to the strings of my heart when he declares, "It is not you who should be grateful, Helena, for you are the rarest gift of submission a dominant could ever hope to enrapture. I am truly enamoured by you. So you see, my precious," he finishes, "it is I, your dominant, your lover and your future husband, that should and always will be the one thanking you... I will always convey to you the politest expressions of gratitude because you are the one and only true, beautiful person that I will ever, ever adore."

I'm left replete by not only my euphoric suspension but also by the honesty and the integrity of his latter words.

Interlude

'Love in an after mist.'

Curling into Darius, as I listen to the strong metronomic rhythm of his heartbeat lulling me into a trance-like stake, as its timely rhythm sends me drunk on the mind-altering ramifications of after-love, I flicker my lashes open. On seeing the hues of the late morning's haze, peeking through the shimmering grey voiles that grace our four-poster bed, while each soft, ray of calming light, cossets us both in Mother Nature's innocent glory, I am left feeling as if I am actually laying on the damp grass of an early spring's meadow surrounded by an abundance of tiny blue flowers, and I am not actually laying replete upon the sex-infused, crumpled silk sheets that lay scrunched and tousled beneath us. Closing my eyelids, I envisage that each tiny floral creation is enveloped in its own individual thread-like, green bract, and I as I do, I know that I will always be entwined for eternity with Darius, dreamily swathed in the never-ending allure of his delicate dominance.

Chapter Eight

Boxing Day ~ Popcorn and Dom Perignon

Languishing on Darius's bare chest, I relax into him, and take a generous sip of Dom Perignon champagne. Placing my chilled flute down onto the side table, as the delicate flavour of the liquid warms me inside, I place my hands together. Upturning my palms like I am opening a book, I survey the blemishes that have been left imprinted around the circumference of each of my wrists. While I do, Darius runs his hands down my forearms and breathes into my ear, "Oh dear... I'm really sorry that there are marks left imprinted upon your neck and wrists."

"It's fine," I dreamily say. "They'll fade in time."

"Tell me, how are you feeling really, Helena?"

"I must admit," I answer, "that I am feeling a little tender in some areas... some more than others."

"Mmm..." he trails, "Any particular place more delicate than the other?"

I shake my head from side to side. He in response leans around me and gives me such a sensual, sexy look – a look that I have become so accustomed of late, that I do believe that I may know exactly what he is thinking.

"Well, Helena?" he asks while planting a series of delicate kisses all down the side of my love bitten neck.

"Stop it!" I ask at his next touch.

"I don't want to stop," he breathes into my ear. "I never want to stop pleasuring you."

"And I never want you to but right now I have to tell you that I can't possibly take any more *punishment* sex or even the delicious, sweet vanilla sex today."

"Shame." He sighs while stroking my hair in a loving fashion, and I finish, "Even though I adore having either rough or soft sex with you, at present, I have to give in to defeat and declare that I'm dead beat after you had to have me again this morning!"

"Ahh..." he breathes, "love-in-an-after-mist."

It's as if he has just read my mind.

Wrapping his arms around me, he nips my earlobe and I shiver as he lightly murmurs, "Good... So I am done in too!"

"Are you truly replete?" I ask, knowing full well that this man of mine's sexual appetite for me could never be sated

He chuckles under his breath, "Kind of!"

"I thought so," I breathe. "I love you, Darius," I then lazily say.

"I love you too... So how about this for an idea? How about we do something sensible instead of considering me banging you senseless again?"

See, he's never sexually replete where I am concerned.

"Like what? What do you suggest?"

"I propose that we eat!"

"Eat?"

"Yes, eat!"

As he slithers out from behind me, he leaps up and nearly bowls me over in his quest to provide me with food.

"Where are you going?" I ask to his muscle rippling bare back.

He rubs his hip and replies, "I am going to find my love-bitten queen some food."

While I watched him slowly amble off in the direction of the kitchen, I hoped that he would while there take his meds. Minutes later he returned wheeling what I can only describe as a maid's serving trolley. As he pushed it to a halt, I noticed that laid out upon the surface were two bowls heaped high with a mountain of popcorn. I inhaled and my tummy rumbled for I was in much need of a welcoming sugar rush. Next, he bent down, placed a bowl into my lap and said that I definitely sounded like I needed to eat! I did. Finally, he settled opposite me too with his flute of champagne but no snack. As we slipped into this quiet moment, the soothing sound of the fire crackling merrily away in the hearth, I watched as his lips curled around the rim of the glass. Mesmerized at him slowly taking a sip of the cool pale liquid as I watched his eyelids close and him revel in savouring the taste, I warmed inside. Next, on seeing his Adam's apple move in response to his swallow, I couldn't help but let out an obvious sigh. Placing his drinking vessel onto the stone floor that surrounds the hearth, he swept the rogue corkscrew of a curl that was dangling over his right eye to one side, and asked, "So, Helena, tell me all about your life before you had the glorious fate of falling head over heels in love with a devilishly handsome, and sexy screen god that is called me!"

I looked up from my bowl of toffee coated delights and our eyes locked. Giggling girlishly at his words, I replied, "Well Mr Carter, I must divulge that my life was pretty much normal... It was how shall I say, sedate and serenely uncomplicated to say the very least until the moment when you signed my premiere programme."

His eyebrows shot up, and quickly dropped into what I can only describe as a thinking frown. While I carried on chomping on the knobbly morsels that were sticking to each other in the bowl, I halted eating when he tentatively enquired, "Do you like the changes that have occurred in your lifestyle since we met?"

Glancing at the ring on my finger, I smiled widely, looked up directly at him, and placed the bowl onto the carpeted floor in front of me. Wiggling my ring finger at him, I responded, "Yes I do. Do you?"

He broke into a boyish grin, and told me that yes he does like the changes that have evolved since we met very much indeed. Picking up my bowl, I offered it to him and asked, "Want some? They taste lush!"

He leant forward, dipped his thumb and forefinger into the bowl, and extracted a popcorn. Tossing it high, high up in to the air, as it plopped into his lap, he looked down at it and while his mass of thick curls tumbled over his face, he chuckled, "Not as lush as you taste!"

I shake my head at hearing his sexual retort, and am focused again upon him when he suggests, "I bet you, my queen, a delicious, long, tongue entwining and extremely long, lingering kiss, that I can catch the next popcorn in my mouth!"

"Bet on!" I smile. "I would love to give a kiss to my King!"

Again he leans forward, again dips his thumb and forefinger into the bowl, and extracts another popcorn. Tossing it up in to the air, I watch as the light brown corn reaches its peak, and then begins to descend. I rouse him, "I bet you anything you won't be able to catch it!"

Within a split second he is laying flat on his back with his mouth wide open, and said popcorn has made it, landing! It is in fact balancing right upon the tip of his tongue! While he closes his mouth, and noisily munches away, he rolls onto his side, swallows loudly and turns to face me while winking, "I told you so!"

"Yes, you did," I admit with joyous defeat.

"So considering that I've very easily won the bet, how about you come close to me, and bestow me with that owing kiss?"

Before I could answer him, within a flash, he had me beneath him. Firstly he took my left arm and stretched it above my head, repeating this action with my right arm. Pressing his body into mine, as I revelled in feeling his cock twitch through his sweatpants, he groaned, "I just can't get enough of you, Helena. You strip me of all my hard trained, discipline. You have become like a drug to me, and I constantly need fix after fix of you... You... you..." he whispers into my parted lips, "you my darling, are my rush!"

Responding to him that he too is my lustful medicine, as he dips his tongue into my mouth, and while the taste of his sweet popcorn infuses me, he slips his hands underneath my buttocks, and hushes over and over that right now, he truly needs to be inside me. I too need him. As the moment unravels, we discard our clothes and without another word spoken lose ourselves within each other's bodies. Slowly, passionately and with such a timely rhythm he brings us both to the precipice of our climaxes. He pauses, stares intently at me and utters to me one word. On hearing the word 'Mine' my body quakes and quivers over him in an uncontrollable fashion, and as I breathe 'Yours' into his mouth, we simultaneously release the most powerful, earth shattering orgasms. The only sound apart from the crickle crackles of the fire that was left to be heard was the ins and outs of two people's breathing returning to their normal resting state. Rising and resting upon his elbows, he kisses me lightly on the tip of my nose and sweetly whispers, "I bet you..."

"No... No... No..." I protest, "Please, no, not another bet, Darius. I for one am totally spent."

Nuzzling into me, he soothes, "Too bad, baby, because I bet you my heart and my soul for eternity that by the way we both climaxed if you weren't on the contraceptive pill we would've just created a new life."

Stroking his damp tresses, as I toy with the rogue curl at the base of his neck, I dreamily reply, "If I wasn't on the pill and we had created a life, would you want to get married before or after the baby was born?"

"Why do you want to know such a thing?"

"I think it is kind of wrong to have a child out of wedlock, don't you?"

Rolling off me, we both roll onto our sides and gaze at each other.

Propping himself up on his elbow, he says, "You surprise me, Helena."

"Why?"

"Because..." He breaks into a warming smile, "You're so very old fashioned in your thoughts, and so very..."

"What's wrong with being old fashioned?" I interrupt.

"Oh nothing... Nothing at all.... I find your thoughts, your values and your ideas very refreshing indeed."

"So now we have established that you like the way in which I tick, what do you say to the possible idea of getting married soon anyway?"

His face full of amusement, he laughs, draws back from me a little. "I'll consider your offer of getting wed soon if you ask me for a kiss."

"Kiss me, Darius?"

While his eyes twinkled in such a mesmerising way, as he leant into me and brushed his lips along mine, I became enraptured and enamoured by the response that fell from his lips.

Chapter Nine

Monday 8 January 2018

Six a.m.

The Condo/ Lift – London

After completing the tenth and final lap of this luxurious swimming pool that graces Darius condo, I climb the three steps up the ladder and look up to see Darius standing before me. He looks like he could do with a shower down after his daily morning workout! Taking a pristine white, Egyptian cotton towel from the top of the pile, he fluffs it out and offers it to me. I accept. Wrapping it around me, I snuggle into its softness and say, "Feeling good after some non-sexual exertion, Darius?"

"Oh, I always feel good after exercise, sexual or otherwise." He winks and then adds, "Actually, Helena, right now I'm feeling on top of the world... And how about you? How are you feeling today?"

"Great!"

While I pat my arms and legs dry, he perplexes me by stating, "You do know how important it is for you to keep fit don't you?"

"Of course I do... What a daft question!"

"It's not daft," he huffs, "it's a very sensible question."

"Well isn't it obvious that one should look after their body?"

"Yes it is, Helena, but this particular question of mine has a double edged meaning."

Almost warmed and dry, I continue, "Illuminate me as to what you mean then."

Rubbing his workout towel around the back of his neck, he launches, "You should not only keep fit for your own well being, but it is imperative that you exercise daily because when we do enter into a more intense form of D/s play it is imperative that we are both fit and healthy."

"Why?"

"To be unfit and unhealthy could result in not only physical and mental traumas but it could also result in low stamina levels and thus ending play before the euphoric rise takes you over and you enter the next undiscovered sexual level."

"Understood, and duly noted, sir!" I reply with a smattering of flippancy in my voice.

Lunging at me, he holds me firm around my waist, and as the scent of his raw manliness enraptures my senses, he whispers into my ear, "Don't be so lax with me, Helena."

"Why?"

"Just, don't" he repeats, with a smattering of a warning tone trailing through his voice.

Puzzled, I reply, "I'm not being inattentive with you."

"It doesn't sound that way to me."

Diffusing the situation, I ask, "Kiss me?"

Drawing back from me, he narrows his gaze, and slithers his towel from around his neck. I am now looking to his left hand. The towel is pinched tight between his thumb and forefinger, and is moving in such a way that I visualise that it is in fact a flogging implement and not the towel that is being held in that grip of his. He just glares at me in such a way, I begin to excite inside. Not breaking eye contact with him, I drop my towel to the floor. Next, still holding him in my gaze, I peel down the straps of my Speedo swimming costume, and shimmy it down past my breasts, revealing my erect nipples. He takes in a whoosh of breath and I note that the bulge in his groin is increasing in its volume. Next, I loosen my costume down over my waist and hips, and finally past my buttocks. Stepping out of the clingy, black, Lycra fabric, I then stand upright. I am now naked before him, and him, well he has that sensual, dark, wolfish aura surrounding him.

"What would sir like me to do?" I lead. "Would he like me to kneel before him? Or would he prefer it if I bent over the chaise lounge over there? Or would he actually prefer it if I met him later on in our personal room of pleasure?"

I am astounded when he replies, "None of those... I wish for you do to none of those things."

"But... but... I stutter, I thought... I thought... you wanted to chastise me for being remiss with you."

Offering me another fresh, warm towel, I take it from him and while I cover my nakedness, he astounds me by answering, "I don't want to reprimand you for being heedless with me."

"But I thought by the way you were looking at me, and the way in which your digits were twitching, I thought you... you...wanted to spank me."

"Oh, I did and I still do, Helena."

"Then what's gone wrong? Why are you not taking me as you wish?"

He steps close to me, places his finger under my chin and angles my face up to him. "My dear, sweet, Helena, I love you so much."

"I love you too," I reply with confusion. "But why won't you..."

After kissing me lightly, he explains, "Right now I would like nothing more than to caress that beautiful peachy arse of yours in between each stinging whip of my towel."

"So why won't you?"

"Right now I have no choice but to exercise my control, my discipline."

"Why?"

"Quite simply because today we go back to work and you having a smarting bottom all day long wouldn't bode well for you now would it?"

"I guess not... But it would remind me of whom I belong to."

He chuckles with glee at my statement and while he says, "Yes... You do belong to me," he snakes his hand around the back of my neck. He holds me firm and finishes, "But later tonight, I have just decided that you will be either horsewhipped or sated in such a manner that you will be left..."

I shudder at hearing the word *horsewhipped* and I enquire, "Left what?"

"You will be left wanting, left needing and left craving to delve a little deeper into the world, the world of BDSM."

"So what you're actually saying to me is that my punishment, whatever it is, will be more intense, more severe than of late?"

"No, it will be none of those things."

Baffled, I groan. "Then what are you trying to say to me? I truly don't understand."

"I can't explain it. You have to experience it with me to understand exactly what I mean."

Exasperated at him, I quietly ask, "You won't hurt me. Will you?"

Aghast he replies, "No, you know I wouldn't ever hurt you and you also know that BDSM is not about causing pain or injury to the submissive in play, don't you?"

"Yes I do."

"So now we have gone all around the houses and are back to square one, how about a shower together before we take breakfast?"

"Which would you prefer?" I smile, "A romantic showering experience together, or a just-fuck-me-until-I-can't-take-no more-shower?"

"I'd like the former," he wistfully breathes against my lips.

"Sure?"

"Sure."

The former it was.

Seven-forty-five a.m.

As the lift descends, I look to Darius who is casually leaning up against the shiny, steel wall. He looks so attractive this morning – actually he looks captivating and charismatic every single morning if truth be told! Not only is it his stunning facial features that always mesmerize me, it's his whole stance – his entire aura. Today he has chosen to go casual and is wearing the following: a dark blue, baseball cap with no logo, a long sleeved, black t-shirt and black drainpipe jeans. A heavy weave, midnight blue coloured pea coat hides his taut body.

He has accessorised it with a soft, azure blue, cashmere scarf which drapes in folds around his neck. On his feet is a pair of Bottega Veneta camel suede Chelsea boots.

"You look far too sexy dressed like that." I smile. "You'll be turning heads as soon as we walk out of here together."

"I know," he says with an air of confidence. "I look like a man of deep, dark mystery don't I?" He grins broadly while popping on a pair of dark, tinted Porsche sunglasses. "And I must say Helena," he then removes his eyewear, "From where I am standing you look pretty hot too... actually you look like you need to climax again!"

I do?

And then as he slowly bats his long, curly, dark lashes at me, and adds, "It won't be me that will turn heads when we make contact with the world, it will be you."

I smile at his kindness, for I know that he will really be the one who turns the heads of both men and women... *It has to go without saying really - doesn't it?*

"Tell me, Helena; are you by any chance wearing a pair of cock-hardening stockings underneath that sensible woollen dress of yours?"

Pursing my lips, I momentarily pause and then reply, "Maybe... I am... Or maybe I'm not!"

Stuffing his glasses into the top pocket of his coat, he gives me that knowing look, and within a flash he is upon me. Both my arms he has grasped, causing me to drop my handbag to the floor. Quickly pinning my hands above my head, he pushes his body into mine, and with such a low, throaty growl, asks, "Are you?"

"I might be!"

"Answer me you little temptress!"

"Why don't you go ahead and find out for yourself?"

"Answer me!" His voice is stern but rather playful at the same time."

"Maybe..." I tease.

"Helena!" he grumbles, "Tell me..."

I narrow my gaze at him and reply, "Yes, Oh Great One, I am!"

"Fuck, baby," he breathes into my mouth. "How am I supposed to make it through the entire day knowing that you are dressed so sexily underneath your wintery work frock?"

"I guess you'll just have to try very hard not to think about me then, won't you," I retort triumphantly.

"Impossible." He drawls along my lips while sliding his hand up my thigh. On feeling my garter belt through the fabric of my dress, he moans,

"I need, and I... what I mean... what I want is to see you thrash out an orgasm for me right now... I want to linger upon the memory all day long...The vision of you coming undone right here in this lift!"

"No..." I mildly protest. "No, not here. I can't possibly do that!"

"I can halt the elevator," he says with toying mischief. "You only have to say you will let me make you climax and I will punch the button!"

"No, baby..." I try to wiggle free from his grasp. "It's... I... I can't...."

"There's no such word in our vocabulary as 'can't, is there?"

"No, there isn't." I sag with a little smattering of defeat.

"You don't want me?" He says in a little-boy-lost manner which actually makes me want him even more.

"I always want you."

Now mentally arousing me, with his words, he nips my ear lobe and whispers, "Even though you had me before breakfast?"

"Yes, even though I had you before breakfast."

I bleat at his, well just him, and as he slips his finger into the side of my panties, rimming the lace trim, I shiver. "I had you, as you so eloquently put it, less than an hour ago and not only am I a little tender between my legs, if I let you touch me again, I know that I'll never make it into work today!"

His face lights up. "Exactly how tender are you?"

"Sensitive enough that every time I move today, I shall be reminded of you."

"Good." He nips my bottom lip, while performing a, how shall I say, check to make sure that I am indeed a little delicate between my thighs.

"Ahh ...." I whisper between his warm, spaced lips. "Darius.... Please... No... Yes... No... Yes... No."

"Yes or no, Helena, which is it? Do you want me to bring you off before this lift lands? Make a snap choice, Helena."

I ponder briefly and then let out a long, drawn breath. "Yes," I can't help but shamelessly admit. "You have me... take me?"

Devilishly smiling at me he extends one arm, and punches the halt button hard.

"Pull that delicious, sensible day wear panty of yours to one side and let me play with what is mine."

I do and he begins...

Crushing his lips to mine, as he begins to work me with his fingers, I take no time in reaching the precipice of my orgasmic peak for it is not just the physical act that's making me ache to come so quickly; it was the following words he said during his labours.

"Just the mere thought of the scent of your musky sex lingering on my fingers... Just the mere thought of when I am in a script reading and your horny fragrance envelopes me... All this... you... your lust, your love for me is now making my cock so fucking rock hard, that I promise you, I am going to have to jerk off before we get out of this lift!"

"You wouldn't dare!" I bear down upon his fingers and mewl. "You... you wouldn't do such a thing, would you?"

"Yes, I would and I will... Well actually," he muses, "I am going to have to because my balls are aching hard for a release!"

"Baby, please..." I wail..."Make me climax right now!"

"It will be my pleasure," he murmured against my trembling lips.

With his thumb now circling my swollen clit and my wetness slicking over his digits, I came, hard and fast and all I could do was slump to the floor and fade into recovering from my surprise climax. He then leant back against the wall, promptly unbuttoning his jeans and I was stunned as he sassily winked at me and then extracted his cock from within the confines of its dark holdings. I look to him and panted, "You're not... You're seriously not going to masturbate in here are you?"

"Yes, I am," he replied without a hint of shame. "And I'm going to relish in performing this act of erotica right in front of your very eyes!"

"You're so very badly behaved, Darius!" I reprimand.

"I know."

Next, he smiled widely and I searched in my handbag for a pack of intimate wipes. As I located them and extracted a single tissue, again I looked over to him. He, the impish devil is already in the throes of masturbation!

"Do you want me to...?" I offer.

"To what?" he interrupts and growls through his teeth while roughly fisting his cock like it needed a firm punishing!

"To assist you...?" I reply while readjusting my attire. "Would you like me to suck you off or join you in that rather vigorous and sensuous bout of hand-fucking you appear to be performing like a man possessed?"

"No!" he snaps, while cupping his balls in his right hand. "I want you to watch me and watch me only!"

"But... But... I..." I protest.

"No buts!" he hisses and I adhere.

Now standing, I was left amazed at his display, and while his eyelids fluttered and flittered and tiny beads of moisture began to form along his upper lip, his lips curled up in the most delectable 'O' and as his pace increased up his thick, veined shaft, I couldn't help but wish that that beast of a cock of his was actually sliding in and out of me and not just being pleasured within his large hand!

"Oh my, Darius." I stepped towards him, and placed my hand over his. Let me..."

He was now somewhere else and as I began moving my hand in time with his, I encouraged, "You look so beautiful like this... Come in my hand? I want to feel you spill over us both."

"Yesssss..." he drawled with such a sexual deviance. "Yesssss... one more touch from you baby and I will spill!"

Rising onto my tiptoes, I pressed my lips to his and dipped my tongue into his warm mouth. While the fresh, minty taste of his morning routine tingled upon my tongue, he snaked his hand around the back of my neck, breathed into my mouth that any moment now, he was going to give us both a luxurious treat and he was extremely close to exploding."

"Let it go, baby," I coaxed.

And as he did, his thighs trembled against my svelte body, he racked, "You made me do this! You made me be so bold! Fuck, Helena, you strip me bare."

"I did? I do?" I kiss him again.

"Yes, you did. You make me lose all discipline, Helena. You make me lose all self control... You are deliciously dangerous and I am never going to let you go..."

"Good," I reply, while slowing my hand in time with his, "Good... because I don't want you to ever let me go."

Now with his breathing decreasing, He releases me from his hold and I take a step backwards.

"Fuck, baby." He sheepishly grins while looking down at his deflating manhood, "You've just managed to not only empty my balls but also to blow my mind!"

Extracting two wipes, I offer him one. While he takes it, I bite the corner of my bottom lip while cleansing my hand on a fresh wipe and say, "You, Mr Carter have blown my mind too with your unashamed lift antics!"

"You can always rely on me to expand and elevate the impossible!" He chuckles.

I roll my eyes at his choice of words, and he smiles beautifully at me but a tad too triumphantly! After we have both cleansed ourselves and readdressed our attire, he dangles his wipe in the air and chuckles. "So you bad, bad girl, what do you propose we should do with these used wipes?"

Tut-tutting him, I try to swipe it from his fingers. "Give them to me, I'll dispose of them."

Snatching it out of my reach, I simper when he finishes, "No, I'll do it." He then wickedly chortles and stuffs them into his coat pocket!"

Shaking my head from side to side, as he punches the halt button and the lift swings back into motion, he floors me by saying that this lift is now full of the scent of our post masturbatory sex!

Yes it is! Whoops-a-daisy!

Before the doors opened, he placed his sunglasses on, yanked his baseball cap down over his eyes, grasped my hand in his and like he was hiding from trouble, he hushed, "Quick, quickly, Helena, when the doors open, we have to make a run for it!"

I giggle. "Why on earth do you suggest that we have to run for it?"

"Because we've left the scent of our sex lingering within the confines of the lift... You and I, well between us, I think we both may have committed a very naughty sexual crime!"

"You think so?" I titter again.

"Oh, Helena," he laughs. "We just may have been caught on camera in the act!"

"Oh my goodness..." I gasp with shock. "You are not serious."

As the lift doors separate, I glance to the camera in the corner.

Its red light is blinking!

Boo! We've got you!

So without another moment's hesitation we squeezed each other's hand tight, and scarpered out of the foyer. On heading towards car that was already waiting for us parked outside alongside the kerb, he teased, "You my queen are a very bad girl leading me astray back there!"

"And you," I jested back, "Are a very wolfish and very naughty king indeed!"

"I know, I am... And you love me like this!"

I do!

137

Chapter Ten

Eight-forty-five a.m.

Pulling up alongside the pavement, Darius switches off the engine, applies the handbrake and turns to face me. "Are you feeling all right, Helena, after our lift shenanigans?"

"I'm very all right, thank you Darius. And you?"

"I'm perfect!"

Yes you are....

"Do you think we were recorded? As we fled, I noticed that the red light on the camera was flashing."

"Yes."

"Oh."

"Don't fret."

"Why?"

"I shall have the tape erased within a flash!"

"How will you do that?"

"By working my subtle magic!"

"What do you mean, by working your subtle magic?"

"Trust me, sweetheart, I can have anything I wish eradicated or if I so wish I can have it brought to life."

"I don't understand. What do you mean?"

"Let me just say this, a man like me has connections everywhere."

"Everywhere?"

"Everywhere!"

"I still can't grasp what you are trying to convey to me."

"Time is marching on so I'll explain in more detail later tonight, all right?"

"I suppose so."

"Why do you appear to be so dismissive at present, Helena?"

"It's just that sometimes I don't really think that I know who you are, and you... You confuse me"

"Of course you know who I am... I'm Darius."

As I reply, "Yes, but... but..."

He interrupts me by grasping my left hand and placing it to his lips. Kissing each of my fingers in turn, he whispers, "I'll divulge what I meant later tonight over dinner... A dinner which I, the man who can't live without you, will prepare, cook and serve for you."

"That's sounds lovely. I could do with some spoiling."

On hearing my words, his face lightened into a beautiful smile. He breathed, "I will always spoil you to the point of almost ruining you?"

"Ruining me?" I question.

"Yes, I will ruin you in such an atmospheric manner that no other man on this planet would ever dare touch what has become mine... And if another man ever does stupidly try to win you over... or attempt to take you away from me, I will do this to him."

"What will you do?"

"I will wreak havoc upon him, destroy him and leave him in shattered ruins!"

I chill at the intensity of his words and then ask, "Who is yours?"

And without hesitation as he answered, "You, Helena... You are mine."

"And you, Darius? Will you always be mine?"

"Without question, Helena... I will always be yours."

And somewhere within that most strangest of pledges between us, our love gathered speed.

So with the New Year upon us, and so many great plans for our future in the making, Darius and I exit the car. I close the door, and as I take a moment to gather my thoughts, I rest up against the passenger side of the sleek, black Aston Martin – another one of Darius's cars from his vast collection of motors – and as the hectic flurry of Londoners en route to their places of work passes us by, he comes around to meet me. Leaning in close to me, he presses his body into mine. He feels glorious!

Looking down upon me, I blink, snake my hands underneath his pea coat, and cuddle him tight around his middle. He shudders into my touch, and as the corners of his lips curl up into a delightful smile, he so tenderly, so slowly, cups my face in his hands, stroking either of my rosy cheeks with the pads of his thumbs. I become oblivious, unaware of the world scurrying around us, and gaze lovingly up at my darling fiancée. I quiver inside as he leans firm against me. Next, as a rogue curl from that mop of his luscious dark, silky locks bounces over his forehead, tickling my skin, and combining with the sensation of his lips brushing along mine, he asks me if I am going to miss him.

I inhale the freshly laundered scent of his person, and as the memory of our recent lift-sex enters my mind, I weaken at the knees, kiss him soft, and reply, "Of course I am, Darius. That truly does go without saying."

Without any further hesitation, his warm lips settle upon mine. His kiss is so light but so very claiming within its delicacy that when he breathes, "And I'm going to miss you too, my sweetheart."

I tremble with the sensuality that is oozing from his every pore, and filtrating into my being. With my head floating, I dizzily add, "Well, considering we are both going to be lonely in each other's absence, why don't we meet up at say lunchtime?"

Breaking into the most heart melting grin, through his next kiss, he whispers, "That sounds like a lovely idea. Shall I bring us a picnic to your work? Say about twelve-thirtyish?"

"Yes," I softly say, "that would be perfect."

"What would you like to eat?"

"Oh I don't know. Why don't you surprise me? You're the master of surprises."

He creases a thinking frown, pulls back a tad from me, and fleetingly glances at his watch. His mood instantly alters.

"Damn it! I'm already twenty minutes late for the first script reading, Helena." Pulling a grimace, he states, "If I don't leave promptly, Cali will have my guts for garters! I'm sorry baby, I really had better get a wiggle on right now."

And with that, before I released him from my hold, I stepped aside, and he swept a light kiss upon the tip of my nose while declaring to me over and over again how much he loved me. Opening the car door, he quickly seated himself, and the door was promptly shut behind him. As the passenger window wound down, he leant over and whispered, "Thanks for the hand job in the lift! We must do it again sometime!"

Shocked at his open and direct words, I clapped my hand over my mouth as he smirked and then blew me a final kiss goodbye before motoring off. I caught that most precious of kisses, turned around, and with a joyful spring in my step, began the short walk to my place of work. I couldn't wait to see Angelica again, and tell and show her my engagement ring. With my thoughts now chock full of Darius, the Christmas we had just spent together, the way he had proposed to me, the manner in which we consummated our engagement, my suspension, and the rather mind blowing, wall-banging sex we had in the shower this morning, (and the impromptu, masturbatory lift-sex) I am disturbingly brought back to reality when something sturdy impacts upon my left shoulder, throwing me right off my balance. As I reel backwards, wailing out a rather loud howl, my backside impacts with the pavement and a few contents of my handbag spill into the cracks and crevices of the cobbled street beneath.

Dazed, and bottom sore, while I momentarily catch my breath, I hear a soft, gentle male's voice apologise, "I'm so sorry Miss. I didn't mean to bump into you let alone angle you right over onto the ground."

Scrabbling up onto my knees, I don't look up at the man who wasn't looking where he was going either; instead I focus upon gathering my strewn belongings.

"It's all right. It was my fault." I mumble under my breath. "I wasn't looking where I was going. No harm done."

Now having located the last of my items, a tan leather gloved hand appears in front of my eyes and a palm upturns; his fingers wiggle while he enquires, "Are you sure that you're all right, miss. You look quite shaken up to me."

I am disorientated, so I decide to accept his hand. I am aided to my feet, and while I look directly at him, mentally imprinting his youthful, facial features into my mind, I respond.

"I'm okay."

Next, I am taken by surprise, when he leans forward, and as I see it, attempts to grasp me by my right arm. His fingers briefly touch my person, and I immediately recoil from him – No man touches me – no one except Darius. If Darius was here, and he could see this man who had just attempted to touch me, this stranger's life wouldn't be worth living – would it? Instinctively shrugging him off, I take a defensive step backwards, and blurt, "How dare... How dare you consider consciously touching me! Who on earth do you think you are? And what gives you the right to... to...?"

I don't finish my sentence because his face has crumpled into a bemused state, and his dark-grey irises are flashing with a painful, hurtful look. While he hastily regains his composure, I stiffen in response to this peculiar situation, and he in turn soothes this weirdest of scenarios by stating, "It's all right, miss, I promise you I wasn't going to do anything untoward to you. I was just making sure you were steady enough to be on your feet... After all, you did fall down rather hard."

I sink inside. He's only being kind. Where are your manners, Helena... say sorry? Darius is your fiancé not your keeper.

"Sorry.... It's just... just... just that..."

Furrowing his brow, he runs his hand through his mass of blond curls, and places his finger to his lips, musing, "There's no need for you to apologise to me, miss for in this day and age every woman has the foremost right to be cautious of a total stranger, especially one who sends them flying to the ground."

"True..." I half smile... "I think I shall have to agree with you on that matter."

"And, now that you've smiled at me," he adds, "I am now left wondering if you would like to go for a coffee with me... Let me at least say sorry for being a blinkered oaf... and also for scaring your wits just now."

I frown. Should I?

He smiles crookedly, albeit a charmingly warming smile, and I soften, and for some peculiar reason. Is it the little-boy-lost smile that he's projected? I then begin to feel a little ashamed for being so brusque with him previous, and before I can answer, he places his hand over his winter jacket covered chest and like a true gentleman stoops a bow, asking, "Wouldn't you at least give me the chance to make sure that you are completely fine before we resume our separate day? I would never forgive myself if I left you in a tizzy."

My head is now in a spin from his question – maybe I am in shock from the fall – a cup of sweet, sugary coffee does sound tempting? One coffee couldn't do any harm, could it? Darius then enters my mind, and as I toy with the idea of calling him up – just because I want to hear his voice – just because I want to tell him that I love him, I recall that as he was dreadfully late for his script call, I decide that it would be prudent not to bother him, so instead I find myself replying to the mystery man,

"I must admit that my nerves are a bit jangled, and I do suppose a double shot of espresso would certainly help in steadying my manner."

He smiles a tad too... too... maybe triumphantly for my comfort – or maybe I'm overanalysing this man and his stance?

I muse.

He interrupts my thinking...

"Maybe you'd like a Danish pastry too or a pain au chocolat perhaps? A sugar rush will help you get over the shock of me accidently bumping you over."

As I missed a complete breakfast this morning because Darius – well let's just say after the romantic shower sex, he had to have me again, but that time, he teased that he fancied plain old, vanilla style sex. So being the dutiful fiancée that I am, the missionary position came into play, and oh my, oh my, while I watched his eyes dewy with love, and while I felt that divine man of mine fight his climax until he couldn't hold back any longer, I was lost within his heart and his soul. However, when he did release, relax, and then recover, I promise you that I'd never seen him look so peaceful, so sedate, and so entirely stress free. His face was a remarkable picture, and is an image that I shall behold in my mind until the day I draw my very last breath.

I am brought back to reality when I hear, "...Time for a coffee and a pastry?"

With my sugar level about to hit an all time low, on the thought of food, my tummy rumbles, and I have to agree, "Yes, coffee and a pastry... sounds delish."

"Well, now we've agreed on an innocent coffee, and a pastry," he laughs, "I'm pretty sure that a while back, I've seen a barista bar just around the corner."

"Oh, I know the one you mean.... Connor flits through my mind and then he fleets away. It's called, 'Mario's'. The atmosphere in there is really pleasant, welcoming and comforting."

"Ah, that's what it's named." He nods. "So, miss, shall we go now to Mario's?"

I then look up at the clock outside the jewellers shop across the road, and I note the time, nine a.m. "Just the one coffee," I sigh, "or I'll be even later for work than I already am."

And as we walk in unison, I begin to feel more relaxed in his presence because I am guessing that he must have to be somewhere too shortly.

After all 'Time' keeps us all in order, doesn't it?

On reaching the street corner, we pause on the edge of pavement waiting for a black van that is heading down road a little too fast to pass us by. But it didn't pass us by. As it halted directly parallel to us, and a side door slid open, before I could even comprehend what may be occurring, my phone buzzed – Darius? Dipping my hand into my coat pocket, as I went to retrieve my phone, I felt something sharp sting me on the side of my neck, and whatever had penetrated my venous system instantly caused my eyelids to become heavy. While they dragged, and the world around me began to descend into darkness, the last sound I heard was the muffled voice of a man congratulating Mr Innocent-coffee on successfully duping me into his lair.

On coming around, I am disorientated, dazed and confused.

...I see two men in the next room sitting opposite each other, and it is their conversation which left me scared, and in a terrific, blind state of panic. Nevertheless, I manage to raise my head from the pillow beneath me. My temples are thumping hard and I feel as if I have been out all night binge, drinking heavily. I note that the curtains to this room I am ensconced within are drawn. In the dim of the artificial light, I carefully survey my surroundings. I come to the conclusion that I am seated on a large bed in what appears to me to be a rather luxurious hotel suite. The room is vast, too huge for a single person alone to dwell in, and it is lavishly decorated in an art deco style. As I rub the left side of my neck, I wince on touching the sore spot where I was *stung.* My head continues banging like nothing I have ever felt before, and I feel as if this artificially induced, hangover will never end. My mouth desperately is dry, and I look around for a glass. What has recently happened to me? Where am I? And who do those strangulated, gruff voices I can hear belong to? With all my might, I shakily rise from the bed, and go in search of my handbag – I have to call up Darius – He'll come and get me from wherever I am. Unsuccessful in my quest to find my belongings, I gingerly walk in the direction of the voices, and peer through the crack of the hotel room door. I see two men in the next room sitting opposite each other, and this is their conversation which left me scared, and in a terrific, blind state of panic.

Unfamiliar voice: "She didn't give you any trouble then?"
Trouble, me?

Mr Innocent-coffee: "No... No trouble at all. Fooling her into thinking that I accidently knocked her over, and coercing her into going for a coffee was as easy as eating the sweetest Danish pastry!"

Mr Innocent-coffee, that's you?

"Good." The unfamiliar voice replies. "And how's our Mr Carter coping at present?"

What does he mean, how is Mr Carter coping? Coping with what?

Mr Innocent-coffee: "Well considering she never made it to her place of work and her boss, Angelica hadn't heard from her at all today, he's been climbing the walls for the last couple of hours or so."

147

Darius... Oh Darius... My poor, poor Darius.

Unfamiliar voice: "Keep on monitoring him. I want to know every single move of his from now until contact – and after contact too. I want to know when he's online, who he's phoning... I want photographs of him looking like a frightened little baby rabbit... I want to break him for a short while... I want him to feel what it's like to have the one you love torn from you... and I want to hear how petrified he is of losing her."

Losing me... No... No... No... Please don't lose me again, Darius.

Mr Innocent-coffee: "No problem, boss. I'm already on it."

Unfamiliar voice: "Give him another few more hours of complete mental torture and then I'll make contact at six p.m. He should be ragged by then, and willing to pay handsomely to have her safely back in his arms."

I flew back to the bed, lay down, and began to hug onto a pillow. You see, when I heard 'pay' it quickly dawned on me that I have been abducted, and that Darius at present is totally unaware of not only this, but where I have disappeared to. He must be more that beside himself, he must be fraught with a gut twisting fear. As I inwardly plea for him to find me, my body begins to rack. I nuzzle my face into the soft, downy pillow and begin to sob. After what seems like an eternity of tears has left my soul, I take a deep breath, and I am startled back to reality when I hear the door to this room that I am imprisoned within open. Instinctively I curl up into a protective foetal ball, not daring to look at who has entered the room. Still as a church mouse, I feel a presence settle onto the bed, and my hair is swept away from my aching neck. I am left strictured and terrified.

"Just another little pinprick," I hear Mr Innocent-coffee whisper. "One more little pinprick, Helena, and I promise you that after you have slept like a baby for the next few hours you will feel refreshed and invigorated when you next awake."

I going to be drugged again... help me God please?

While he leans over me, his stubble grazes the side of my face, and his foul, cigarette infused breath manages to creep up my stuffed up nostrils. On his touch, his aroma, I retch hard but considering I haven't eaten since last night, nothing purges from my stomach except the bitter secretion of bile. As the taste fills my mouth, I swallow hard, almost regurgitating it back. Next, as I feel something that I can only describe as an ice cold swab sweep across the skin on my neck, he leans in extremely close, too close, and while the syringe of artificial liquid is once again inflicted upon my venous system, he with a chilling sarcasm in his tone, hisses, "There, there, Helena, don't fret now, for I assure you that if Darius meets my employer's demands, when you next open those pretty little peepers of yours, you will be looking directly at the man who has just parted with some serious, hard cash for your return.

I never left him you... you... bastard! You stole me away from him!

I awake again feeling worse than before. I shuffle up onto the bed, draw my knees up to my chest, and begin to hum for Darius. While I rock back and forth like a disturbed and lonely child, once again I hear voices on the other side of the adjoining door. I am instantly alert.

"Put him on the speakerphone."

When I hear Darius's voice rage through the airwaves, "Where is she, you fucker?" my heart splits into a million painful shards, and I yearn for the safety of his cosseting arms.

"Now, now..." Unfamiliar voice, cuts in, "There's no need to be so rude, Carter, when I am in possession of something as precious as your Helena.

"Where the fuck is she you fucking excuse for an arsehole?" He rages like I have never heard before. "Where the fuck is *my* girl?"

"If you carry on conversing to me in that manner, slating me, Carter, consider this; you may never see her again."

Deathly, deathly silence... and then...

"Taking what's mine?" Darius angers, "You must want to die an early death!"

"Empty threats, Carter?"

"There is nothing empty about my warning... it's just, at present, its unfulfilled, and trust me I can assure you that if you hurt one single hair on her head," he asserts, "I will hunt you down and when I have you in my clutches, trust me, I will spear you, and you in response will howl like a stuck, squealing pig that is begging for its mother to save it from its predator!"

On hearing the deathly threat, the depth of desperation in Darius' voice, I shake and shiver like I have just been stripped to the bare, plumaged frantically into an ice cold bath several times, cast to one side, and left on my own to fend for my survival.

"Empty warnings, Carter, will only make matters, how shall I say, more expensive?"

Quiet reigns, and I quiver.

"You see," unfamiliar voice continues, "This experience is not about hurting her; I can assure you of that."

"Then what is it about?"

"It's payback time."

"Paying back for exactly what?"

"You'll see one day in the future."

"Don't fuck with me whoever you are. I promise you that if you toy with me, you will regret it!"

"Oh, I'm not toying with you, Carter. I'm deadly serious in what I want."

A long pause occurs followed by Darius coolly asking, "How do I know that she's there? That you have Helena?"

"Stay on the line, for in the next moment you shall know, Carter."

On assuming that I may now be able to speak with Darius, my heart takes a leap, and I take a small icon of comfort in knowing that he now knows that I am somewhere. While I try to clear and clarify this situation, I am snapped back into this insane scenario when suddenly I am hauled off the bed, and dragged into the next room, halting only when I am roughly plonked down into a chair. With my vision blurry due to the stinging tears that have been continually falling from my soul I can't make out the features of the man who is sitting opposite me. I hear a thudding tap of a finger on the desk surface, and I am told to drink the glass of water that it situated before me. My mouth is so dry that I know if I don't take a few large gulps, I won't be able to speak, so I drain the entire contents of the glass, and the tumbler is taken from me. I am then informed that I now have fifteen seconds to speak out loud to Darius.

"Darius... it's... it's... me," I sob. "Please... Please... come and get me? Please find me..."

"Helena... Helena!" his tone is as scattered and desperate, as is my own heart. "Oh my God, Helena, stay strong... I'm coming to find you right this very second! Has he... have they... There are two? Have those fucking bastards dared... no-one has touched you, no-one's hurt you... have they? Please tell me they haven't?"

"No," I pitifully cry... "Please... find me, Darius... I... I... he... he... he's going to... to..."

We are cut off from each other when "Time is up!" is roused roughly through the air.

On the shock of having Darius once again torn away from me, I snap my mouth shut. I remain firmly rooted to my seat and listen.

"Well, now you have confirmation that she is here, Carter, I am now going to explain to you exactly what you have to do for her safe return."

As I hear Darius, his tone eerily calm, say, "State what you require for me to do." I am then again dragged up by my right arm, and with all physical and mental strength now drained from me I let myself be guided back into the suite. En route, I mumble, "I need... I need to pee. I need to use the bathroom."

Not a word is responded from my captor, I am silently guided towards the bathroom, and while I use the facilities, I am not left to do so alone. Mr Innocent-coffee just perches himself upon the rim of the washbasin and scans my every move. When I am finished, I turn my back towards him, and quickly pull up my skimpy panties. After smoothing my skirt down, I flush the toilet and turn. He's brooding. And I am scared witless. I step towards the wash basin. He takes one step aside, but as I wash my hands, he continues watching me from behind in the mirror. On seeing my reflection, I barely recognise the woman staring back at me. She looks haggard, older and paler than pale can be. In fact she looks starved of energy, starved of life. I am. I dry my hands on the white hotel towel and with my hands trembling; I leave it where it falls.

Now being shepherded back into the bedroom, I glance over to the table by the window to see a tray resting upon the shiny glass surface.

"Eat," was the only word Mr Innocent-coffee said to me before he exited the room, locking the door after him.

On reaching the tray, I picked up what appeared to be a glass of freshly squeezed, orange juice and I took a sniff. With my defences heightened, I wondered if the chilled, fruity liquid has been infiltrated with a poison of some kind. I return the glass to tray. Next, I tentatively removed the cloche from the plate beneath it, and I saw a sandwich lain out, and I too wondered if its filling had been tainted. Just staring at the fodder, it then dawned on me that what these men want from Darius is a substantial amount of money for my exchange. They aren't going to murder me off. They don't look like life takers – either of them, do they? While I remain static, staring at the food before me, debating whether to taste the juice and bite the white bread delight, I hear the door unlock, followed by Mr Innocent-coffee saying, "Eat. I promise you it's all good nourishment."

Spinning around, my mood frayed to the hilt, I snap, "Why on earth should I believe you?"

"Because..." He cracks a dry smile, and ambles towards me. His eyes are flashing with a sense of threat, and as he stills tall in front of me, he gives me another unnerving smile, and through that salacious grin of his, I detect a necessary sense of to-be-on-your-guard-Helena. While the adrenaline begins seeping into my bloodstream and my heart reciprocates to this natural flight-or-fight hormone, my heart thumps vividly in my chest. He takes a step closer to me, and I cringe when I feel his hand snake around the right side of my neck. Leering into me, as I think he's going to attempt to kiss me, my spine stiffens... And I am more than relieved when he doesn't take that liberty with me, and instead whispers into my ear, "... Because your boyfriend has, in the last ten minutes, stumped up a whopping one million pounds for your safe return, and you need to keep up your energy since you appear to be such a beautiful, frail little creature."

Trembling, I stare hard at him, and bravely throw in to the conversation,

"He's not my boyfriend, he's actually my fiancé, and when he finds you and your boss, you will both so very much regret abducting me."

Taking my hand, the one that my engagement ring is placed on, he places my hand to his mouth, and as he kisses the heart, shaped solitaire while hissing,

"Well, whatever he is to you," he hisses, "I really don't give two hoots."

I sicken inside. Curtly snatching my hand away from him, and as I go to raise my knee to power it into his groin, and scream for him not to touch me, it's all too late. His hand is secured over my mouth preventing me from speaking, and his other, well, his other hand is snaking underneath the hem of my woollen dress. Holding my quaking thigh extremely firm, he snarls, "Are you waxed? I bet you are for I've heard that a pristine man like Darius usually likes his women free of any pubic hair."

On hearing his words, my eyes widen in fear, and I churn and I yearn, I long for the safety of Darius's arms.

His voice turns callous and dreadfully urgent, "Nod for me if you are bare."

Even though it's none of his business whether I am waxed or not, to placate his manner, I point my lashes down, and just weakly nod to signal a yes. He purrs in response muttering dirty, rich, whorring slut under his tobacco scented breath. As his hot hand travels higher, I whimper out against his palm for him to stop.

"Shhh..." he claims, "I only want a little touch of that smooth, million-pound worthy pussy of yours... I can't wait to feel how beautifully tight that expensive cunt of yours is, and I am looking forward very much to seeing how moist I've made you when I finished filling that dizzy little mind of yours with a barrage of erotic words."

My stomach now violently churning, as his bony fingers locate the top of my garter, and he starts to caress the silk of my stocking hem, he whispers to me that Darius is a very, very lucky man to own such a woman, such a slutty, dirty, filthy, whoring prostitute like me, and especially one who wears such expensive, almost non-existent underwear outside of the bedroom. I whimper again, and as I do, he presses his body into mine. My buttocks sweep across the pelmet of the bed and I flay backwards. He makes no hesitation in covering me with his body, and his weight presses down on me; I recoil on feeling his cock that is straining at the fabric of his trousers pressing into me. His mouth is lingering above mine, and the smell of his breath is acrid. As he glares down upon me, I move my head to right, avoiding him, but has me held firm in his grip. Clutching a clump of my hair, he jerks my head hard so I have no choice but to see him, and with hate dripping from his mouth, his next words twist into me like a searing blade.

"What do you think Darius would do if he knew that you were laying here underneath me, willingly letting me touch you? Do you think he'd forgive and forget that you, his precious whore of a submissive had revelled in the joys of being heightened by another man? Do you? How do think he'd feel knowing that you would soon be begging for my big cock to fuck that precious tight cunt of yours, eh?"

I'm terrified beyond belief, for his grey irises are alight with a dark, devilish stare, and the tips of his fingers are now dangerously close to the black silk crotch of my panties. I start to sob, imploring for him to let me go... to stop invading me. But he doesn't. He starts grinding his crotch into my centre, and the vile sounds that are warbling from the back of his throat are positively spine chilling. Finding my voice, I fearfully plead with him to stop. He stills, jars my head again, and I squeeze my eyelids shut.

Whispering into my ear, "Do you think he'd still worship you, his tart of a submissive, or do you think he will discard you like he once ditched her?"

Who did Darius ditch? Does this man mean, her, Alice?

I mute. I freeze. I cry... I die inside.

And while I feel his breathing increasing, and he reaches the inner lace band of my knickers, I try so very hard to blot out every single atom of his being. If he is going to... to... rape me, then I have to mentally shut down.... I must... So I begin to mediate... And he continues invading my person.

"Mmm," he lowly purrs. "It seems that you were telling me the truth. Your skin feels so beautifully smooth, and so invitingly soft. I am hoping that a whore like you is on birth control?"

After squeezing my thighs so hard, he lets go of me, and I wince as he grabs both of my wrists tight, and raises my arms above my head. Nastily breathing, "Well, let's hope for your sake that you are on the contraceptive pill, for I am not a fan of using condoms or of unplanned kids for that matter!"

Fear prevents me from uttering a single word in defence or for that matter moving a single muscle. My flight-fight response is dead. With one hand, he holds both my wrists firm. Next, I hear the rash unbuckling of a belt, followed by the hurried unzipping of trousers, and as the hem of my dress is raised, fully scrunched up around my midriff, he demands for me to open my eyes. I don't. I won't. I do not wish to see either him or his horrid face or his body part! "Fucking open your eyes, bitch" he rasps. "Open them you bad, naughty girl or I'll have you on your knees in a flash ready to serve me in another way!"

If you do, I'll latch on to you bite you in half!

I don't obey, and within a split of a second, he has manhandled me onto my knees, spun me around, and I collapse forward onto all fours. While I stare at the carpet beneath me, lost in this most horrific of moments, hearing him say that for my disobedience, I deserve to be gagged before being flogged and fucked like a whore, I begin to retch hard. Next, he begins to wind my hair around his fist, and I yelp! Straddling over me, he looms down over me, and dangles his yellow tie in front of my face. As he cackles into my ear that he is going to gag me with his tie, and after he has done so, he will take extreme pleasure from hearing my muffled cries when he pounds his cock into me. The cheap synthetic fabric of his tie is being pulled hard against my lips, and as it chaffs my face, I hear the door to the room that I am being abused in, wildly cast open, followed my abductor's booming voice enveloping the room. Instantly, Mr Innocent-coffee releases his hands from me, taking his tie with him. As we both spin around, I, without hesitation spring onto my feet, and I scamper towards the corner window. On reaching the window, I slump my back against the sill, and sink to the floor only to see my assailant bolt upright facing his boss.

With his voice cross, his boss demands, and I may add, slips up terribly when he reveals Mr Innocent-coffee's true name, "What the fuck were you attempting to do to her, Marcus?"

Marcus.

Ignoring the fact that his boss has revealed his identity, Marcus tousles his dull, blond hair, and begins tucking his manhood away. After he redressed himself he flippantly started to restyle his tie, while asking for a smoke.

"I said, Marcus, what the fuck were you going to do to her?"

Laughing, Marcus replies, "I was only playing with her."

"That's not what we agreed. You weren't supposed to touch her in any other way than knocking her to the floor, and the injections."

With his next two statements, I retch when I hear him seethe, "Well, boss, I guess all this was her fault... you know, me having to touch her in a sexual way."

With exhaustion in his voice, his boss sighs and asks, "Why, Marcus? What did she..." He looks at me in a condescending fashion. "What did this poor little defenceless female do to you to make you break our one golden rule?"

Raising his eyebrows, he looks directly at me and lies through his tobacco stained teeth.

"She enticed me into having a little play. You see, she started crying for me to let her go, and when I told her I couldn't, she cried harder, she threw herself into me. She stuck to me like glue! When she finally stopped snivelling tears, she took me by surprise by starting to stroke my crotch, and my cock couldn't help but stiffen. I told her to stop but she didn't. She continued rubbing..."

Raising his hand to Marcus to stop him mid-sentence, Marcus quickly snaps his mouth shut as his boss shakes his head from side to side and mumbles under his breath, "All of that, Marcus, I find very hard to believe."

"Anyway, boss," he gloats while staring menacingly at me, "I bet you a million pounds she was far too tight to take every inch of my impressive dick!"

Knotting his fists on the sides of his hips, his boss angrily states, "Enough is enough! Get yourself straight in your head, and get moving out."

Winking at me in a way that abhorred me in so many connotations, he then finishes, "Anyway, boss, I don't do film stars' leftover whores any more."

Film stars' leftover whores any more?

Tapping his wristwatch, his boss frowns at me, and looks at me like I have now become an annoyance to him. I am now truly scared of what may occur next, and as I hear him inform Marcus to meet him in the basement car park in twenty minutes, I cringe when I see him extract a syringe from the inner pocket of his suit jacket. As the door is closed behind Marcus, I curl up into a foetal protective ball and wait to once again to be introduced to the sharp end of a needle.

It's dark. Pitch black in fact. Not even a minuscule chink of light to guide me. Where am I? Am I still dwelling in this living nightmare? Are those men coming back? Even though I am bewildered and perplexed, my survival instincts have become heightened; I realise that there is not a whisper of a sound, and that there is no fragrance within the air. I blink - it's still inky black. I shift a little and hug my own body. I hear shrill noises in the distance. Sirens perhaps? While my heart pounds in my chest, the noises of rescue become louder and more defined. Has someone been looking for me? Is someone coming for me? Is Darius coming to find me? Or are the emergencies for someone other than me? My questions are answered when the sirens cease, and within a few minutes – the longest minutes of my life – I hear a barrage of footsteps thundering close by. As each footstep becomes more urgent, more intense than the last, abruptly they halt... I sicken. They're leaving me? They can't find me? I hear my name called clearly called. I open my mouth to respond to the caller, but no words come out, and I just start rocking to and fro. I'm terrified that the footsteps will fade leaving me here all alone. The next sound I hear is the battering, the desperate ramming, and finally the destruction of wood splintering in all directions. As light begins to illuminate the room I am in, I place my hands to my tear stained face and gingerly open my eyelids. I blink several times, peek through the gap in my fingers, until a tall figure eventually comes into my focus. The figure kneels down next to me, and I am swept up into his arms. While I try to speak, confusion reigns and I close my eyelids and plead, and protest in earnest for Marcus to put me down and to please not to touch me again.

"Look at me, Helena," the man whose arms I am in asks.

On opening my eyes, I focus upon this man's features. His face is ashen in colour. I look to his hair, and I notice that it is its usual mop of an unruly mess. His beautiful, alluring blue eyes have lost their enchanting sparkle. They are dull – one could say almost lifeless, and they are rimmed red raw. A whisper of, "I've found you, Helena," falls against my cheek. And my heart does a small leap.

My voice hoarse, I manage to squeak, "Is that really you, Darius?"

While his tears mingle with my own, he so lightly breathes, "Yes, baby, it's most definitely me."

My whole body sags with relief, and I can't prevent myself from going limp in his arms. As he cradles me, I bury my face into his chest, and inhale the scent of his manliness.

"Darius," I whimper against his thumping heart, "I knew you'd come for me. I love you."

"I love you too, Helena," he mumbles into my matted hair.

While we remain like this in hold for what seems to me to be for hours upon hours, a kindly male voice interrupts, "Sir... sir... You must let the paramedics take her from you now. We really should get in her in the ambulance."

Darius grip tightens on me, and as I hear his reply – that no, absolutely no-one is going to take me away from him ever again, followed by that he is going to be the one to carry me to the ambulance – And, he adds, that he never again will leave my side.

While I am carried to safety past the emergency services and hotel staff, he orders to the air, "Keep the paparazzi at bay."

"Yes, Mr Carter," a male's voice responds, "we will do. And take the lift right down to the basement where we can slip you both into an unmarked emergency vehicle."

While the rest of the emergency crews all look bemused, they manage to give Darius and I their best sympathetic smiles. Without uttering another word to anyone, Darius then heads towards the waiting lift, all the while breathing to me, to any one around us that can hear that he will never leave me ever again. As we entered the small space and the doors closed, he looked adoringly down upon me, and told me that whoever abducted me, whoever they happened to be, from this moment on, their lives would not be worth living.

The wrath of Darius had now been ignited.

POST HELENA'S ABDUCTION

Day One
After several hours spent in a private hospital room during which Helena encountered several physical health checks, she was now back at the condo with Darius. He tenderly bathed her, dressed her in a set of pyjamas and settled her down into their bed, whereupon she slept for twenty-four hours, only to briefly wake once when she muttered to the air that it was raining furiously in her mind. As she slipped back into a slumber, he never left her bedside once. He never untwined his fingers from hers at all, and never stopped reassuring her that he loved her.

Day Two
It was around ten-thirty a.m. when she finally stirred. Darius was still present. Everything for her was groggy, but recognisable. They talked. She wanted to stay here she was because she felt safe. She didn't want to leave the condo – ever. She explained to Darius as best as she could, that it felt as if the rain in her brain was easing up, and that the heavy droplets of warm water had now begun to turn into more of a tepid, light, pitter-patter of soft, summer rain. After she fell back to rest, Angelica as asked by Darius, took watch over her best friend. Darius left the room and kept himself very, very busy!

Day Three
Six-thirty a.m.

The rain had finally ceased.

Helena awoke to feel tenderness in certain areas of her body. Angelica had left and Darius had returned. He was holding her hand. After mentioning to him that she was hurting, a look of deep concern crossed his face. He asked her to show him where the pain was. She drew back the covers and shimmied down her pyjama bottoms. Revealing the bruises upon the flesh on her inner thighs, Darius immediately let go of her hand and exited the bedroom. Angelica who was waiting outside in the hallway promptly returned. Helena curled up into a protective foetal ball, and as she sobbed herself to sleep, Angelica stroked her hair, soothing to her that everything was going to be just fine.

Day Four

Angelica left and Darius returned. Approximately one-thirty in the morning, Helena experienced a chilling nightmare. Darius continually mopped her brow, and she slept fitfully until eight a.m. Next, he gently lifted her into his arms and seated in i the chair next to the bed. As the sheets were changed and the bed remade for her, by their housekeeper, he cosseted her by rocking to and fro. He sickened inside as he witnessed her sweat soaked body intermittently convulsing and cramping against his torso. She shook, she cried until she was void of any emotion. It was then, when the demons who had been dancing in circles in her mind finally left, she was able to sleep peacefully in his arms.

Day Five
At last... The sun came out from behind the stormy clouds.

Day Six

Darius was not in the room. It was just Angelica and Helena, and this is the brief conversation that followed.

"Did Marcus touch you, Helena?"

"Yes."

"Are you going to tell Darius?"

"I think he knows already?"

"... How?"

"He saw the bruises on my inner thighs."

Seven-thirty p.m.

It is just Darius and Helena in the room and this is the conversation that transpired.

"He did what to you, Helena?"

"He... he assaulted me."

"He's going to die."

"Is he, Darius?"

"Yes."

It's as simple and complicated as that.

Day Seven

One p.m.

Helena was curled up on the sofa and she had covered her lower body with a blanket. Surrounded by an array of glossy magazines, which she was not in the slightest bit interested in flicking through, she looked over to Darius who was standing by the floor to ceiling window, looking out at the rain-soaked, London skyline. His back was facing her and his hands were stuffed into his faded, jean pockets. He had been silent for some time. While Helena surveyed him from the top of his head to the heels of his bare feet, drinking every part and piece of him, the silence between them was finally broken. He bowed his head, looked to the highly polished floor beneath his feet and soulfully declared, "We should go home you know."

Whisking the blanket away from her lap, she rose to her feet and walked over to him. Rising onto her tiptoes, she settled her hand upon his left shoulder, and rested it there while asking him why he wished for them to return to their chalet in Inverness. He turned around and when she saw the dewy glaze in his dreamy blue eyes, she faltered. Next, as he took her hand in his, he draped them around his neck, dipped his head low, and nuzzled noses with her.

"We should go home because," he paused. "...Because it's much safer there for you."

She looked up to him and he dipped his lashes.

"Look at me baby," she softly asked.

He does and Helena explains to him that it doesn't matter where they are because as long as she is with him, she will always be safe. He sighs, shakes his head from side to side, and when he responds informing her that until Marcus and his boss had been caught, tried and punished according to their crimes, he would not settle and therefore they would be flying back to Inverness tonight, finishing by adding that there was more room for debate on the subject.

"Tonight... you seriously want to go tonight?"

"Yes," he murmured along her lips. "I want us to be cosseted in our own home for as long as it takes to... to... to bring...?

Darius doesn't finish his sentence for two reasons; the first being that Helena silenced him with a lingering kiss, and the other because he knew that through her kiss, she knew exactly what he was trying to convey to her.

Chapter Eleven

Nine-thirty p.m.

As the beautiful, sexy tones of the saxophone with the composition of big blue overture by Eric Serra soothes and calms us both, I sink back into the passenger seat. Darius presses his foot to the pedal and the Porsche Cayenne motors off. While this luxurious vehicle purrs along the country roads, I close my eyelids and listen to the music until the moment it timely fades to its end and we reach our destination. As the gates part and he steers the car up the winding path, I place my hand upon his upper thigh and give him a light squeeze. He shifts a little in his seat for this is the first time – apart from the one kiss we shared earlier today – I have made a sensuous gesture towards him since my rescue. I remove my hand, and he immediately reaches out for me, grasping my fingers mid-air. His voice, almost a whisper, asks, "Touch me again, baby."

I do as he asks, and I settle my hand. He lets out a long deep sigh. Quiet now surrounds us. Focusing on our home which is now coming into view, I have to say that I'm not surprised to see that this stunning looking home of our is well lit, so brightly illuminated that I am sure if it was a reasonable possibility, one could spot our domain for the outer rims of space. The car halts, and Darius applies all the necessary motions to the car to end its journey, and I am then asked, "Ready to go inside, Helena?"

I nod. While I unbuckle my seatbelt, he is already by my door opening it. Offering me his hand, I take it and when I feel the warmth, the strength in his hand as he curls his fingers around me, I momentarily close my eyelids and imagine that I am beneath him and he is consuming me with his body while offering me his soul.

Ten p.m.

After Darius had so tenderly undressed me out of my jeans and t-shirt, and he too is stripped bare, he placed his shaky hand in mine. Curling my fingers around his, I let him lead me in the direction of the wet room. Standing opposite him, he gave me a crooked smile. I sighed, and the water began to flow. While the jets of soothing, warm liquid cascaded over us both, he tentatively leant into me, placed one arm by the side of my head, and rested his body weight upon the wall. With his other hand, he took a dark, blue bottle from the cosmetics rack, and with his thumb and forefinger, flipped open the lid. Stepping back from me, I watched him squirt a generous amount of Chanel Bleu gel onto a buff coloured, natural sea sponge. I relaxed my body, leant up against the charcoal granite wall, and splayed my arms out wide – baring my naked body to him. Taking his time, he began to soap me from head-to-toe, starting at my outstretched neck. While I looked down upon him, and he intermittently glanced up at me, I focused upon his adorable eyes. The love, the tenderness I saw within his steely-blue irises melted me to the very inner of my core.

"I love you," I moaned into the damp, fragranced air. "Keep me safe?"

Looking up at me, his entire look saddened, he rose, nuzzled noses with me, and pressed his lips to mine. Responding, he breathed into my mouth, "I will always keep you safe from future harm. I promise you that with every fibre of my being I will protect you from danger."

Holding back my tears of extreme relief, he then knelt down before me, and breathed, "I would never recover if I lost you."

Neither would I, Darius.

Wrapping his arms around me, he then affirmed, "I love you too, Helena."

As he kissed the jewel that was adorning my tummy button, again I had to hold back my tears. Extending his arms upwards, as he began sensually soaping each one of my breasts in turn, circling my nipples, I felt slightly bereft because I knew I was showing no obvious signs of becoming physically aroused by the man I love. As much as I wished that I could respond to his presence, truth be told, I was so mentally drained from my return to him after my abduction. So, after he had cleansed my whole body – even the fleeting touch of his fingers between my thighs didn't alight any passion from within me – I was coldly numb in a sense. Next, he punched the faucet button hard, ceasing the flow of water, and as I yawned loudly. I found he was already wrapping me in a queen sized, Egyptian cotton towel. I was then carried like a precious cargo towards our bedroom. Finally after laying me down on our bed, he climbed in next to me, and coiled his body around mine. With us now both feeling calm, and extremely sleepy, he obscured us from the tainted world, by covering us with the grey, cotton covered eiderdown that was adorning the bed.

And while he soothed me to sleep with make believe stories of all good things that were soon to come, I dreamt of the moment that he had asked me to marry him, and thus I fell into a most welcomed, nightmare free, slumber.

Chapter Twelve

Inverness

February – One month later.

Just over four weeks it has been and I have yet to physically reconnect with Darius. Today, I feel that I may be ready to do just that – for him to take me tenderly.

Last night, I dreamt that is our wedding night, and that Darius for the second time in two hours, was again making slow, sweet love with me.

"I adore you, Mrs Carter," He breathed, in between his slow rocking into me.

I adore you too, Mr Carter," I whispered, in between my clenches around his throbbing cock.

"Climax with me, Mrs Carter?" he asked between his deepening breaths.

"Climax with me, Mr Carter?" I implored between raking my nails down his sweat-sheened back.

And we did indeed orgasm at the exact same moment and the room around us fell away. He relaxed over me, rolled us both onto our sides, and with his cock still throbbing away inside me, he broke me into a fit of girlish giggles by suggesting that it would rather ladylike of me to let him have ten minutes rest before he could go again!

I, being the perfect lady, did as he asked.

Ten minutes later...

He being my husband, gentle dominant, my lover and my soul mate did exactly as he promised.

I awake from my dream with my hands placed over my breasts. My nipples have hardened, and as I softly caress them, I shiver, imagining that Darius is running his tongue around each of my tightening buds in turn. I feel so sexy and as a deep tingle begin to collate at my centre, I whisper out, "I want you Darius. I am ready for your gentle love." Smiling warmly to myself as I reminisce upon my dream of last night, I roll over on to Darius's side of the bed. He's not here at present, and by the aroma of freshly brewing coffee that's infiltrating through the air, I gather that he must be in the process of creating us one of his luxurious breakfasts. Snuggling into his spot, as the warmth that is impregnated within the sheets, the warmth that his Adonis-like body has left behind comforts me from the mental trauma of my abduction, and I notice that there is a single red rose laid upon the dent in his pillow. Darius, forever the romantic, my romantic. Inhaling the perfume of the flower, I lose myself within the delicate fragrance that is infused in the velveteen softness of each one of the delicate, fresh petals.

After the last few weeks back together, and with my dream as a positive indicator, I now feel wholly ready – I want to become as one with him again, and while I reflect upon the thought of his steely-blue irises gazing lovingly down at me while he is the throes of a climax – a climax that I know he has been fighting back against for the best part of the last half an hour, I am brought back to this most precious of mornings by the sound of his bare feet padding over the oak wooden floor.

Flopping onto my back, I shuffle up and draw the sheet with me. While I rest up against the sumptuous, white pillows, I stimulate even further when I see him lightly gliding towards me. He looks positively morning sexy! He is carrying a breakfast tray that is laden, yes, heavily strewn with an over-the-top breakfast that comprises of a pile of freshly baked croissants, and a bowl crafted high with strawberries, blackcurrants and blueberries. Alongside the pastries and fruits are a jug of iced cranberry juice, and a tall cafetiere of dark, almost jet black, infused coffee, along with two, tall blue mugs.

Carefully settling the tray down onto the ottoman that it situated at the end of the bed, he looks over at me, smiles, and then asks me if I am hungry. I am – For him! I twiddle with the rose, waiting to be asked what I would like to eat first, but as I notice that his sweatpants are slung way low, and that the centrally aligned, dark patch of hair that is peeking at me over the waistband of his, coupled with twitching of his lean hips as he straightened his torso, I instead find the following sentence tumbling out of my mouth,

"I'm very... ravenous... indeed..." and then I can't help but tease... "But on this occasion, this particular moment, Darius, I do not desire for food."

He frowns with, well with an ache of concern and asks, "If you do not wish for food then, Helena, tell me, exactly what are you craving for?"

"You..." I say over the brim of the rose. I'm... I'm..."

With his face full of disquiet, he says, "You want me?"

"Yes, I do."

I peel back the sheets covering my upper body down to reveal my breasts."

"Oh!" he gasps, "so you want do want me."

Hiding behind the rose, as the soft petal brush along my lips, I whisper to the flower, "Yes, I do. I want hot sex first and breakfast later."

On hearing me say hot sex, he grins widely and replies, "Well, Helena. If it's hot sex you want, then hot sex you shall have."

"That's sounds wonderful, sir!" I jest.

As the word, sir, filters through his mind, his look immediately changes from one of a man who is about to make dreamy love to his fiancée, to one of a broodier, darker, more dominant strike.

"Basement?" he quizzes. "You can't possibly be ready for the basement."

Laughing, I throw my pillow at him, and he successfully manages to dodge out of its way!

"No... No basement... Not at this moment in time.... I really just want... want... you."

"Thank goodness for that," he breathes. "Even I don't think that I am ready for a full on session of deeper soul findings!"

I tilt my head to one side, and while I process his last sentence, trying to decipher the delicacy within his words, the lightness within his dominance, he picks up the pillow at his feet, tosses it back at me, and I catch it full on. He's now smiling, and by the lustful look in his eyes, I can tell that he is aware that I am actually in the process of peeling my panties down with one hand. As I achieve my aim, I watch him pick up a blackcurrant, flick it into his mouth, and devour it. While he flashes me a knowing wink, my eyes widen as I see him quickly step out of his attire, revealing his already semi-hardened cock. He then coils his fingers around his girth, bestows upon it a caressing tug, and I have to press my thighs together because he has just broken into the most alluring, delectable grin imaginable to woman! Now craving him to the point of a maddening insanity, I place the rose on the bedside table, and slip back down under the covers.

"I'm coming for you, Helena." He whoops with delight!

"Good!" I say against the sheeting that is covering my face – while resisting the temptation to call him sir.

Before I could contemplate, I felt his hands curl around my each of my ankles and hold my lower body still. The manner in which he began the most sensuous of foreplay, completely left me with the notion that when his body was aligned with mine, if he so much as whispered a single word of erotica into my soul, I would have no choice but to climax without him having even entered my body! We are now together – I am now so sexually charged. I am laid beneath him waiting, wanting, and needing to feel him inside me, and I can tell that he is in thought by the furrowing of his brow. He is focusing intently upon me, and while his eyes bored through to my very soul, tugging at each one of my individual heartstrings, I relaxed on hearing him declare, "I love you, Helena. I always have and always will. I will never let anyone hurt you ever again."

Without a single moment's hesitation, I reciprocated, "I love you too, Darius. I always have and I always will too."

Before he lifted me into him, he whispered, "Are you sure you're ready for me... for me... to... to... for us to..."

"I'm more than ready, Darius, for you and I to make love."

"Sure?"

"Sure."

"How sure are you? On a scale of one to ten, tell me?"

"I'd say... Mmm... I'd say..."

"Baby, answer me..." he pitifully wines.

I giggle – *I haven't giggled in quite a while*

"Ten."

With my arms now draped around his neck and his torso locked between my thighs, I tentatively arch my back and push my body into him. He groans sensually, sweeps his lips along mine and murmurs,

"Which would you prefer? Still desiring hot sex or would you settle for soft sex instead?"

I've changed my mind – "I wish for soft."

"Good, me too, so being your fiancé, your lover, and man who adores you more than you will ever know shall grant your wish, so soft it will be."

Spreading my legs, I whisper, "Thank you."

He dips those curly, long, dark lashes of his, And without another word crossed between us, I wholeheartedly welcome his body into mine. We to-and-froed in only a way that two lovers who are oblivious to the world locked out from them can. With every fibre of his being, when I saw him fighting against the peak of his pent-up climax, my heart did a series of cartwheels. There is much stored up trauma within his soul past, and his eyes misted over, and his eyes opened, with the imploring look in his steely blue irises that indicated to me to hold back my own climax and to release with him. I managed to do just that, and finally when his entire body racked with a powerful series of lunges, I cried out in passion... in lust... in love, and within the depths of my own release, once again he had found us. He's now buried deep, deep within me, and as I mentally and physically chart the typography of every ripple of his body aligned with mine, I know that neither of us are lost any more...We are... how shall I describe? We, through our act of lovemaking have managed to relocate each other's souls. Finally I lock my legs around him, holding him firm, and loop my hands around his strong neck. As we both gasp an airless breath simultaneously, he breathes out my name in such a fashion that it is as if I have never heard 'Helena' breathed by being another before. We pause... we move... we still... we move a little... we halt. No words... Just the sound of our breathing returning to its normal rate... At this particular sensuous moment in time, there is no need for the exchange of twenty-six mixed up letters of the alphabet...

Silent thoughts have now turned into fresh memories that will always, always be in the making.

Chapter Thirteen

Five months later

17 July 2017

"Happy birthday to you, Helena..." Angelica sings down the phone, and finishes with, "Happy birthday, dear Helena, happy birthday to you."

"Aww..." I smile. "Thank you my honey."

"So tell me, what's Darius bought you?"

I pause. "Nothing at present. I'm not even sure if he remembered it's my birthday because he's not said a single word about it all morning."

"I wouldn't be too concerned; I expect he's going to lavishly surprise you!"

"Mmm," I muse, "Do you know something that I don't?"

"Maybe..." she giggles..." Maybe Darius has shared a secret with me way back."

"Tell me," I wail down the phone..."I need to know."

"Nope..." she says adamantly. "You'll just have to wait and see... and anyway I want to know. How are you feeling, Helena, after... you know?"

"I'm feeling much better as each day passes, Angelica."

"And you?"

"I'm just peachy fine."

"And how's our adorable, top London barrister, Xavier?"

"Rampant as ever and smashing at being illegal between the sheets!" She laughs wildly at her own humour. "I can barely keep up with him, if you get my drift!"

"I understand... Like brother, like brother!" I giggle.

"In all seriousness, Helena, how are you coping with the aftermath of... of...?"

"It's all right, Angie, you can say the word... It won't upset me."

"Well, I won't say it because we both know what I am asking, don't we?"

"Yes, I guess we do. I'm coping well. Darius has been my rock just as I was to him when he had his..." I pause, take a deep breath and finish, "his motorbike accident."

"You make a great team, you and Darius."

"And so do you and Xavier by all accounts! So how's life been treating you both in my absence?"

"It's been pretty dull without you here, but Xavier, well I have to admit that my feet have barely touched the ground since he came into my life."

"What do you mean? Do you mean that you have spent most of your free time with Xavier laying on your back thinking of good old England?" I tease.

Laughing, she replies, "Well yes, a lot of time reclined on my back, among various other positions that I never even thought were possible unless one was a bendy-doll... And I can assure you, Helena, that I was never thinking of good old England during the hot sex that Xavier, that he... he...!"

"Whoa!" I stop her there mid-sentence. "This is fast becoming way too much information for us to share... well over the phone..."

"Is it?"

"Not really." I titter.

"Want to know some more then?"

"Yes, but only when I see you and we can talk face to face. When I come back you should come over to the condo. We can have afternoon tea, and I can show you around Darius's movie star pad!"

"Afternoon tea would be lovely... What's his place like?"

"Considering it's his place, it's sort of an almost sterile representation of his personality."

"What do you mean by sterile?"

"It's hard to describe, but I think you'd fathom what I mean when you see the place."

"Fair enough... So when do you think you will be coming back to London, to your apartment, and more to the point, have you and Darius thought about setting a date for the wedding yet?"

"My apartment's on the market, I don't need it any more."

Her voice aghast, she wails, "You're not coming back to live here? You're not coming back to work with me?"

"Of course I am. I'm just going to be living here at the condo with Darius... or without him when he's on locations."

"Oh," she breathes with a sigh of relief.

"Answering your previous question, probably in a few weeks we'll come back to London."

"That long?"

"Well yes, Darius has taken another month off from filming, and as for a date, no not yet. I think the past trauma has overshadowed any thoughts we've had about our wedding."

"Give it time, Helena."

"I miss you, Angie."

"I miss you too, Helena."

"Enough of this 'I miss you' mush... At least we have our sexy men to entertain us!"

"Entertain? That's rather a timid description of Darius and Xavier's sexual behaviour, don't you think?"

"I wasn't talking about their bedroom activities; I was talking about them just being here, for us."

"Sorry, Helena... I guess I've just got sex on the brain morning, noon and night!"

I laugh! "I do like sex!"

"I adore sex, especially with Xavier... God he's so.... Soooooooooo....."

"He's so what? Spill, Angelica for you've got me intrigued!"

As she begins to garble something rather personal about Xavier, I jump out of my skin because I can feel Darius's hot breath whispering into my ear, "I do like sex too... In fact, Helena, the rougher the better in my book!"

While he starts nibbling my earlobe, telling me that his cock is rock hard, and he'd love nothing more than to hear me swallowing his cum – *be careful what you hope for, Darius* – I groan into the phone, "I desperately, urgently have to go, Angie."

"You sound funny, Helena. Are you okay? Why so desperate? Do you need to pee?"

And Darius whispers that very soon, he is going to have his wicked way with me by fucking me senseless in the shower. With my sexuality aroused, I whimper down the phone, "No pee... I'm very, very, all right, Angie... It... It's... It's just that..."

"It's just what?"

"It's Darius... He's... He's right here! And I mean very close!"

"Well, can't you talk with him in the room?"

"I can... I could, but he's doing something to me that is rather distracting to say the least!"

A brief pause...

"Ah..." she trails, "I think... I think I get it! No problem, I'm off! Enjoy the delights of your man... I'll text you later, and I will be expecting some good tips!"

Before I can try to say goodbye, Angelica has terminated the call, and Darius, well he is heading upstairs while throwing his shirt over the banister. I followed his trail of discarded clothes until I reach our bedroom, and as a waft of his shower gel wafted under my nostrils, I quickly stripped bare.

My back is now flush against the shower wall, and I am supported by Darius who upon my urgent request is powering his taut body into mine. I want him to take me hard, fast and deep, and by the way I am openly begging for him to fuck me until I go limp, coupled with way that he's obliging my ask, shows me that he knows I need him to make me never forget his name – As if I could! The words of pure erotica that are falling from his lips don't perplex me, they don't phase or even embarrass me like they used to do – each word, each manly grunt that comes from his inner being, just makes me feel alive, and not as if I am just breathing. After our recent slow, sweet love making, the hunger for sex upon sex suddenly consumed us both in a way like no other. This precise moment, (and the ones that followed) were ones of a series of the pure carnal desire to fuck each other like wild ferocious beasts. I guess it was our way of silently informing the past that we won't allow it to be kept as a memory – we won't give in to blackmail, extortion and kidnap or any other form of the invasion of our lives – we just won't! He's now lifting me deeper into him, and I am clenching his cock with every ounce of energy I possess. Grabbing onto his thick silky curls, I yank his hair hard. He doesn't flinch an iota, he just stares deep into my eyes and I meld into him.

"Fuck me, harder!" I scream into the heavily, perfumed air. "Fuck me until I can't take any more of you!"

"Yesssss, baby," he hisses between his clenched teeth. "I'll fuck you wildly until you use your safe word."

"I won't need to use my safe word," I wail as he drives deep into me, and my back rides up along the marble wall.

"Yesssss... harder..." I trail into his mouth... "More..."

His strong, muscular thighs are trembling against me, and his cock throbs so prominently inside me. He momentarily stills, knots my hair in his fist, and then growls into my mouth, "How much harder do you want it, Helena? How much more of me wall banging you with this kind of ferocity do you think you can take?"

"Fuck me as hard as you possibly can... as ferociously you want!" I yell, and then with gusto, wildly declare, "I can take every inch of you whole!"

He narrows his gaze, and thrusts hard into me while whispering into my ear, "If I do give you my all, I know I will accidently hurt you in here... You're... you're still... you are so very fragile."

"I don't care!" I shout out. "I just don't care if you... you... hurt me! You won't be hurting me, you'll be pleasuring me, and I want you harder right now!" I demand. "Give it to me!" I finish while screaming like a banshee.

His voice full of devoted concern, he glares hard at me, and I hear him say, "I will never hurt a single hair on your head. Do you understand?"

I nod, and sag. He's now supporting me by the buttocks. He parts my cheeks, and his fingers lightly tease my aperture central. As the new sensation of his light probing, arouses me even further, without thinking, "I trust you, sir," just comes out of nowhere, and with my declaration fast filtering through to his mind, he takes me by total surprise, withdraws from me and sweeps me up into his arms. His face is beaded with a mixture of water and manly sweat, and his eyes are dancing with the most wicked merriment imaginable to woman – One could say that he is appearing almost devilish in his desire for a more wilder, a more wanton, and sinfully, uncensored sex.

I look up at him and quiz, "What are you doing?"

His face is unreadable. And when I hear him answer – "Basement," I don't question because something within me has fired, and I am aching to the very inner of my core to see him in all his dominant glory, while I offer him the most precious of gifts – and that gift is my submission.

Interlude

I, Darius, am seated in the chair in the centre of this room. A few months previous, Helena and I had baptised this room – our room of pleasure... secretly, I took a silent liberty and double christened it by also naming it a room of well, of pleasurable-pain...

This room of pleasurable-pain is somewhere that only Helena and I will ever know. On narrowing my gaze I hear what I can only describe as a set of high heels tip-tap-tip-tapping upon a highly polished surface. The floor of the basement. I fleet up a glance to see Helena slowly, and so sensually, walking towards me. I remain blank faced, all the while hiding my most agreeable pleasure. Spreading my leather clad legs a tad for her, I lounge back against the support of the chair, and effortlessly stiffen my upper body – that was not the only part of my body that hardened when I saw what she was or was not wearing! She was naked except for a pair of black, Christian Louboutin heels that not only elongated her already long legs, but held her stature in such a beautiful, feminine form... I must admit, right now I am more than exceptionally glad that I was conceived as fully red, blooded male!

And as that those most heavenly divine pair of red soled shoes caused something dark within me to surface she stood still, smiling at me, and as she teetered on her stick-thin heels, I thought...

So what are you waiting for, Helena?

Safe, sane and consensual has previously been agreed by us both and now the scenario was about to begin.

After giving the door that allows entry to the basement the lightest of shoves, it opened, and when I clapped eyes on Darius who was gracefully and erotically languishing upon the leather chair that was situated in the centre of the dimly, candlelit room, truly, I tell you, I had to try extremely hard to catch my breath. The reason for my surprise was that this gentle dominant of mine was clothed only in a pair of tight, black leather trousers and nothing else. His hands were placed over the tightly, weaved, inky-black coloured flogger that I had previously chosen as the implement for this lesson in my art of submission. While it rested safely in his lap, he lolled his head backwards, letting his curls fall where they lay, and as he outstretched his bare, firm torso to its fullest capacity, I felt a series of tingles radiate through my hips and collate at my naked centre. I mentally counted every striated, toned planked muscle that graced his chest, as they flexed as if to say – I'm all yours Helena... all yours to play with. I was excited at the sight of my adorable sexy, dark-haired man, and I couldn't help but focus on the pinking scar that lay off central to the left of his sternum. As I pushed that particular past memory to the base of my mind, the once frightening memories of him fighting to breathe, scrambling for a mere soupçon of oxygen still jumped forth and I had to blink back the tears that were threatening to pour out from the depths of my heart.

I promised him I wouldn't ever cry again at the events that occurred upon that almost fateful day, didn't I?

Refocusing my thoughts, I was aroused as I saw that the zip of his trousers was midway low. As my vision travelled along his muscular thighs, a warm sensation flooded through my veins because this man of mine was barefoot.

-Per-fect-tion!

I was suddenly broken from my erotic scenario when I heard his voice splice through the vanilla infused air. The tone was alluringly low and so heavenly syrupy, and he slowly drawled, "I know you are there, Helena."

I hushed back through the gap in the door. Peeking around the door, I then asked,

"How do you know that I was already here, sir?"

"I know," he purrs, "because from where I am sitting, the arousing scent of your bare sex is infiltrating every pore of my being."

On seeing that the flogger was now firm in his left hand, I trembled inside when he dropped his arm to one side, and the soft, leather tassels of said flogger flayed. Each strip of highly polished, animal skin was tempting me into their darkened world of pleasurable pain, so I placed my hand on the brass knob of the door, curled my fingers around it. "Well, Helena," he questioned, "do you propose to stand out there all evening in the hallway ogling me, or are you likely to come in anytime soon and please me, your lover and your dominant? Which one is it to be? "

Without hesitation, I again gained entry, and stepped inside. This is the account of what transpired after I had made my presence known:

I am standing approximately five feet away from Darius, watching his actions. The flogger in his grasp is at present motionless. My eyes widen as I see his free hand that is laid upon his right thigh shuffle, and settle upon the zipper of his leathers. While he slowly pulls the tab of the zipper down, I feel that powerful tingle once again radiate through both my hips, and collate at my now aching centre. He continues this alluring tease by freeing his cock from its dark holdings, and curling his fingers around his hefty manhood. While he strokes it to a peak of erectness, making the most sensual of sounds, and I see it pulse strongly between his fingers, I wonder whether I should approach him without being asked – I choose not to. Glancing at the tassels of the flogger in his left hand that have now begun to gently sway, I decide to remain in situ until I am asked to proceed over to him. What occurred next had to be the most, yes the most erotic act I have ever encountered with Darius to date.

Looking straight through me, he doesn't blink; he just parts his lips, opens that delectable mouth of his, and while he begins to circle the rim of his crown with the pad of his thumb, he, through his enticing groans, hushes for me to come over to him. Not being able to take my vision off the clear moistening of pre-cum that is coating his thumb, I excite even further at thought of what his liquid will taste like, and I take the necessary steps forward, halting directly in front of him.

He stops arousing himself. And I shamelessly focus upon his cock.

"Kneel," was his only command.

I knelt.

I am now submitting before him with my hands gripped onto his leather clad thighs. His torso is exceeded to the maximum, and I can't see his face for his head is dropped right backwards. All I can see are the bulging veins in the sides of his neck pulsating with every beat of his heart. His Adams apple is extremely prominent. So while he winds my ponytail secure around his fist, he moans as he angles his cock towards my mouth. As it sturdily throbs against my red painted, lips, he steers my head via my hair closer to him. I part my lips, and take a deep breath. The thick, purple crown of his splendid manhood is now probing at my mouth, and as I take him, slowly, inch by inch, I can't help but gag as suddenly his hips gyrate and the spongy circumference of his cock impacts with the back of my throat. He growls – with delight I think! I suck. He hisses wildly. I suck even harder. He thrusts again. I gag. He rasps out my name, and tells me that the sound I just made is greatly to his liking. I accommodate him as best as I can – He's too much for me like this. While I devour him, he makes sounds that I have never ever heard fall from a man's mouth before. He pulls at my hair harder. I'm now craving, wanting more and more of him! I taste – It's a unique flavour – him. I lick. I nibble. I nip. I swathe him with my mouth and barrage his pole of blood gorged muscle with my tongue while pumping him with my fist. Soft leather trails down my back. I nip him hard, and his legs jerk forward. I gag strongly. He thrusts powerfully. The leather leaves my skin only to return its slithering in waves that feel like tiny, little, puncturing bee-stings. He locks me between his thighs, holding me firm with his lower body. Leather smarts against my bare flesh, and I mumble into his cock, "Mmmm."

His torso racks hard. I contract the muscles of my lips and mouth to make a partial vacuum, and I siphon on him as if my life depends upon my performance. His breathing is rapid. Lash upon lash urges me forth and my jaw begins to ache. Another lash, and as it abated from my skin, I welcomed the first of a generous swallow. Leather lashes, gentler than of late, but still reminds me of this lesson in my art of submission. His thick-opaque cum floods copiously in my mouth and I consume his flow, drinking every drop until a sexual silence reigns over us. He unknots his fingers from my hair, and I slowly slide him out from my mouth. He places his palms flush to either side of the chair arms and grasps on tight. His knuckles have whitened, and to me, it seems as if his entire body is beginning to elevate.

Taking me by utter surprise, he warns sharply, "I'm going to climax again!"

He is?

He shudders, and wildly grasps out for me and I take him again full on – How I managed to accommodate him the second time round, I have no idea – While more of his pearlesque warmth spewed like a geyser intermittently releasing its warm pent up earthly fluid into my mouth, I keep consuming every drop until I felt his taut balls begin to soften and relax into my cupped palms. On gently sliding him out of my mouth, I rested back on my haunches to see his torso covered in a glorious sheen of sweat. Taking a huge gulp of air, I wiped the dew from my eyes, followed by the small dribble of his cum that had trickled down my chin. Panting I asked, "Are you all right, Darius?"

He doesn't initially answer. After a few moments pass, I rise from my position, turn and with the intent of leaving him in situ, and I start my exit from the room. On making it almost to the door, his voice echoes around the room,

"And where do you think you are going, Helena?"

I want to rile him for a bit of fun so I turn and answer, "I'm going shopping!"

And while I must have been en route out of the room, he had stripped out of his trousers and is now reseated with a large cotton towel wrapped around his midriff. Snapping the flogger into his palm, glares at me, and asks, "And exactly what are you proposing to purchase? Some more shoes for me to go crazy over?"

189

Flicking off my *fuckable* heels, they spin across the over primed floor, and spin, halting in front of him; I flinch on hearing the flogger crack hard into the air.

"No, I'm not wishing for another a pair of shoes. I'm actually intending to buy a new dress."

He shakes his head from side-to-side and with a tad of irritancy within his voice, he retorts,

"You do know that you are being extremely flippant with me and for that reason I am telling you my precious, you," he snaps the flogger again, "you are not going anywhere this instant, but across my knee!"

"Really?" I taunt. "Well if you want me across your knee, you are going to have to get your sexy, pert arse up from your chair and attempt to catch me first!"

"Be careful, Helena!" he roars with an edge of playful warning! "Be very, very careful with the way you are attempting to provoke me."

"Why?" I laugh. "You're just a pussycat wrapped in a towel! There's nothing for me to be frightened of, is there? "

"No, of course there isn't!" he blurts aghast. "After all you know," he chuckles. "You know that I am really just a sleek panther swathed in a fluffy towel!"

I start to giggle uncontrollably at his description of himself, and he in turn ruffles his curly mop of hair while looking boyishly bemused. When my tittering finally show signs of abating, I slap the left cheek of my arse, and nonchalantly reply, "I'm going shopping, so for you, my dear dominant, a spanking will have to wait until another time."

His eyebrows shoot up, and he quizzes, "Why on earth do you need another dress? You have rails upon rails of them."

"I want to look special for you this evening."

"Why?"

"Because, in case you have forgotten..." I drop my lashes and then raise them to meet his gaze. "It's... It's... my... my..." I drag out.... "It's my..."

"It's your what?" he urges. "Tell me..."

"Today it is my twenty-first birthday."

"Oh fuck it!" he mutters loud enough for me to hear, and then swears some more, "Oh fuck-fuck-fuckety-fuck!"

He's forgotten?

"Oh fuck, by any chance, Darius?" I jaunt.

He half smiles, and we both fall about into soft merriment when he walks over to me (still holding the flogger), skims his lips along mine, and tells me that I taste very nice indeed. I warm, and reply that's because I taste of him. He presses his body into mine, and I tremble on feeling his cock once again ready for action!

"I... I... don't think I am quite ready to take you in my mouth again just... just yet."

"Why?"

"Because..." I rub the left side of my face, "at present my jaw is aching from the previous oral!"

"Oh dear, sweet, Helena... I don't want you to take me in your mouth again – Well not just yet – This time I want to make love to my birthday girl. I want to show you just how much I love, want, need and cherish you."

"Where do you want to make love?"

"Not in here."

"If not in here where do you propose to make love to me?"

"Mmmm" he whispers into my ear. "You'll see soon enough."

"But I don't think I can wait any longer," I breathe into his mouth."

"Really?"

"Truly"

"Tell me you love me first and I might just take you right here."

"I love you," I quickly say.

"Well, considering you love me," he laughs, "how about that quickie in here? Do you think that will be enough to suffice your insistent sexual urges until a little later on?"

Cheeky devil! It's him that is sex-crazy not me!

Picking up the hem of my imaginary skirt, I bob a curtsy, and reply, "Absolutely, kind sir... I am looking forward very much to bonking with you."

He tips his head back, roars with laughter and then proceeds to roll a bow to me. Offering me his hand, I place mine in his, and he pulls me close to him. With his free hand he fumbles under his towel.

"What are you doing?"

"Turn around, Helena."

"Why?"

"Just please stop being so inquisitive, and turn around."

I do.

"Close your eyes."

My eyelids blackout...

"Move your pony tail to one side.

I swish bunched hair aside.

"What do you feel?"

"Well apart from your forever-at-your-service-cock nudging me between my buttocks, I feel something cold settling around my neck."

"I make no apologies for my cock's behaviour, but yes, I'm sorry that whatever's around your neck is cold, but I promise in a few moments it will warm from the natural heat of your flesh."

Pushing my rear into him, I ask, "What is it?"

"Open your eyes and look down, and then you will see."

I do both and when I see a fine gold chain weighted by an opalescent pearl, as the jewel nestling between my breasts, I gasp out in wonderment. Kissing the side of my neck, he mumbles against my goose bumping flesh, "You like it?"

I turn, "Like it? I absolutely love it."

"Perfect..." he kisses me again and swirls me around to face him. Looking adoringly at me, he breathes, "Happy twenty-first birthday, Helena."

Fondling the smooth, pink blush pearl between my thumb and forefinger. "You didn't forget after all."

Skimming his lips along mine, he tenderly replies, "How could I forget something as momentous as your key-of-the-door birthday? I'd be a fool, an incomprehensible blind, stupid idiot not to have noted it wouldn't I?"

In all my nakedness I blush throughout, and he grins with happiness.

"So now you have present number one," he quips, "fancy a quick, hard fuck before you receive your next gift?"

There are to be more gifts? Isn't this enough?

I am stunned, because this towelled, sleek, panther never, ever fails to amuse, excite and intrigue me, so as I let him lead me to what I can only describe as a bespoke crafted lounger specifically designed for sexual purposes. Pointing at this piece of furniture, I ask, "Will you be giving me a birthday seeing to fast and hard over that creation?"

"Since it's your special day, and you do give one hell of blinding blow job, I will fuck you, my Cinderella, however and wherever she wishes."

I giggle at him referring to me as Cinderella, and question, "Can I have three wishes, my fairy godmother?"

He guffaws with amusement at me calling him the fairy godmother, and gleefully replies, "You can have as many wishes as you like."

After I stood on my tiptoes, and whispered wish number one into his ear, I ran my fingers along the rim of his towel. While I loosened his towel to reveal his nakedness, he gave me such a carnal look, and then like Prince Charming, he knelt down, and slipped my heels in turn back onto my feet.

And all that is left for me to say, is that my first wish was promptly granted, performed, and savoured within five minutes flat! My other two wishes on the other hand...

After our heated sex session in the basement, we are now bathed and dressed. A few moments previous, Darius has blindfolded me, and I am now deadly curious as to what he has in store for me next. Holding my hand, he guides me forth and tells me that to take three steps in front of me. I carefully step down until I am on solid ground.

"Where are we going?"

"We're not going anywhere."

"What do you mean?" I ask and then question, "I don't understand."

"We're not going anywhere because we are already here."

"Where is here?"

He's now fumbling with the knot at the back of my head and as he releases the blindfold that has been obscuring my eyes, he sings, "T'dah!"

I stand still.

"You like it?" He kisses the side of my neck.

"That's... that's..." I stutter. "That's for me?"

"It most certainly is, Helena." He grins broadly dangling a set of keys with a Porsche fob logo attached."

Looking adoringly at the red Porsche Boxster, which is tied up with an enormous red bow, I exclaim, "I can't... I can't accept that... It's way too generous of you."

"You can and you will," he says with such precision.

"Why must I?"

"Because my darling, sweet, inquisitive, Helena, I love you... It's as simple as that."

I swing around and lunge myself at him, planting a series of light kisses all over his face.

"Stop it!" He tries to playfully fight me off. "You're making me all wet!"

"I love you... I love you." I chant over and over. "I love you sooooooooo very much!"

"I know." He smiles with boyish glee, and then totally bowls me over, by wrapping his arms around my waist, drawing me close to him, and suggesting something rather indiscreet!

"You want me to do what with you in my car?" I utter.

"I want you to..." he whispers, "to pull your panties to one side, slide down on my stiff cock, and ride me."

"What if I don't want to ride you in my new car?"

"Then maybe you could suck me off instead?" He shrugs.

"Darius...!" I scold. "You are insatiable to say the very least!"

Brushing his lips along mine, he tickles me when he replies, "I am quite wolfish, quite predatory, aren't I?"

"Yes, you are very a ravenous fiancé indeed." I kiss. "And I love it!"

"I like that." He smiles.

"You like what?"

"I like you calling me your fiancé."

"Why?"

"It makes me feel special."

"You are special."

"And you Helena are *my* special."

As I plant a light kiss upon his cheek, he asks, "So which is it to be, Helena? Do you wish to ride you fiancé, or perform fellatio upon him?"

The thought of having sex with him while the smell of newness in my car envelopes my senses, I groan, "Ride..."

"Mmmm... Perfect."

"When would you wish for me to ride you?"

Pushing his body into mine, as I feel his cock twitching against me, I ask him the question again, and he responds with, "Now."

Now it was.

Seven-fifteen p.m.

After assessing my outfit in the mirror, I pick up the black stole laid out on the bed, and I wrap it around me.

After exiting the bedroom, I walk down the stairs and into the lounge. I see Darius standing by the hearth sipping upon a glass of champagne. He is dressed in a black tuxedo, and he looks positively sexy to say the least! On seeing me, he places his flute of Dom Perignon down onto the mantelpiece, lets out a shrill wolf whistle and states, "You look dangerously hot in that dress. I think you should take it off!"Knowing full well I do look scorching hot, I flippantly reply, "Do I?"

"Yes," he answers while prowling towards me. "Take it off right now!"

"Excuse me?"

"I said take it off!"

"No!"

"Take it off, Helena, or I will have to take it off for you!"

"No!"

He's now almost with me, and by the look in his eyes, I think he might actually be going to take it off for me! He is with me now, and my stole I have discarded. Tipping his finger under my chin, he looks into my eyes, and without a single word exchanged between us, I quiver, as his fingers locate the large bow of the halter neck, and a sharp tug jerks around the back of my neck. Still staring intently at each other, while the soft black silk floats down over my chest, revealing my naked breasts, he holds me in his stare. His lips meet mine, and as the taste of expensive, vintage champagne infuses my mouth, I feel his hands grasping onto my hips. Pressing his body into me, my breasts swell against his highly priced suit, and my breathing increases as he sexily breathes into my mouth, "I've ordered us dinner in."

"What are we having?" I exhale while his hands explore my spine.

"Kusshis oysters..."

"I've never tasted an oyster before." I whine as his he nips the thin flesh that coats the side of my neck.

"You'll love them." He bites again. "They taste of the ocean."

With my body aching for him, he confuses me as he grasps the ties of my dress, and begins to redress me.

"I thought you wanted my dress off?"

"Later..." he smirks.

"You are a wicked devil!" I say.

"I know." He grins. "The wicked wolf of a boyfriend – That's me!"

"Why are you teasing me in this way?"

"Because I adore playing with you... I love seeing you come undone... I love putting you back together and then unravelling you over and over."

"Do you?"

"Yes, and right now the look on your face is a picture to behold!"

"You are so roguish!" I lightly chastise.

"Oh I am much more than just roguish." He chuckles. "I am impish, and my sexual appetite for you is positively unquenchable!"

"I hadn't noticed," I say while trying to stave off the arousal that he has just inflicted upon me. Cocking an eyebrow at me, while he expertly reties the bow back around my neck, and it settles back to its original state, he skims his hand over my left buttock. Suggestively caressing me through the silk of my dress, as his cock stiffens against my lower body, I moan into his mouth,

"What does Kusshis mean?"

"It's Japanese for Precious." He smiles. "Precious like you and that pearl necklace that's nestling around your neck."

"You speak Japanese?"

And as he so sensually hushes along my nude, glossed lips, "Yes, I do among many other tongue twisting languages."

I feel like I am about to dissolve right into his arms or elevate onto another level.

"And did you know," he adds that oysters are rich in amino acids that trigger increased levels of sex hormones."

"I didn't know that. You must have eaten heaps of them in the past then!" I giggle into his mouth.

"Yes, I have. I can't get enough of them in the same way I can't get enough of you."

"You really can't get enough of me?" I say, hoping for an, 'I love you, Helena,' but instead he caused my heart to swell when he enlightened me with the following:

"Helena," he says with conviction, "You are a powerful magnetic force and even if I wanted to... even if I wanted to forget you, which I don't, I know that I never ever could be without you. You, my precious make me whole. You are the rarest of pearls which resides within the most luxurious oyster shell ever discovered by man. It is as if I have been waiting for you to arrive from the first day that earth was created from out of nowhere."

Now stunned into silence, and feeling so very emotional at his speech, I reach to him and start to remove his jacket. He shrugs out of it and it lay where it fell. Resting up against the rim of the back of the sofa, as I started to fiddle with his black bow tie, he quizzes, "What are you doing?"

"I, my beautiful Adonis, am attempting to undress you."

"Why?"

"Just because..."

"Why do you want to strip me bare, Helena?"

With his tie now draped around his neck, as I turn the wing tips of his starched collar upwards, he tilts his head to one side, and looks adoringly at me.

"Why, Helena? Why do you feel the need to disrobe me?"

I stay quiet, and as button by button, as cufflink by cufflink, is unravelled, I pull open his shirt to reveal his dark, curly haired chest. Gently guiding his shirt down over his broad shoulders, past his biceps and releasing it from his person. I then kneel before him and begin to unbuckle his trouser belt.

"Baby," he leans over me, and whispers into my hair. "Talk to me?"

I stay quiet, and as his dress pants are loosened, he lifts his backside a tad off the sofa and I peel them down over his pert buttocks. He rapidly discards his shoes and steps out of his attire. He's now stroking my hair with a soft affection.

"Helena?"

I look up.

"Yes, Darius...?"

"You stun me."

"I know I do."

I kiss him there on his prominent bulge. His cock twitches strongly. I kiss him again, and again, and again until the crown of his cock protrudes over the waistband of his silk boxers.

"Baby?" he whimpers.

I look up.

"Yes, Darius... What is it?"

Looking down upon me, he breathes, "I love you."

"I love you too."

I draw down his boxers down over his hips, and curl my fingers around his pulsating girth. While fleeting my tongue along the smooth, spongy circumference of his purpling crown, he hisses through clenched teeth,

"I love you more."

"I love you equally."

His body is beginning to tremor and now he has no choice but to aid in steadying himself. With his hands gripped tight onto my hair, as I take him within my hands, and devour him with my mouth, my tongue and my fingers, his thighs tremble, and the sounds that warble from the back of his throat are so positively delicious, that throughout the future, they never left me... ever.

"I'm going to shoot!" he warns. "Take me?"

I slide him out of my mouth and reply, "I've hardly touched you..."

"Yes... I know, but I can't help wanting to burst!"

"Try to hold back..."

"I'll try." He breathes hard, "but I can't promise you that I won't spill!"

I chuckle at his choice of word for climax, and then encourage him to go ahead release by lightly sucking upon his left testicle, and when done, I take the other. He almost collapses forward but has the inner strength to control his stance. While I consume his sexuality, I tingle deep while revelling in the warmth of the most delicate parts of his body (apart from his scarred heart – that's truly fragile... truly breakable). He covers his hand over mine, encouraging me to stroke his shaft faster and faster. As I roll his generous length from its sturdy root to its sensitive tip, swirling the moisture that has come from my mouth and the moisture of his sweet pre-cum with the pad of my thumb over his now throbbing crown, he does finally *shoot* and his cum pulses upwards in jets; it spills in abundance over both our hands and he wails to the air, "Ahh... Fuck that's almost too good!"

It's better than good, Darius – for where I'm at, it's looking divinely heavenly!

I lick him there, here and everywhere tasting in his offering, tasting in his saltiness, and as I do, he pitifully whispers down to me, "Don't ever leave me again, Helena."

His body tremors once more and then he sinks to his knees. Cupping my face in his hands, he crushes his lips to mine and as his mouth trembles he droops further, and curls his body around mine. While he gently cries into my arms until there is nothing left emotionally for him to bleed out, I pledge to him with the whole of heart that I will never separate from him again – no matter what.

Chapter Fourteen

It's the middle of the night, and Darius is not in bed with me. Curious as to where he may be, I don my gown and slippers and go in search for him. On reaching the top of the stairwell, I pause to hear his voice coming from downstairs. Following the trail of sound, as it leads me to where he is, I find myself halting at the entrance to his office. The door is ajar. Pulling the sash on my gown tighter, I peek through the gap, and listen to the conversation that Darius is engaged with via the speakerphone on his desk.

With hindsight, I wish I hadn't listened, hadn't understood a single word that had been exchanged between Darius and Xavier, but nevertheless I had, and now this is the heart wrenching story that unfolded.

"How's Helena baring up, brother? Did she have a happy birthday?"

"I think she enjoyed her special day. I've left her sleeping soundly. She seems to be doing all right, but one can never really tell what is truly going on in one's mind, can one, Xavier?"

"No, I guess not."

"I hope that I can help in keeping any demons she may be harbouring.... Truth be told, brother, I virtually cracked up myself when she went missing for all those hours."

"I'm sure if she does have any bad monsters lurking around in her mind, you will be the one to help them fade into a non-existence."

"I do hope so. I'll do my utmost to protect her for any future harm."

Darius sighs and then continues, "So I believe you've called me not only to find out how Helena is, but to give me an update on how the quest to find her abductors/blackmailer is progressing?"

"Correct."

A long, drawn out pause followed, only to be diverted when Xavier divulged to Darius the following:

"Helena's abductor is called Milo Hunter, and the worst part is that he is..."

Another silence reigns...

"He's what, Xavier? Tell me."

"I'm sorry to say this, but he is actually Alice's step father."

-I retch on hearing her name.

Next I hear Darius boom, "Fuck... fuck... fuck!" which is rapidly followed by the sound of his fist ramming into what I can only describe as a hard surface. His voice strained, he then asks, "Is all this information bona fide?"

"Yes. It's a legit. My source is more than competent in her ability to search and sift out information that how shall I say, would not be easily be overturned by the highest court in the land."

"Continue..."

Xavier does.

"His accomplice," Xavier resumes, "Marcus Harvard, has been dating Alice since... Well, never mind when, the point of the matter is that the extortion of money from you in return for Helena's safe return could possibly boil down to having something to do with Alice. She was obviously sour over the demise of your relationship with her, and chances are that she wanted to hurt you, hurt Helena and wanted you to pay the price in more ways than just hefty finance. If she is involved, it would seem that her intent was to make you pay handsomely – emotionally and physically for breaking off with her. She's always made it perfectly clear in the past that you left her for Helena but we both know that not to be true, don't we, Darius?"

A longer, more agonising pause drawls on until Darius says, "Truer than true, brother. I left her because she would never be the right woman for me."

"Where do we go from here, Darius?"

"It's very late now, and I need some time to digest what you have told me... I also must get back to Helena."

"As you wish... But don't stew on it for the truth will out in the end.

"I won't brood upon it... I just want things fixed so Helena and I can move on forward with our lives."

"I understand. Goodnight, and Darius, I am truly sorry for what I had to tell you... especially at this time of night."

"It's alright, Xavier. You have nothing to apologise for. I'm just glad that you took mine and mother's nagging, stuck law school out, and passed the bar."

"I always knew my talents would come in handy one day, but I never wanted it to be like this... To see you and that beautiful fiancée of yours, so hurt."

"We're doing fine. Now go, go back and get into bed with Angelica, and... and... If you love her like I love Helena, and she's not just another notch on the top lawyer's bedpost, then do me a favour and ask the poor love-sick girl to marry you! Can't you see how much she adores you?"

"I adore her too, Darius. I truly do."

"Do you love her enough to make an honest woman out of her?"

"Yes, I do love her enough...Too much to lose her."

"Well ask her before too long... Promise me?"

"I promise, you... Goodnight, Darius."

"Goodnight, Xavier."

With my stomach now churning over at Xavier's and Darius's conversation, my head goes into a whirl, and the memories of my abduction begin to rise. Feeling like I am going to collapse right here outside Darius's office, I lean up against the door, and slide down until I meet the floor. I am unsure of how long I was curled up hugging my knees, rocking back and forth while humming to myself that this is all a dream – a bad, bad dream – and that soon, soon I will awake and this will all be behind me... behind us. If only one could rewind the past, and start certain parts and pieces of life again, wouldn't life be just perfect? I am broken from my thoughts when I hear a loud shattering of glass breaking through the silence. With my nerves all a jingle, I rise from my slump, turn and gingerly push the door open. Darius is quite clearly in turmoil. He is hunched over the drinks bar with his arms splayed out wide. As my vision travels along his left arm, it finally halts at his injured hand. His knuckles are scraped, and his hand is covered in blood. While he curses continually under his breath, at her, Alice, I note his bare back. Under the duress that he is in, the muscles beneath his shoulder blades flex and relax non-stop. I survey him further, and I can't help but notice that his blue-striped pyjama loungers are slung way too low off his lean hips for it to be considered legal! His feet are enticingly bare.

"Bitch!" he growls into the air. "The fucking, self-centred, conceited fucked up in the head, bitch!"

I cautiously take a few steps towards him, and tenderly place my hand upon his shoulder, and say, "Hey, baby...Why don't we pause for a moment and get that hand of yours cleaned up?"

He jumps out of his skin and then stiffens. I trail my fingers down his bulging bicep, resting it just below his elbow. He shudders.

"Please, Darius... Let me help you."

His body sags with a deep sigh, and I again ask for him to let me tend to his minor injury.

"How long have you been here?" he asks.

"Long enough to hear what you and Xavier were talking about..."

"You weren't supposed to hear any of that conversation, Helena. I'm really sorry."

"It's all right." I kiss against his neck. "You and I promised each other that we would never have any secrets, didn't we?"

"Yes, we did and this wasn't intended to be confidential. I was trying to... trying..."

"Trying to do what, baby?"

"I was, I am trying my hardest to protect you from any further mental trauma."

"Well," I begin to reassure, "you've been doing a fine job so far at sparing me the hurt. It isn't your fault I overheard. I woke up and you weren't with me. I was just coming to look for you. I wanted to know where you were."

He turns, and when I see the look of pain, hurt, anger, despair etched in and around his eyes, I tell him that everything will be fine. With his uninjured hand, he brushes a lock of hair away from my damp cheek, rubs the pad of his thumb up and down my cheekbone.

"Do you know that I would be nothing without you, Helena?"

"I... I..."

"You what," his lips brushing against mine... "Tell me, sweetheart."

"I would be nothing without you either." I quietly say, "Nothing at all."

While we lose ourselves in an entwining of tongues, speaking our own magical language, the room around us falls way, and time loses it order.

"I want you right now, Helena," he breathes into my open mouth.

"If you want me, then take me, Darius. I'm all yours."

He needed no more encouragement than my response.

"Slow or fast... Which would you prefer?"

"Slow."

"Then slow it shall be."

Drawing back from me, he grabs his white t-shirt that has previously been draped upon the back of the chair. I am amazed as he effortlessly tears it into a strip and proceeds to make a makeshift bind. Winding it around his fist, he winces a tad as the cotton fabric tightens against the lacerated skin of his knuckles.

"Let me..." I start to offer.

"Look!" He holds his bound fist up to the air. "Look, it's done."

"But... But..." I go to protest.

"No buts!"

"Darius please let me at least fetch some antiseptic and tend to your hand."

"No."

I give in; give up with my efforts to tell him that I really should take a look at his hand before he bound it.

"Don't fret, Helena." He smiles. "It's only a temporary bind. I'll let you play nurse later!"

I tut-tut him at his jest, and before I can retort in any way, He has hoisted me up. I wrap my legs around him, and he carries me across the room. On reaching his desk, he perches me upon the edge, and proceeds to shove my night gown up until my nakedness is revealed to him. Without hesitation, he leans over me, and supports his weight with his injured hand. With his good hand, well let's just say, his fingers did the most arousing talking imaginable!

"Fuck, baby," he hisses into my ear as he brings me close to climaxing, "you're soaking... you're dripping wet."

I lean back almost flush against the desk, and groan, "Make me orgasm like this."

"It will be my pleasure."

While he slides a finger, two fingers inside me, and begins to confidently locate my G-spot, I arch my back and wail for him to... to... to go a little faster.

"I want to taste you," he breathes into my mouth. "I want to feel you explode in my mouth."

I bite his lower lip, and without shame, I pant, "Then kneel and taste."

He crouches to his knees. And I close my eyelids and drift...

"Take me somewhere only we know, Darius," I speak into the air.

He does, and as every part and piece of me unravels before his very person, he blows the lightest puff of air over my post-climaxed clitoris and I, once again am left wanting, needing, and craving for so much more of the man who is looking up at me from between my legs – grinning!

The next morning...

"Please pass me the pepper mill, Darius."

He does. While I grind a generous amount over my scrambled eggs, he asks, "What are you thinking about?"

"I'm not thinking about anything."

"You must be thinking about something."

"Well I'm not," I curtly reply. And then add, "Why do you think that I am thinking about something?"

"Well, from where I am sitting, I can hear those inquisitive cogs whirring around in that over active imagination of yours."

Scooping up a spoonful of the creamy, free range egg concoction that is heaped before me, I say, "Do you really wish to know what I have been thinking about?"

Taking a noisy glug of his freshly squeezed orange juice, he says, yes, he does.

"Sure?"

"Sure."

"I've been thinking about her."

"Who?" he asks, as if he doesn't know!

"Her – Alice"

"For pity's sake..." he sighs, "Helena, why on earth are you letting her get to you?"

"I'm not!" I huff.

"Well it seems to me like you are."

"It's just that last night when I heard Xavier say that Milo Hunter is Alice's stepfather, I can't stop thinking that she must something to do with my abduction."

"It's a strong possibility, I have to agree but you, we can't dwell on this otherwise we won't be able to move forward."

"How do you propose I stop these thoughts?"

He grasps my hand in his and sighs, "I don't know, baby."

"I wish you did," I say with sadness.

"Helena?"

"Yes..."

"It will be all right in the end, I promise you that much."

"How do you know it will end well?"

"Trust me?"

"I trust you."

"Good. Then let's say no more on the subject and finish our breakfast."

I say no more but continue to think an awful lot about Alice.

Chapter Fifteen

Carter and Darlington Solicitors

London – Mayfair

3.50 p.m.

A month later Darius and I find ourselves seated within the luxurious offices of 'Carter and Darlington' solicitors. We are presently waiting to see James Darlington who is not only Xavier's partner within this law firm, but Darius' closest, childhood friend. Xavier is at present not here for he is presenting a case in court.

"Would you like a cup of tea or coffee, Mr Carter?" Loni, Mr Darlington's personal assistant asks.

He looks up from today's copy of the *Financial Times*, and replies, "I'm fine with just water, thank you."

She then turns her attention to me. "Ms Payet, what would you like to drink?"

"Just a glass of iced water, please..."

"Which would you prefer, sparkling water or still water?"

"Still would be fine, thank you."

As she tends to my drink, Darius pushes back the pristine white cuff that graces his wrist, and notes the time on his wristwatch. He lets out a long extension of a breath. Offered the my water, I take it from her, and settle it onto the side table next to me – I'm not actually thirsty. I guess I just ordered it to pass some time.

"Mr Darlington will be ready to see you both shortly," she informs us as she totters off back to her desk.

Darius glances over at me, and I slowly uncross and recross my legs in an alluring fashion. Smoothing down the skirt of my black Chanel suit, I smile at him. By the glint that is illuminating in his eyes, I can tell that he has just registered that I am pantieless. Leaning across the table that separates us, his voice sounding shell-shocked he whispers to me, "Good grief, Helena, this is a fine time for you to choose not to wear any panties."

Rubbing my wrists in turn, I smile. "I'm sorry. I was in a bit of a hurry this morning getting dressed because my dominant kept me suspended for longer than originally intended. Please would you accept my most heartfelt apologies, sir?"

"Heavens, Helena!" Exasperated, he says, "This is not the time to be playing one of our games. Do you by any chance have a pair rolled up in that handbag of yours? Please tell me you have?"

I do have a pair in my bag, but I'm not going to tell him the truth, am I! I mean, where would be the fun in that? Today is so stressful that I have to inject a smattering of playful, light heartedness into this day!

"No, I'm sorry, I don't."

"Well," he breathes with relief, "thank goodness I have a pair on my person."

"Excuse me?" I exclaim.

Surreptitiously extracting out a pair of semi-sensible silk, black lace-trimmed panties from the inner pocket of his dark navy, pinstripe Armani suit, he tells me to give him my hand. I do, and as he presses them firmly into my palm he tells me to close my hand and go to the powder room this instant and put them on.

"Why should I?"

"Because, Helena, as I previously said this is not the time to be flashing me your beautiful wares! And also, now I have to get through this important meeting of ours with the thought of your pussy almost being so easily accessible to me!"

Smirking at his thoughts, I tease, "Why is it not the time? I thought you were adamant about me being free and easy for you!"

"Helena," he groans, "please just be a good fiancée and go and put the goddamn panties on!"

"That's a first," I nervously laugh, "you asking me to put panties on instead of take them off!"

He shakes his head from side to side and slumps back into his seat, and he rests his hands behind his head, giving me a teasing bat of his lashes. I rise. Passing him en route to the ladies, he halts me by grabbing my arm. Gently angling me down so we are eye to eye, he tickles me to the bone when he informs me,

"After this frightful meeting is over, because you've misbehaved, I am going to fuck you fast and hard before we get home!"

"Promise me?" I lark.

"Scout's honour!" he gestures.

"I'm curious... Where do you intend to perform this act of reprimand upon me?"

"You'll just have to wait and see!"

"I can't wait to know! Tell me now!"

Letting go of my arm, I straighten and as I do, he gently slaps me on my arse, and urges, "Go... go and put the panties on."

I head off in the direction of the powder room to return clothed beneath my skirt and with Darius standing tall ushering me forth. I take his arm and say, "Sorry."

"It's all right."

"I didn't mean to behave inappropriately. I guess I'm just nervous."

"No need for sorry."

Before I can respond, Loni appears and we are ushered into the elite, sumptuous Mayfair office. A combination of seriousness and worry now reigns over me. We sit opposite James and he gives me a sympathetic smile.

"Are you ready to begin, Darius?"

"Yes, I am... Would you please proceed, James?"

Turning to me, James asks, "And you, Miss Payet? Are you comfortable if I start?"

I hold on very, very tight onto Darius's hand. My voice a wisp, I reply, "Yes, James. Please do begin."

"Milo Hunter-De'vore and Marcus Harvard are both in custody pending a court hearing."

A strained atmosphere fills the room. Darius lets go of my hand, rolls his chair forward, and rests his elbows on James's desk.

"So you're telling me that the two bastards who abducted my Helena, and extorted a million pounds from me are actually behind bars at present?"

"Yes, Darius, they are. I'm pretty much certain that they will never see the outside world again for a good lifetime of years."

I quake as I see Darius's whole body shudder with a mixture of rage and relief. "And her, Alice?" he hisses under his breath. "Was she involved? If she was I'll murder the bitch with my bare hands!"

James fleets a glance to me, and then to Darius. Looking down at the dossier in front of him, he turns the page. Pushing the bridge of his glasses up his nose, he looks direct at Darius and offers, "I can tell you this much..."

In a lighter but definitive tone, Darius asks, "Please reveal."

"It would appear that Alice was not involved. Her stepfather and her ex-boyfriend concocted the whole sordid idea purely as a revenge tactic for the demise of your past relationship with her."

"It was never a relationship," Darius angers. "It was ..." he looks to me with regret, with sadness in his eyes, and finishes, "it was a poor agreement... A massive error on my part... Once could call it a misjudgement of the meeting of minds."

A silence surrounds all three of us. Next, Darius rises from his seat, and walks the short distance towards the floor to ceiling window. Standing still he shoves his hands into the pockets of his suit trousers and looks out upon the street below. Moments pass and the strained silence is broken by these words; "I should... I should... I wish... I wish that I'd never set eyes upon Alice."

No one offers a response, least of all me. I mean what can you say to the man you love at a time like this? Do you say? 'Oh, never mind we all make mistakes from time to time?' Do you say, 'What manifested in the past, stays, in the past?' Do you say to him 'Yes, he should've passed her by?' No, you don't say a single word. You just be there for him. You say you love him unconditionally? Well then if you do, you must really love and understand him. You don't judge. Deciding what's right or wrong in our particular case is for the walls of the courtroom. The scales of justice for me do not belong within a relationship. You are not the jury, and your partner is not your judge.

He turns and focuses upon me.

"You see this beautiful woman sitting right here, James?"

"Yes, Darius." James nods.

"Without her, I am nothing."

"I understand."

"Without her, I would be a mere shell of a man."

I go to protest at Darius admissions, for if I hear another emotional word from him, I will break down and cry in front of these two men. Thankfully James intervenes by suggesting that Darius and I should not brood upon what has been divulged here. He suggests we should try to move on, and that time will eventually out the truth, and that he is one hundred percent certain that my abductors will serve a sentence far greater than imaginable.

"How can you be sure, James?"

James looks at Darius is such a way that I shift uncomfortably in my chair and something silent but powerful passes between them. Standing James then extends his hand to Darius, leans into him and passes a whisper into his ear. Darius's torso stiffens, and as the two men part, James looks to me. I can't fathom what he's thinking.

"Miss Payet?"

I rise.

"Call me Helena, James."

"Helena, although the circumstances are how shall we say, unfortunate, it has been a pleasure to meet you. Darius is a very lucky man."

"Thank you." I smile. "And I am a very lucky woman."

"Mr Darlington?" Loni's voice comes through the intercom.

"Yes, Loni."

"Your four twenty-five appointment has arrived."

"Offer them both a drink, and tell them I'll be with them soon."

Darius takes my hand in his, place my fingers to his lips, and I waver as he openly kisses my engagement ring.

"It's all going to work out fine," he says with conviction in his voice. "I promise you on my heart."

"I know it will," I bravely say.

"It will. Trust me." James adds.

Knowing full well that neither the three of us in this room can really guarantee whether or not this court case that looms over us will work out fine, I end the meeting by doing my utmost to move on forward.

On reaching the lift, Darius turns to me and asks, "Shall we take the stairs?"

"Yes, I could do with a little thinking time."

"Agreed..."

As we walk in silence, I wonder if he's thinking about her – Alice.

On reaching the underground car park, he grasps my hand in his and I falter inside when he says, "I'm been thinking about you."

"Me? Only me?"

"Yes... only you."

I brave it and push. "So you weren't thinking about Alice as we walked?"

He doesn't hesitate, he just answers, "No."

"Have I always been in your mind?"

"Yes. Even before I was created."

"That's nice to know."

"We can beat this you know."

"I know."

I push it a little bit more. "Do you hate her?"

"Hate is a very strong word, Helena."

"Well, do you?"

"No."

I cringe inside. "Why?"

"I don't hate her because I detest her. I prefer the word detest."

I sag with relief.

"It's quite cold down here."

He spins me around and wraps his arms around me. Snuggling into me, he asks, "Better?"

"Better."

And then the whole past scenario of office to basement is quashed when he tips his finger under my chin, angles my face upwards, and gives me the look that quivers me to my very inner core.

"Did you put the panties on as I asked?"

I shrug my shoulders, and lead, "Why don't you find out for yourself?"

"Mmm..." he muses, "maybe I will, and maybe I won't."

"You are a bounder, a cad, a teaser!" I playfully swat him across the chest.

He fuddles me by replying, "You'll have to wait, Helena."

"What do you mean? Wait for what?"

"As we drove to this meeting this morning, as you surreptitiously stroked my groin through the fabric of my trousers, you said the next time we had sex, you wanted me slow."

"I did and I still do."

"Well, I'm going to give you slow when we get home."

"I can't wait. You left me wanting this morning! Can't we do it – you know – in the car, or at least find a hotel?"

"Yes, you can wait and you will wait."

"No, I can't."

"There's no such word as 'can't' in our vocabulary is there?"

I sag. "No, there isn't... It doesn't matter, I still can't wait."

He grabs both my hands, and raises them above my head. My buttocks sweep against the bonnet of the sleek, black Aston Martin and I melt when he whispers, "Since you can't wait for slow, then you shall have to have it here, fast!

"Here?

"Yes, right here."

"But... But..."

"Stop protesting, Helena, for you and I are going to enjoy this."

"Am I? Are we?"

"Yes."

"You sound so very sure of yourself, Mr Carter!"

"Trust me?"

"I trust you."

"Say your safe word?"

"Checkmate. Why? Will I need to use it here?"

"It's always a possibility when I'm fuelled up with frustration!"

"What are your intentions towards me at this particular moment in time?"

"To fuck you hard over the bonnet of my car, and make you go crazy!"

"Crazy?"

"Yes, sex-crazy."

"How will you make me go batty?"

"By pulling your panties to one side and slowly teasing you."

"How will you tease me?"

"By stroking the crown of my cock against your aching centre. I will soon have you greedy with lust and you will be begging with me to fill you and fuck you hard!"

"If I beg you, will you fuck me hard?" I can't help but ask.

"Yes, I will. It will be my pleasure."

"Why?"

"I'm a gentleman and therefore I believe in pleasuring my lady well! I," "he adds. " I also want it rapid! And I know you, you little femme fatale do too!"

"Why do you want it so fast?"

"Because apart from the fact that I have so much pent up aggression in me right now, I wouldn't mind catching a glimpse of my manhood as it slides in and out of what is mine."

"And why do you want to watch?"

"I get off on watching!"

"Why?"

"Because I get aroused at watching me slide in an out of you while you drench me in your wetness."

"That's very, very descriptive, Darius!"

He chuckles. "That's the abridged version!"

"And what's the unabridged?"

"Do you really wish to hear it?"

"I do."

"Well if you wish to hear it then I suggest you do this: Bend over and pull those expensive, black, lace trimmed panties to one side. I want to feel the lace trim tickling my cock as I slide into you."

"What, now?"

"Right now...!"

"You're kidding!"

"I'm not! Trust me."

Suddenly feeling cowardly, I ask, "Are you really, really sure?"

"I'm sure."

"I'm... I'm... I'm not any more." I admit. "It's a bit risky in this underground car park, isn't it?"

"It was risky back in the lift, remember?"

"Yes, I suppose it was."

"You took the risk though, didn't you?"

"I did, but I wasn't consciously aware of the camera in the beginning like I am," I point to the ceiling, "aware of that camera up there."

"Risk is good for the soul," he says. "And it's good for the eyes, and also good for the blood! I climax so much harder when taking a risk!"

Goodness me, Darius!

Trying to stave off the imminent *car-banging*, I ask, "How hard do you climax?"

"Hard enough to make sure you to feel every single spurt, every single twitch, and every single lingering drop!"

Oh my!

"What about the security cameras?"

"Refer to risk!"

"But... but" again I object. "This is too risky... I can't do this... I... I..."

Within a flash, he has me, and I have to admit I do want him to take me, but here for security to see? My breasts are flush with the cold bonnet of the car, and he aligns his body over mine, my nipples stiffen as the silk fabric of my blouse rub against my bare flesh. As I feel him fumbling behind me, he whispers into my ear, "I'll be extra quick."

"Hurry up!" I urge. "Before I change my mind."

He does hasten by raising the hem of my skirt, and as he sees that there is no need for me to pull my panties to one side as I never adhered to his previous request, a rash unzipping of his trousers is heard, and as promised, he took me. A little slow at first, while explicitly rasping into my ear a cache of uncensored obscenities and the aforementioned unabridged version! As his pace increased, I had to stifle a moan with my hand, because as I climaxed, hot, abundant and powerfully hard, I felt a new sensation penetrate me, higher, between my buttocks.

Breathing fast, he asked, "Baby...?"

"Yes."

"Did you enjoy the fast and furious fuck?"

"I did."

"What did you feel while I was climaxing?"

"I felt something different... but I don't know quite what it was?"

"Do you want me to tell you what it was?"

"I do."

And as we both jumped up, rapidly adjusted our clothing, he mouthed to me what the sensation was; I nearly died on the spot! So while I tried to recover from what he had just divulged to me, he unlocked the car, and stepped inside. I too seated myself, trying to not to only make sense of what he has just told me but also trying to get used to the sensation that was weighing inside me. As the car engine roared into life, he floored me even further by adding, "And next time, Helena, just please do as I ask and wear the fucking panties!"

"Why?" I asked while he reversed the vehicle.

"Well, then I wouldn't have had to insert the glass butt plug for your disobedience!"

I gasp at the thought of a conical shaped glass butt plug that is now weighted inside me, "How... how..." I stammer, "How long do I have to keep the plug thingy in for?"

Devilishly grinning at me, he winks. "Until the moment I decide otherwise."

"So is this my punishment for not putting the panties on as you asked?"

He shrugs his shoulders. "Something like that!"

I sigh, and then slip my hand into the pocket of my suit jacket, and run my fingers along the lace trim of unworn panties. Rolling the delicate fabric between my thumb and forefinger, I close my eyes and try to visualize it through Darius's eyes. On my imagination being, well let's say, successful, I found myself openly pressing my thighs together and having to resist the temptation to slip my hand between my legs.

"I know what you been doing."

"What have I been doing?"

"You've been fiddling with the panties in your pocket while having dirty thoughts about us!"

"How do you know?"

"I saw you pressing your thighs together a short moment ago and now you want to orgasm don't you?"

"I didn't orgasm with you."

"I know."

"Do you still want to orgasm?"

"Yes."

"Then put the panties on first."

"Why?"

He raises an eyebrow, and gives me the look that says don't rile me.

"Just put them on, Helena."

I did... and within moments, as my self induced orgasm ripped through me, intensified by the object filling my behind, I cried out his name with such gusto...

Darius drove, smiling the entire journey back to the condo!

That evening Darius was in an extremely rampant and wolfish mood.

"Bend over the bed for me Helena!"

"Why?"

"Because, my disobedient sweetheart, I am going to screw you from behind while revelling in seeing my cock pulsate as I slowly side it in and out of your tight pussy."

Good grief, Darius!

I do, and while he sensually peels those blessed panties that he has become fixated with down today over my rear, I ask, "When can I take the plug out, Darius?"

"Why?"

"It's getting a little how shall I say, heavy?"

"I might let you take it out after I've enjoyed fucking you senseless!"

"Oh... And why do you wish for me to keep it in while you fuck me?"

Slapping me hard on my rear, he replies, "You'll see in a moment!"

With said panties now dangling off my right ankle, I turn to see him... He has the most dirty, filthy grin plastered across his beautiful face, and by that look of his, I know that I am soon to be devoured by him! As he drove his cock deep into me, he was right... I now fully understood why he had wished for me to keep the plug in situ. Firstly Darius's pleasure was enhanced because as the amount of space in my pelvis had been reduced by the invasion of the butt plug, and as a result of this alien sex toy in my body, he groaned into my ear, that even though I have a perfectly tight pussy, it felt tighter than normal, and he was going to have to fight really hard against his climax. Secondly, I have to say that additional texture provided by the plug made my vagina feel different – and it too made his cock feel harder, longer and wider than it actually is. And so with every stroke of him inside me, pushing me to the hilt, this all felt so extremely pleasurable, that the guilt feeling of having a sex toy plugging my anus vanished from my mind. When he came, he came quickly, and with such conviction. Everything felt more defined within my vagina, and as I wailed my orgasm, it was multiplied and intensified by him slowly withdrawing the butt out from my anus. Collapsing onto the bed, my body all a tender quiver, his cock still throbbing away inside me, as I felt his finger circle where the plug once temporarily resided, I had taboo visions of his cock invading me there while his tight balls slapped against my arse cheeks! As if he read my mind, He flopped on top of me and whispered, "Maybe another time, I'll deflower you there if you wish."

"I wish... Maybe..." I breathed heavy into the pillow beneath me while he shifted his weight against me.

Rolling onto our sides, we curled our bodies around each other's and as his eyelids drooped heavily, I quietly hushed, "When will you grant me my wish?"

As his lashes flicked open, he drew me close into him and soothed against my hair, "When I have explained to you exactly what you and I will experience from consenting to participate in anal sex."

"And when will that be?"

As he began to drift off to a slumber, he murmured, "Soon, baby... Sleep first..."

We slept deeply.

Chapter Sixteen

October

Two months on.

A few weeks ago, after a long and lengthy debate, it had been *proven* that Alice actually had nothing to do with this case. For some strange reason, I silently beg to differ. Where she may be is no concern of mine or Darius's for that matter, but I still have this nagging feeling that she is connected to my abduction in some way, shape or form and I fear that we have not heard the last of her.

Verdict Day

The last few months have been quite simply a living hell. Today, even though it is closure day, I fear in my heart, will be no different than the last time I was brought up to the stand. So here I am again, standing up in court. The judge, the jury and virtually everyone else present is focusing upon me. (Why do I feel like the accused and not the victim as I obviously am?) Darius is seated up in the balcony, along with Angelica. Cali, Darius's stylist/personal assistant is also with them. Over the recent months, with her by Darius's side, supporting him, I have come to trust and care deeply for her.

Milo Hunter-De'vore and his accomplice/my abuser, Marcus Harvard are seated with their respective lawyers. My lawyer, Xavier is at his seat too. While I make eye contact with QC Knightly, I can tell by the fierce look in her eyes that she is eager to put me through my torment – for the final time.

"Recapping, Ms Payet," QC Knightly begins. "On the 6 January 2018, you, Ms Payet were on your way to your place of work, we're you not?"

Focusing upon her, I answer clearly, "I was."

"And as you ambled along, on that fine winter's morning, you say that you were literally bowled over by the accused?" She points to Marcus Harvard and follow her lead. I shiver, and on seeing the salacious grin spreading across his face my stomach churns. I look to my knotted hands and take a deep breath.

"Is this correct, Ms Payet?"

I am quiet.

"Ms. Payet?"

I still remain silent.

"Ms Payet..." Her voice commanding me to respond, "... Is this correct?"

I look from my hand, to Marcus and then to Darius and finding my voice, I reply, "Yes."

She smiles unkindly and continues. "Aforementioned accused, after apologising, and helping you to your feet then proceeded to offer to take you for a coffee. You agreed to this offer of his?"

I again gaze up to Darius who face is full of sadness and with my voice almost a whisper I respond, "Yes, I did."

"Excuse me, Ms Payet?"

My voice now virtually non-existent, I respond, "Yes, I did."

"Speak up Ms. Payet."

I clear my throat and say as clearly as I can, "Yes, I did."

"Why did you agree to his kind offer?"

"I was shaken up... I was unnerved."

"Would it not have been more sensible to say no to having coffee with a total stranger, albeit one that had accidently brought you to your knees?"

"With hindsight, yes, it would've been."

"Do you often make a habit of having coffee on a whim with men off the street?"

Connor... Oh please, don't dredge up Connor. Why do I have this sickening feeling that she is going to drag my Connor into this horrible trauma?

"Objection...!" Xavier intervenes. "My colleague, QC Knightly is attempting to lead my client down the judicial rabbit hole!"

"Sustained..." the judge replies and adds, "Please, QC Knightly, adhere to the facts, and try not to create fiction in my courtroom. This is not a fairy story we are encountering here, this is real life working in motion.

"Apologies, my lord..." she replies with a hint of distaste, and then aims straight for me.

"Ms Payet is it possible that you may have actually created the situation by bumping into the accused rather than him into you?"

No – I die inside.

"If so, one could say that it was you that instigated this whole wild scenario of lies, could one?"

Now filled with a mixture of anger and frustration, I quip, "Why would you think that I would've done such a thing?"

"Please do not surmise, Ms Payet, you are just here to answer the question, and please remember that you have sworn on the oath."

"No, I didn't create the situation," I say with firmness and agitation in my voice. "I... I..." I stammer, "I..."

"Ms Payet?"

"I... I..."

Before I can reply there is a there is a flurry of commotion within the room. And before she is able to resume with her word twisting, a hush descends upon the courtroom. Both Milo and Marcus much to my amazement are quickly ushered out of the room, and I am left shaking and bemused. I shiver as Xavier and Knightly are summoned up to the bench; while I stand *stripped bare.* My mind full of confusion, I raise my lashes and look up to the balcony. I sink inside when I see that Darius, Angelica and Cali are in the process of exiting the viewing area.

Where are they going? And more to the point, what's happening here?

Through the foggy haze now enveloping me, I hear the court being informed that there will now be an hour's recess. The hammer goes down hard and Xavier turns and strides towards me.

"What on earth is happening?"

He removes his round spectacles, leans onto the surface and replies, "I'm not sure at present."

"Xavier? What do I do now?"

He then informs me that I will be directed by the court usher on my next move for he has now to go and reside in the judge's chambers along with QC Knightly. Lightly patting my hand he tells me that everything is going to be fine.

"How can it be fine?" I quietly say. "This is all a mess."

"Ms Payet?" A hand curls around my upper arm.

I turn to see the court usher.

"Please come with me."

"Go now, Helena," Xavier softly urges. "Everything will be all right."

I can do no more but to be taken to where I am *supposed* to be. On walking into the waiting area, I see Darius standing face to face talking with James. Angelica is seated with Cali, and they are deep in conversation. I feel as if everyone is staring right at me. I falter and hold on to the table in front of me. (Why do I still feel like the accused?) As my knees weaken and buckle beneath me, Darius is right with me.

"Hey, hey, baby," his voice caring and considerate, "steady on there, I've got you."

"You've got me?"

"I'll always have you."

Thankfully.

"What's going on, Darius?" I anxiously ask. "What's happening? Why did the accused get escorted out of court and why are we at present in a recess?"

"We've..." he gestures to James to come over. "We have no idea, but shortly I am sure that we all will."

"Do you think that I will have to go back in there again?"

"It's a possibility."

"I can't... "I cry... "I don't want to see their faces ever again."

"You have to sweetheart, it's the law... It will be the last time – I promise."

"How can you promise me that?" I rage. "Death will be the only guarantee that I will never see either of them again."

"Helena... Please..." he softly says while attempting to hold me in his arms.

I jump back from him and without reason say, "Don't you dare touch me!"

Reeling backwards, he, after taking a few steps back from me, shoots me the most bemused look, and I wilt inside. James intervenes by grabbing his attention, and I stand alone for a few painful minutes, until finally I am approached by Angelica. Putting her arm around my shoulder, she soothes, "Come on... don't be so hard on Darius... He's finding all this extremely difficult too."

"Hard!" I shrug her off and unreasonably exclaim, "he wasn't the one who was abducted was he! He wasn't the one who was a hair's breath away from being raped, was he? He wasn't the one; he isn't the one who has been left mentally traumatised by those thugs, is he?"

"No, he wasn't any of these things you mention," she sympathetically replies. "But my angel, he was terribly distraught beyond belief for the duration of the whole time you were missing. He thought he'd lost you forever... And so did I."

I am so close to a mental breakdown that I don't think I can take much more, and as desperation floods through my veins, the foyer suddenly fills with another rush of commotion. I try in earnest to search out Darius, so I ask, "Can you see him anywhere, Angelica?"

"No, but he can't be too far away."

I grasp her hand in mine with the full intention of leading her with me to find him, and as our hands grip tightly onto each others, I sway as I see the sea of people part and Darius striding towards me, closely followed by James. Angelica tightens her grip on me, and I on her.

"What's happening?" I whisper to no one in particular.

On reaching me, Darius's eyes have misted over, and the stressed look that he has carried with him of late appears to have abated a little. Angelica lets go of my hand, and Darius takes my shaking palm in his.

"What's happening?" I breathe up to him.

Taking both my hands in his, he presses his forehead to mine, and I begin to quake with the fear of the unknown.

"It's all over, Helena. It's all over."

"I... I..." I stammer. "I don't understand what you mean – over?"

Drawing back a tad from me, he smiles briefly, and explains, "New conclusive and immovable evidence came to light during the time you were last on the stand. The judge felt it only correct to exercise his supreme right to bring the case to a close and pass a sentence. I am in awe when he also tells me that the punishment for their crimes cannot be divulged at present but what has been weighted upon both men is more than substantial."

My head in a spin, I weakly mumble, "I still don't understand."

"Helena," he breathes with desperation, "it's over. Please try to grasp and accept the fact."

"How can it be over?" I sob. "There has been no guilt found in the open court."

"Helena, I understand you're confused and emotionally drained. We both are. But my darling, it's over."

Why do I have a feeling that Darius, James and Xavier all together had something to do with the case suddenly being brought to a head? If they had, and it was all three of them who aided in steering it towards an abrupt ending, I ask myself two things: One. How did they work *their magic*? And two. What would Darius not do for me? *Kill* – my mind shivers and I fall as if I am inebriated, into the safety of his arms.

233

With his upper body now wrapped around me, he holds me tight, and explains to me that when we get home, he will divulge everything to me in detail, and then I will most definitely understand how the trial concluded.

"But... but..." I demur.

"Hush," he soothes into my hair. "Just go with the flow, Helena, and I truly promise you that everything is going to work out just fine."

I am so drained and as a feeling of a sense of utter relief sinks right through me, I choose to do as Darius had suggested, and as we hold hands and walk together towards the exit, the chitter-chatter around us fades into the air. We step out into the world and onto the steps of the courthouse. The paparazzi as expected are waiting for their daily dose of gossip and photographs. The noise is phenomenal and I am not sure if I can take much more.

"Take a deep breath, Helena."

I do.

I am now held tight around the waist. Darius has put on his professional, movie star stance, and is at present delighting the paparazzi and the general public with his presence. A female reporter rushes forward, nearly tripping over in her eagerness to reach him, to reach us, and without a breath taken, she launches straight into me with the following question. I recoil.

"So how does it feel, Ms Payet, to know that the men who abducted you... The men who extorted a million pounds from your..." She hesitates and looks goggle-eyed at Darius. "Your delightful and gorgeous husband-to-be..."

Back off Missy! runs through my thoughts...

Fleeting a glance at Darius, she bats her heavily mascara swept lashes at him, who in return gives her the most intense warning glare imaginable. "And," she then unkindly adds, "how does it feel knowing that the man who nearly raped you, a film star's fiancée, along with your blackmailer, have both finally been sentenced?"

I feel sick. Her inappropriate question hits me like I have just run head first into a brick wall, and I look to Darius for some kind of help. He furrows his brow, and as a series of blinding flashlights obscure my vision, suddenly I feel the floor beneath my feet begin to move. It is as if I am floating through the air. Darius grip around my waist has tightened and he is with one arm guiding me through a make believe path that leads towards our waiting car.

"Darius... Darius!" a barrage of news hungry reporters shout, "Over here... Another picture of you and our heroine, our woman of the hour, Ms Payet?"

Me. A woman of courage?

He is expertly ignoring everyone around him, and I am fast failing, and as the next question bombards, it really hurts beyond a belief.

"So, Darius, can you tell us where your ex-girlfriend, Alice De'vore, fits into the story? Do you think that she was secretly behind Ms Payet's abduction and the extortion of money from yourself?"

I believe she was I want to shout out so very badly! But if I did no one would hear me would they? If they did, would anyone actually believe me? I doubt it.

"I feel dreadfully nauseous," I say to the air.

"Hold onto me tight, Helena. We're nearly at the car" he assures. "Just try to blank everyone out and keep moving forward."

"What about Alice?" A woman's voice asks again. "Come on Darius, tell us. Was your jealous ex-girlfriend behind everything?"

"I'm going to be sick, Darius." I gasp.

"No you're not, Helena. Just take a huge breath. I've got you."

More flashes are followed by further chants of, "Where's Alice? Where's Alice...Where's Alice."

No comment." Darius coolly says to into a microphone that has just been shoved between us by a tall, stick-thin redhead.

"Well," she huffs, "there's no smoke without fire, Mr Carter!"

"No comment!" he rages again, and as she triumphantly hisses back. "So come on, Darius, we all know that you are one for creating dramas, so come on, don't be shy and spill the beans! You of all people *must* know where she is!"

He doesn't offer another word. We move rapidly, and as microphone after microphone is stuck in our pathway, we start to move quicker.

"Tell us, Mr Carter." Another question splits through the frantically barraged air. "When did you last see Ms De'vore? Recently was it?"

"No comment!"

But this time his answer is filled with a sense of threat and within a moment, an eerie hush briefly crushes over everyone close by. As the safety of our escape vehicle comes into my view, our view, I gasp a much needed gulp of air, and flood with relief when I see Giorgio holding the passenger door open. On reaching the open door of the black Bentley SUV Darius literally shoves me in first. As he joins me, and Giorgio shuts the door behind us, we both sag back into the seat. The noise is faint, but apparent enough for me to realise that the paparazzi aren't going to abate until we leave.

"Step on it, Giorgio." Darius orders with an unbelievable unique calmness.

And as the car motors off and accelerates, I'm left with the ringing in my ears of the last reporter's question - *'Tell us, Mr Carter, when was it that you last saw Ms De'vore? Recently was it?'*

It was the morning after the night after the verdict...

Rolling onto my side, I gaze at Darius, and ask, "Darius, did you have anything to do with the case being brought to an abrupt end?"

The corners of his eyes crinkle up. "Ask me no questions," he sighs. "And, Helena, I assure you that I will tell you no lies."

"Well, did you?" I ask again while running my finger over his bottom lip.

Kissing the tip of my finger, he enquires, "Why are you so keen to know, baby?"

"I want to know the exact truth. I've never hear of a court case ending in that way... they just don't finish in that way."

"Some do. Some have." He flutters his lashes at me.

"What do you mean, some do, and some have?"

"Please, would you just drop it, Helena?"

"But..."

"Look, sweetie, the main point is that those men are behind bars for a good portion of their lives and you and I can now safely and happily move on forward with our lives."

"You did, didn't you?" I say with definition. "You actually had something to do with the outcome, didn't you? You did something to quash it didn't you?"

"I may have," he suggests. "And then again I may have not."

"Why are you being so twisty with words? Why won't you tell me the truth?"

"Helena," he sighs, "could you please, please just let this subject matter drop."

"Why?"

"Drop it for there is nowhere to go with this conversation!"

"What will you do if I keep asking because you know I will keep badgering you until I get a concrete answer from you, don't you?"

"I won't do anything at all. I just won't confirm an affirmative answer to you."

"Why?"

"Enough." He rolls over, sits up and snaps, and I look up to him and carry on probing.

"Did you bribe the court?"

"No I didn't... for that's not at all possible."

Now trailing my finger along his midriff, I ask, "But you had tried?"

He groans at my touch. "A resounding no to that ridiculous idea of yours too..."

"Then why on earth did it end in the way that it did?"

Gritting his teeth, he runs his fingers through his mess of morning curls and firmly answers, "It just did."

"I don't accept that answer."

"Well, you'll have to."

"Why?"

"All I can say is that it ended because I know someone who knows someone who knows someone with extreme power."

"Like who?"

"I am not at liberty to say."

"Why?"

"Helena?

"Yes?"

"Shut up."

I don't quiet.

"Did you do anything illegal?" I enquire while lightly kissing his tummy button.

"No." He responds, shifting under my touch.

"Then what did you do?"

"I didn't do anything."

"You didn't do absolutely anything at all? Swear on your life?"

"I swear on my life." He taps the scar over heart and I soften. "I did nothing at all."

"Promise me?"

"I promise... now will you let it go?"

"Yes."

"And you promise me that we won't mention this again?"

"I promise."

"Good."

"Darius...?"

"Yes Helena?"

"Thank you for making everything better."

He looks to me, and I melt inside when he smiles,

"It was my pleasure."

"Talking of pleasure..." I lead, "Pleasure me?"

He slips down the bed, rolls on top of me, and slowly pins my arms above my head. Holding both my wrists with his left hand, she smiles wistfully. Focusing upon me, as his eyes mists over, his lips hover above mine. "By god do I love every part and piece of you... Even the most stubborn and annoyingly inquisitive pieces of you. You never fail to leave me breathless."

"I love you too." I meekly say as he spreads my legs with his knee.

"How would like me to pleasure you...Slow or fast?"

"Slow...very slowly."

And as he penetrated my body, slow it was.

One month on....

Wednesday 21 November 2018

Nine a.m.

Facing each other, as the soft autumn light streams in through the skylight above us, I pull the sheeting over us obscuring us from the world and ask, "Do you like your birthday gift then, Darius?"

"I adore it." He smiles while running his fingers lightly over the 18k white gold/ceramic 'Trinity de Cartier' bracelet that has recently graced his left wrist. With curiously in his voice, he enquires, "Where did you purchase it from?"

I can't help but smile as the memories of our once-upon-a-time heated, sexual exchange in Selfridges lingerie cubicle come forth... "Selfridges" I answer.

He grins... "Ah yes, Selfridges. I love Selfridges, especially the lingerie department!"

"I know you do," I giggle. "But are you sure you like my gift to you?"

"Of course I'm sure. Why on earth wouldn't I be?"

"Well, considering you bought me a pearl necklace and a Porsche for my birthday, my gift seems a little... A little... lost in comparison?"

"Don't be so silly, Helena. I love it. It came from you, so what is there not to like or love about it?"

"Nothing, I guess. Do you want to know the significance behind it?"

"Yes I would."

"It is a symbol of my undying love for you. It is a token of my affection."

"Baby...?"

"Yes."

"It's perfect."

"Truly it is?

"Truly it is."

"So now we have established that you are happy with your present, fancy a birthday snuggle-cuddle before I bring you a lavish breakfast in bed?"

He twiddles with the bracelet, grins and then looks directly into my eyes. "I wish... I wish..."

"What do you wish for?"

"I wish for you to hop on and ride me instead of a snuggle-cuddle."

Giggling at his choice of words, I say, "You'd rather I rode you than cuddled you? How very surprising to say the least!"

Rolling onto his back, he grasps his cock in his hand, and I fall about into more chirpy titters for he had just said to me, "Hop on to my stiff cock, and while you pleasure this birthday boy, I shall take an enormous amount of pleasure in lazily laying back and watching you enjoying riding me!"

His wish was promptly honoured, and I must say that we both luxuriated in a long, slow birthday ride!

Six p.m.

We are laid out on the cushion strewn sofa of the condo lounge, and are both naked. I am coiled around Darius's body. He is bearing down upon me, with love lighting up his beautiful blue irises. We are post-coital; the half-eaten Tai takeout, that he chose as his birthday meal is strewn across the glass top table. And our chopsticks are scattered where they lay. The smattering of ceiling lights that are dotted around the room had been set to dim, and the over sized television that virtually takes up the entire wall of the condo lounge is on low, and is still showing the movie, *Meet Joe Black*. I turn my head to the right, run my fingers lightly down Darius's sweat sheened back, and glance at the screen; it's showing one of my favourite parts of the film...

The swimming pool love scene – 'Death's deflowering'.

Joe (Death, the entity, who has been temporarily residing in another man's body throughout the movie) is making love for the first time to Susan (Who believes that Joe is in fact the man she met at the beginning of the film, in the coffee shop.) – This love making scene is full of sweetness and wonder, and the sensual abandonment to the physical act of lovemaking is so delicate that it takes my breath away. – In the same way that Darius has just made love to me as if it was both of our first times.

I love movies that you can't do without – don't you?

As I focus upon the scene unfolding, my heart goes into an irregular rhythm when Darius props himself up on his elbows, blows a light puff of air in an upward motion so the rogue curl that has fallen over his forehead bounces up in the air only to settle where it organically laid. He smiles widely, and then launches into the following quote: "Love is passion, obsession, someone you can't live without. I say, fall head over heels. Find someone you can love like crazy and who will love

242

you the same way back. How do you find him? Well, you forget your head, and you listen to your heart. And I'm not hearing any heart. Because the truth is, honey, there's no sense living your life without this. To make the journey and not fall deeply in love, well, you haven't lived a life at all. But you have to try, because if you haven't tried, you haven't lived."

I look up to him with tremendous warmth in my heart. "Tell me you love me now, Darius."

He looks down to me with an equal quantity of undying love and murmurs against my lips, "I love you now, Helena. I have loved you always."

"Tell me again..."

"I love you now, Helena. I have loved you always."

"Again..."

He presses his lips to mine.

"I love you now, Helena. I have loved you always."

I run my fingers through his silken, messed up curls, and breathe into his mouth, "You are my passion, Darius. You are my obsession. You are someone that I can't, I don't ever want to, live without. You drive me crazy. You make me forget my head, so I have no choice but to listen to my heart."

His cock twitches inside me, and his taut midriff stiffens against my middle.

"Tell me again, Helena."

I squirm beneath him, and stare deeply into his eyes. He moves inside me.

"You are my passion, Darius. You are my obsession. You are someone that I can't, I don't ever want to, live without. You drive me crazy. You make me forget my head, so I have no choice but listen to my heart."

"Tell me one more time... but slower..." he retreats and returns into me.

"You are my passion, Darius... You are my obsession... You are someone that I can't... that I don't ever want to live without... You drive me crazy....You make me forget my head, so I have no choice but to listen to my heart."

"Ditto, baby..."

And as he buried his body as deep as he possibly could into mine, and took us both to the edge and back, when he finally climaxed, hot, hard, and powerfully into me, the only word I heard was the repetitions of my name falling from his bowed lips and settling upon my fragile heart, followed by him once again asking me to marry him before the year was out.

Chapter Seventeen

Thingvellir National Park – Iceland.

Four weeks later

Friday 21 December

It was a magical day, our wedding day. It was low key, almost secretive in a sense, and it turned out to be just perfect. We'd chosen to get married in Iceland – How we came to choose the venue was that we, unbeknown to each other had always as children, had a passion to visit the beautiful country of Iceland. Another reason was that we were also hoping that within our seclusion, the paparazzi wouldn't be able to find us, to hound us on our special day – And luckily, I think we may have got away with it. Darius and I had agreed on a quaint, little church situated in the Thingvellir National Park. Our guest list was as follows: Xavier and Angelica, and Cali, along with her boyfriend, Ed... That's all.

Angelica steps out of the hired Porsche Macan first.
"Here," she offers, "take my hand."
I do.

Stepping out onto the salted encrusted short pathway that leads up to the church, I turn to her and ask, "How do I look?"

Tugging at the lapels on my crème coloured, faux fur box jacket, she replies, "You look beautiful, Helena."

"Do you think Darius will like what I am wearing?"

"Well if he doesn't," she giggles, "he must need his brainbox testing!"

I laugh at the bizarre thought of Darius having his head examined!

"I can't believe that this is really happening. Can you?" I ask as she adjusts the rear of my veil.

"No, I can't, but I am so very happy that it is. There," she claps her red satin gloved hands together. "You are good to go, Helena."

"I'm really nervous." I whisper. "What if... if..." I stammer, "What if he's not... What if he's changed his mind?"

Linking her arm in mine, she assures, "Don't be daft! He would follow you to the ends of the earth and back. He'll be there, you'll see, and everything will be fine."

I take a deep breath and as we proceed to the entrance of the church, the world around me fades and all I can think about is my husband-to-be waiting inside the church. We climb the three stone steps, and halt at the open door.

"Are you ready to walk the walk of love, Helena, and become Mrs Carter?"

"I am. I'm very ready, Angelica."

Through the fine mesh of my pearl encrusted veil I look straight ahead. Seated are Cali and her boyfriend, Ed. They turn to see me, and I smile. Next, I look to the centre and on seeing Darius dressed in his groom's attire, my heart does cartwheel after cartwheel. He is wearing a Prince of Wales fine check suit – An attractive shade of azure blue which compliment his irises perfectly. In his lapel is a single red rose. As he turned sideways, and saw me, his eyes sparkled so prominently, that I faltered against Angelica.

"Blimey, Angelica," I gasp, "he looks so handsome. He's just taken my breath away."

At which Angelica responds, "You both look perfect."

Darius then beams at me the most delightful smile, and I melt inside.

"Shall we go?" Angelica whispers.

"Let's do this," I quietly say. And with that, I squeeze her arm, and we both take the mini walk in unison. When we have completed our passage down the aisle of this petite church, she unlinks from me, takes my small bouquet of blood-red coloured roses and steps to one side. Next, she latches on to Xavier who has been standing next to Darius from the moment Angelica and I entered the church. Both Xavier and Angelica take a few steps back – It is now just Darius and I, and the priest. A few timeless moments pass, and as the simplicity of our joining unfolds, within a short while, we become as one in the eyes of our god.

"You may now kiss the bride," Father Jorgenson softly instructs.

I dreamily look up to my husband, and while his fingers skim along the delicate rim of scallop edging that crafts my veil, and as the light catches the central diamond of the platinum ring that moments ago I placed upon his finger, he so slowly peels back my veil from my face, and I tremble on the anticipation of our first wedded kiss. He's close. But first, before that momentous sealing of mouths, he takes my left hand in his and places it to his lips. As he bestows a kiss, firstly upon the ring he had just placed upon my finger, and then secondly upon my engagement ring, he leaves me breathless by softly saying, "I love you so very much, Mrs Carter." He spoke to me and the rings. And as he continued staring deeply into my eyes, I mirror his words,

"I love you too, Mr Carter."

Stepping as close as he possibly could to me, he cups my face in his hands, and while he, while we seal our vows, our marriage, and our eternal love for each other, with the lightest but claiming of kisses from him, he breathes into my mouth that nothing, absolutely nothing on earth could top this moment.

"...Nothing?" I smile against his warm lips.

"...Nothing," he assures into my heart. "Absolutely nothing at all..."

"Not even the birth of our first child?"

He looks stark, and whispers,

"You're... you're pregnant?"

I giggle, and divulge, "No... But I most certainly can't wait to get practising as a married woman!"

Running his hand through his thick mass of curls, he gave me such a roguish look, leant forward and well, what he suggested that he was going to do to me, with me and for us later this evening left me completely astonished! So with happiness bursting from both of our hearts, we turn, and tae the first step as a newlywed couple who are eager to embark on an uncharted future.

The cosy bar of this charming, Icelandic hotel is bijou to say the least, and it's just perfect for all six of us to celebrate not only our wedding, but also Xavier and Angelica's engagement too.

"Everyone," Xavier chirps. Raise your glass the newlyweds!"

As Cali winks at Darius, she chinks her glass with Ed's, and announces, "Wishing much happiness upon our sexy screen god, Darius, and his beautiful bride, Helena, the flower girl! – May nothing ever come between your love for each other."

We all laugh at her description of Darius and I. Next Angelica chinks her flute of Dom Perignon with Xavier's and then offers her toast.

"Congratulations to Mr and Mrs Carter. May all your future joys be little ones!"

Darius and I too clink glasses, and as we take our first sip of the ice cold dry champagne, we knowingly smile at each other.

"To us, Mrs Carter..." He smiles, while placing the rim of the glass to his lips.

"To us, Mr Carter..."

And, he turns, raises his glass high in the air, toasting to Xavier and Angelica's engagement, and then thanking Cali and Ed for being a part of our special day. With the formalities behind us, all six of us dine out on a selection of canapés. Throughout the late afternoon, we laugh, we jest, we share jokes, until time ebbs and dusk envelopes us in her snow covered purple aura of light. Xavier yawns rather loudly.

"Time to retire to one's bed I think?" Angelica asks with hope, with longing in her voice.

He leans into her, and I hear him answer."Yes, my darling it is, but I'm not thinking about sleeping in the bed!"

Her face lights up and I giggle into her ear, "I think the man's up for hot, drunk sex with you!"

She titters back, "And this lady's up for hot, drunk sex with him!"

We laugh so hard at the conversation that unfolded between us that as Darius tried to join in, I shot him a look as if to say – girls only allowed! He bats his lashes at me, wistfully smiles, and then floors me when he points to his groin and mouths to me that his cock is twitching! I arouse at the thought of my husband's cock standing to attention for me, and whisper,

"I think my man's also pretty hot for me too, Angelica!"

Giggling she asks why and I tell her exactly how Darius had just teased me! As we fall around in laughter, sharing teasers of secrets to each other, Xavier stands up and wobbles on his feet!

"I think I'm in need of a strong coffee or two..."

Looking at me, Angelica winks, "Room service!"

I laugh, and nod in agreement.

After the departure of Angelica and her rather tipsy love, closely followed by a champagne-infused, giggly Cali and an equally inebriated Ed, Darius suggests that we too should retire to our room. I quite simply let him take the lead.

Hitching up the train of my silk wedding gown, I drape it over my arm. Holding on to Darius, we begin the two flight climb to our room.

"I think you are going to be pleased with the room, Helena."

"I'm sure I am."

We promptly reach our destination, and I wait while Darius reveals from his suit pocket a brass ornate key.

"That's an intricate design," I say.

"It's rather ornate," he replies, as he twirls it between his thumb and forefinger before inserting it into the keyhole. As the door unlocks, and he gives the rustic pine door a shove, I step forward. Immediately I am blocked by his body.

"No... No..." he says, aghast. "I must carry you over the threshold. It's bad luck if I don't."

"Be my guest." I smile.

Within a flash, I am lifted into his strong arms. As we enter the room, he kicks the door shut behind him, and finally we are alone. Settling me onto my feet, I balance and then drink in the decor of my surroundings. A log fire flickers away in the hearth. The light is low, inviting and calming. The fragrance within the air smells of a combination of woody embers, and freshly laundered linen. The room is not vast or expensive looking in any way, shape or form. It is beautiful in its rustic simplicity. The bridal bed so-to-speak, is the centre focus of the room. It is of a four poster design, draped with luxurious purple, chiffon voiles. The bedding is too of the same shades of purple. The walls are crafted from knobbly stone and they are left unpainted. There is just one lead light window, and as the streetlight outside flickers in the dark, the dancing embers of the synthetic gaslight highlight the beauty of the twirling snowflakes that have been continually cascading since I awoke this morning.

"Do you like the cosiness of the room, Helena? Would you have preferred a more opulent, elegant room?"

"Oh Darius," I gasp, "This is just perfect."

"Sure?" he asks with a slight hint of doubt in his voice.

"Oh I'm sure. It's warm, cosy and romantic.

He draws me into him, and the heavenly scent of his manliness hits me like a strong force gale.

"I love you." I nuzzle into his chest.

Stroking my hair beneath my veil, he whispers, "I want to make love to you, Mrs Carter. I want to make love with you while you are wearing nothing but those cock-hardening, thigh length boots and your veil."

"I want you naked and on top of me," I honestly say.

"You want it missionary?"

"Yes, I do. I want it good old fashioned vanilla style!"

He chuckles deep, and says, "Then sweet vanilla you shall have!"

Releasing me from his hold, he begins to loosen the Windsor knot of his dark, blue tie. I step forward and begin to aid him with his undressing. On undoing the second, third and fourth pearl buttons of his dress shirt, I pull open the pristine, white fabric, and firstly I with delicacy brush my lips over the scar of his past trauma. A whoosh escapes from his lips, and his thighs begin to tremble. I keep planting little peppery kisses all over his torso, trailing my tongue low, until I reach the top of his suit pants. I kneel and focus. The outline of his erection is so very prominent against the fabric, and I can't help but place my mouth to his bulge. I kiss him there twice, and as his cock pulses through the weave and against my lips, his fist knots in my hair, twisting my veil with it. I look up to him. His eyes are flashing with pure sexual lust.

"Stop..." he moans down upon me.

"Why?" I kiss him there again.

"Stop..." he says with more conviction in his tone.

"Why?" I quiz. "I'm your wife... Surely I am allowed do anything I wish to you, with you."

"You may be my wife," he lovingly says, "But I am your husband, and I want... I want..."

I kiss him there again, halt, and rise until I meet his mouth.

"Because..." he whispers, "I want to be found inside you right this very minute."

I turn.

"Unbutton me?" I ask while sweeping my veil to one side.

He does. I step out of my dress, and turn back around, revealing to him my choice of bridal lingerie.

"Wow... wow... wow... wow!" He focuses and mesmerizes upon my underwear. "You look so, so... so very..."

"I look so very what?"

Hastily undoing the last button on his shirt, he then offers me his wrist covered cuffs, and while I proceed to unfasten his cufflinks, he whispers into my ear, "You look so very fuckable in that pearl G-string, Mrs Carter."

"And you," I tease, "always look fuckable, Mr Carter."

He winks at me, and within a flash he's discarded the rest of his clothing, and is standing tall in front of me.

"What are you waiting for, Darius?"

He grasps his cock in his hand, sharply tugs it, and devilishly says, "I'm waiting for my wife to lie down on the bed, spread those beautiful leather clad legs of her and plead with her husband to slowly ease this throbbing beast of a cock into her while she angles her hips upwards and takes me..."

As I focus upon his generous girth, I nip the corner of my lip, and a strong tingle radiates from my hips and collates at my centre. I then shudder when he slaps his erection against his palm, and so wickedly finishes, "... extremely deep inside her."

My back is now flush with the mattress. He, without hesitation, aligns his perfectly toned body with mine, and as his cock slides into me, stretching me, filling me, his eyes glimmer like never before. After the deep, inarticulate sound he made while entering me trails away, he then exclaims, "Mrs Carter... You appear to be beautifully dripping and slickly wet for me already."

"It's you," I gasp and arch my back, and he begins to set a timely rhythm between us. "It's you...." I kiss against his strong neck, "You do this to me... you always have... and you always will."

He sighs with such satisfaction. I lock him between my legs and as the soft leather chaffs gently against his sides, he makes another inarticulate but pleasurable sound. With my veil crumpling all around us, I look to him. The concentration on his face is a picture to behold. The tiny beads of sweat are glistening within the creases of his brow, and his lashes are damp with salty emotion. With each claiming thrust into me, the muscles in his jaw pulse.

"This is magical," I breathe as his whole body tightens against mine.

"It's perfect," he barely whispers in between curling his hands underneath me and holding my buttocks firm.

"I love you, Darius."

"And, I." He stills, strokes the side of my cheek with his finger. "And I." He gyrates his hips. "And I love you too."

I grin goofily, and as his body heaves and the rising and falling of his chest against mine becomes more intense, coupled the sounds that are warbling from the back of his throat, I can tell that he has to fight hard against his impending climax.

"Helena... Helena... Helena..." he whimpers as his orgasm threatens to unleash into me. "I love you to death and I know for sure that there is life after death."

"You do?" I mewl as my thighs begin to quiver against him.

"Yesssss..." he drawls. "My accident... I died... I walked through the tunnel of light with Mr Snuggles, But you... you brought me back to us..."

Mr Snuggles?

As tears begin to well up in the back of my eyes, I toy with the rogue curl at the base of his neck, and dip my lashes. While I soften into the cotton covered mattress beneath my back and I let my body become as one with his, he moves me in a way like no other by completing his sentence.

"And when the day arrives and we meet again in the afterlife, in that most magical and mystical of places." He pants hard, and fixates me in his steely-blue irises. "I ... I..." he pauses, dips his lashes, and as he retreats and powers deep and hard into me, I feel the first of his warm ejaculation emptying into me. I clench him tight not wanting to let him go, and while the emotion of his passion, his love for me, his love for us envelopes and reigns over me, he openly begins to weep, declaring to me...."I will love you always; I will love us for eternity."

And those words he so sentimentally shared with me were the trigger for me to give in to my climax. After my orgasm flowed, reducing me to the near point of exhaustion, he began starting to rotate those agile hips of his, and by that motion of his, his body burrowed into mine again. But this time each convolution of his hips seemed to have more power in them, and this particular act of love was harder, faster, and more urgent than of previous. This sharing of bodies, was so very carnal to say the least because as his cock pistioned effortlessly in me, he began whispering a scenario of what he would like to do with me in D/s situation. My own thoughts rapidly turned to one of a submissive, and the mere thought of me giving my gift of submission to my husband, to my dominant was enough for me to let go for the second time in succession. He kept powering me over and over, and I kept giving back until we both were splayed out flat on our backs and gasping for air. One could say that at present, if you had painted this picture of us, it would be one of art...

Two lovers lying in a tangled heap of soft white veil on a bed that had been drenched in the power of love.

22 December

Seven-forty-five a.m.

Wrapping my body around Darius, I watch him slowly wake, and I warm as I feel him adjust to the new day.

"It's still snowing," I whisper against his lips,

"Mmm?" he sleepily responds.

"I said it's still snowing."

"Great!" He stretches out and yawns loudly. Relaxing around into me, he mumbles, "Perfect."

"Why great? Why perfect?" I ask while stroking his stubbly cheek.

Pushing his body into mine, he murmurs, "Because I have always had this kinky fantasy about you!"

"Enlighten me."

While his erection swells against my belly, he opens one eye, and peeks at me. "Because, Mrs Carter, I have always fantasised about banging you in the snow!"

I tut-tut him and say, "If you did, wouldn't that be rather detrimental to your cock?"

"What do you mean?" he frowns.

"Well." I peck him on the nose. "Wouldn't it be too cold for you to get aroused?"

Flipping me onto my back, he shoves his knee between my legs, and prises my legs apart.

"Maybe it might be." He winks. "And then maybe it might not be!"

"You are such a wicked tease," I laugh. "I love you so very much."

"I know I am," he chortles, "and you love it!

"I do." I kiss against his lips. "I love your sexual humour!"

He kisses me back hard, and I quiver when he bears down upon me and declares, "Since I have a morning glory." He points to his cock! "I'm now going to make love to you very, very slowly."

I charm at his description of his morning erection, and muse. "Really, you are?" I jest while running my fingers down his sides, tickling him. He shivers at my touch, nods, and I jibe, "Well, aren't I the lucky one, Mr Carter!"

Narrowing his gaze, he, grasps my hand and rests it on his throbbing cock."Guide me?"

I coil my fingers around him, and he pulses hard against my palm.

"Take me inside you, baby."

I do exactly as he had asked and while he does indeed give himself to me extremely slowly, he fills my mind with the most romantic of lines of poetry, and it takes no time at all for me to climax over him.

"This is for you baby... Let every part and piece of you unravel into me, Helena."

I do. And as he let's go too, he so delicately hushes, "You are beautiful, Helena."

"And so are you." I breathe into his curls... "And so are you."

Twelve-thirty p.m.

Yanking on my Ugg boots, I pause. The reason for me halting is that I am focusing upon my husband pulling on his leather jacket over a v-necked, white tee shirt.

"You look too, too sexy in that attire." I smile.

Angling his head low, as his curls bounce over his forehead, he secures the top button on his faded, denim jeans, and looks up at me. Ruffling his mop of dark, luscious hair; he winks at me and boldly replies, "I can never not look too seductive for you!"

I groan at his response, and as I carry on pulling on my boots, he kneels down before me, tips his finger under my chin and holds me in his dreamy gaze. Batting his lashes at me, he then settles his hand over my right breast. Teasing me with the briefest fondle, he grasps the front zipper of my dress, and whispers, "When we are in-flight, I am going to slowly pull this zipper down, and have my wicked way with you, Mrs Carter!"

"Just how wicked are you going to be, Mr Carter?" I ask with sexiness dripping from every pore of my being.

"Naughty enough for you to be left craving for more after I brought you to climax not once but twice before we touch down!"

"You sound so very sure of yourself, Mr Carter," I delicately say.

"I am...." He sweeps his mouth along my lips... "I'm always very sure where you are concerned."

I roll my eyes at him, and he, well he gives me the look – A look that assures me if we had the time at present, I would now be naked, kneeling in front of him while patiently waiting for his first move... But alas, as our flight back to England leaves in a few hours, and that thought, that delicious thought of him naked and proud before me, I have to sadly put on hold for much, much later.

Hurling our cases into the white Porsche Macan, Darius urges me to hurry up, jump in the passenger seat and buckle up. I do.

Within a couple of hours we are seated on board our private jet, and the craft has now levelled off. As the seatbelt sign pings to signal to us that we may now be free to roam the aircraft, Darius asks while holding my hand, "How are you doing, Mrs Carter?"

"I'm doing just fine, Mr Carter," I reply while feeling his fingers running over the rings on my wedding finger.

"What do you suggest we should do to pass the time on this short flight back to Heathrow?" he smiles.

Making no hesitation, I stand up in front of him, and while unzipping the front of my red, woollen dress, I allure, "I suggest we should join the mile high club!"

His eyes alight with merriment, and in turn he starts to unbutton his jeans while smirking. "Would you like to ride me all the way home?"

"Maybe..." I whisper while shrugging out of said dress revealing the lingerie I bought from Selfridges way back. Now wearing just the sexy, skimpy lingerie ensemble and a pair of Ugg boots, I look to him.

"Oh my, oh my, oh my," he breathes while slipping his hand into the opening of his jeans, "you look so very delicious, and so very fuckable."

"You approve, sir?" I say with sensuality.

Raising an eyebrow, he points at my feet, and muses, "Sir is not too sure that those boots complement with the lingerie."

I giggle. "I like them... They're cosy."

Caressing his cock, he bites his lower lip, and moans, "Well if you like them, how could sir not possibly approve?"

I grin.

"And," he adds, "there is nothing more erotic at this moment than seeing your pert breasts heaving against the white, trimmed lace of expensive silk."

"And the matching G-string?" I ask turning my back to him so he can see the curves of my buttocks. "You like?" I ask while wiggling my arse.

"Don't you dare move a single muscle!" he says with firmness in his voice. "Don't move a bloody single inch!"

I stay put, and on feeling the first sharp sting radiate over my left buttock, I outstretch my neck and an "Ahh..." escapes from between my lips. I wiggle again... anticipating the next arousing impact of his hand upon my flesh for my disobedience, but I am not fulfilled with another slap because he has risen and his front is now flush with my back. His breathing is heavy and his cock is prominent against the central parting of my bottom.

Nipping my earlobe, he chills me with excitement with the following, "I should spank you for jiggling when I instructed you not to move, shouldn't I?"

"Yes, sir... You should chastise me for my misbehaviour," I taunt while pushing my rear into him.

With that, I am scooped up into his arms and carried the short walk to the back of the aircraft. Kicking the door open, I see the bed strewn with blood red rose petals and a glistening pair of jewel encrusted handcuffs nesting on my pillow – now that's so much more fun than seeing chocolates left upon ones pillow, isn't it! – I look to him and can't resist requesting,

"Please would you be so kind as to cuff me and then spank me, sir?"

Beaming triumphantly at me, he settles me upon the bed. I reach to the pillow, and slowly pick up the handcuffs, and dangle them above my face, assessing the precision curves of cold, yet inviting metal. He looks at me quizzically and assures, "If that is what Madam wishes, then a cuffing, followed by a generous spanking she shall have!"

"Thank you," I submissively and demurely replied while hatching a turn-the-tables-on-you-sir plan!

"Lay with me?" I request while tucking the cuffs safely behind my back.

"I thought you wanted a spanking right now."

"In a minute I do, but first I want to cuddle with you."

"Is my submissive feeling a little vulnerable?"

"A little bit, sir."

"Does she need her sir to be tender with her first?"

"She does."

"And if her sir is gentle at first will his submissive take her punishment like a good submissive and make it all the way past the tenth lash?"

"She will."

He nods with satisfaction.

"Then sir shall lay down with you."

Quickly discarding his converse trainers, he roughly removes his tee shirt, shimmies out of his jeans and silk boxers, and lies down next to me. Wrapping his arms around me, we silently embrace each other for a few moments until I nudge him firmly, and say, "Lie onto your back for me."

"Why?"

"Because I want... I want to suck your cock before I submit to you."

Without hesitation, naturally he assumes flat-back position! He's now in allurement of me and I have him exactly where I want him! As fast as I can, I straddle over him while grabbing his right wrist. Before he can even contemplate what is happening, I have his arm suspended above his head with his wrist cuffed to the bedrail!

"Fuck! Fuck!" He tugs hard against the cuff. "You are an underhand little minx!"

Scolding him, I say, "There's no need for foul language is there, sir?"

"When I eventually break free," he playfully roars, "you are going to be in for so much more than a buttock reddening spanking!"

"Jolly good!" I say lightly. "I quite fancy something new and exciting to inspire me!"

"Oh trust me." He pulls against his restraint. "There will be nothing jolly when I have you at back at home in our personal room of pleasure, gagged, bound and spread on the Crux Decussata."

"Explain Crux Decussata?" I say with bewilderment. "And I add, what do you mean by spread?"

"Uncuff me and I will divulge exactly what a Crux Decussata is and then you'll understand what I mean by spread."

"Nope..."

"Why?"

"I'm quite happy to wait and see what the Crux thingy is!"

"Helena!" he gasps.

"What?"

"Please be a good girl for me, and unshackle me?"

"No."

"Why?" he growls.

"Because..." I giggle. "This bad girl likes you like this... all naked, cock hard ready, and delightfully submissive to her."

A look of aghast spreads across his face, and he mummers,

"Jeez... she's got me! She's only damn well got me!"

"I do have you," I laugh, "and I'm most certainly going to enjoy riding you all the way!"

Stunned, his eyes widen and he then burst out, "All the way? You're going to need heaps of stamina for that epic task!"

"Don't worry," I whisper. "I won't fail."

"Are you sure, all the way? Maybe you'd like to swap positions halfway through?"

"All the way..." I emphasise, not giving into him. "All the way to the hilt until there is not a drop of your hot pent up fluid left inside you."

"Okay," he sweetly agrees. "This sounds like it's going to be exceptionally good fun! I'm going to enjoy watching your folds glisten as you slide up and down on my big cock!"

"Oh, it will be fun... for both of us... I promise you that."

As his cock twitches hard against my belly, I lean over him and look deep into those stunning blue irises of his while asking, "Are you ready to be embarked on the ride of your life, sir, while flying high above the clouds?"

Snaking his free hand around the back of my neck, he knots his fingers in my tresses, draws me even closer to him and breathes into my mouth, "Oh my darling, darling, bright little fragrant minx of mine, I'm very ready for you to fuck me, and drain my balls that are aching to be emptied.

"Funny that..." I giggle again while caressing him at the root of his erection. "So am I ready!"

And with last retort exchanged, I delicately cupped his warm, smooth balls in my hand, grasped his gorgeous, thick veined throbbing cock at its base, and rubbed him teasingly against my moistening folds.

"Take me," he groans, "Hurry up and take me before I explode in your hand."

Next, I slowly impaled myself down upon his inches, and as his girth stretched me, and his length filled me, I slowly rode him all the way to the hilt, until the moment he bucked so powerfully against me, and thrashed out his orgasm while cursing my name to the conditioned air of the aircraft.

During the entire act of our love, he never once let go of his hold around the back of my head, and I never stopped staring into his mesmerising, blue eyes.

Chapter Eighteen

Monday, 24 December 2018

Eleven-thirty a.m.

"It was inevitable, Helena."

"I guess it was, Darius."

"It's a good photo of us."

"Let me see."

As we wait in the foyer for the lift to arrive, I muse, "I wonder how they got the picture. I never saw anyone hanging around the church or the hotel, did you?"

"No I didn't, but trust me, the paparazzi, they always have their ways, their methods of seeking and searching out..."

"Does it bother you, Darius that we are now once again in the public eye?"

"Not really." He shrugs. "I'm used to it, and I expect that you'll get used to it over time too it was inevitable, that they'd get a snap of us, Helena."

"I guess I will become familiar with being in the public eye every now and then, and that a photograph of our special day was inescapable."

Holding up the newspaper in front of me, he smiles, "It's a good photo of us, don't you think?"

I study it. The snow is cascading all around us, and Darius is holding me in a falling embrace. I am languishing back in his arms, looking all the part a radiant bride. There are smatterings of snowflakes dusted within the spirals of his curls, and his lips are lingering above mine. The smile on my face is virtually off the scale, so to speak. We look so dizzy in love with each other – well we are, aren't we?

"Yes it is," I agree. "It sure paints a thousand words."

"It does," he concurs as the lift finally arrives. He then offers me the paper, and I fold it in half and tuck it away into my tote bag. Stepping into the lift first that will leads to the condo, Darius then follows pulling our luggage behind him. As the doors close, he punches the button for our level, leans back against the wall and closes his eyes.

"Are you all right, baby?

"I'm fine, Helena. I just want to get inside, and relax with you."

"So do I," I say as gravity leaves beneath us. "So do I."

On making it inside, we step into the lounge, and as we see that the room has been strewn with bouquet after bouquet of flowers, mountain upon mountain of unopened gifts and an abundance of cards, I say, "I am guessing from the picture in the newspaper, the whole world now knows that we are wed."

Quietly, he replies, "Yes, so they do."

"How do you think all these flowers and gifts were able to filter in here?"

"Maria – you know – our housekeeper?" he replies with amusement in his voice.

Feeling foolish, I say, "Oh yes. I almost forgot that you... that we have a housekeeper."

Then out of the blue, he asks, "Where do you most feel at home? Here or Scotland?"

"I love the condo, but it still seems as if it's yours... As if it will always be yours."

He turns, cups my face in his hands and takes my breath away when he asks, "Would you like a new home of our own right here in London?"

"Yes, I would," I breathe against his lips... "But could we keep the home in Scotland? I do so love the house."

"Well, my intention is to have Scotland, one day..." he pauses, kisses me delicately, "to have it evolve into our family home."

Now feeling heady at the thought of Darius and I having a family, I dreamily admit, "That sounds absolutely perfect to me."

"Good because it sounds perfect to me too."

Toying with the rogue curl at the nape of his neck, I brush my lips along his and murmur, "So when do we go house hunting?"

He smiles against my mouth and quietly says, "We don't."

I draw back from him a little and quiz, "What do you mean, we don't?"

"Come..." He takes my hand in his. "Come with me for I have something that I wish to show you."

Leading me towards the sofa, we sit and he picks up the remote from the coffee table, angles it at the television and the screen comes into focus. As the picture before us unfolds, I gasp out with amazement, for it appears to me that Darius has already been house hunting, and he has purchased us a house in the rather expensive, upper class and beautiful area of Holland Park right here in London.

"Home number two!" he chirps with boyish glee. "You like your wedding present, Mrs Carter?"

"I like very much," I stun, "but I haven't bought you, my darling, anything."

Shaking his head from side to side, he looks endearingly at me, and I am swept away when he replies, "Helena, you have given me everything I desire by becoming my wife. You are the ultimate gift any man could ever wish for."

"I don't know what to say."

"Then don't say anything at all... Just kiss me."

I kiss him.

And as he lifts me in his arms whispering that it is now time for us to christen our bed in *this home* as a married couple, I look into my husband's stunning eyes, and feeling like the luckiest woman on the planet, I tell him over and over that I adore him.

He just beams with pride and I rise and lead him in the direction of our bedroom.

25 December
One-thirty-four a.m.

For some peculiar reason, I am feeling rather restless. Darius is sleeping soundly, so I head downstairs with the intention of making myself a cup of herbal tea which may aid me in relaxing. As I pass the lounge, the potent, floral scent of mixed flowers that is drifting through the air entices me into the room. For some strange reason I am drawn to an ostentatious bouquet of white, stargazer lilies that has been placed upon the grand piano by the window – who would send white stargazer lilies as a wedding congratulation? This variety, this colour of bloom I know is most often associated with funerals. Lilies also symbolize that the soul of the departed has received restored innocence after death. I begin to feel unnerved. For moments I stand staring at the flowers, deep in confused thought until I notice a small green greeting envelope lain next to the vase. I gingerly pick it up. The outer just has my name scribbled upon and strangely not Darius's too

I breathe deep and as I proceed to open it, I hear his voice, "They're bothering you, these flowers, aren't they?"

Without turning around to face Darius, I shove the tiny envelope into my gown pocket, and I nod to signal –Yes, the stargazer lilies are perplexing me.

I can hear him padding lightly towards me and en route he whispers, "Would you like me to get rid of them for you?"

I nod again. He comes around, grasps the vase in two hands, and walks off in the direction of the kitchen. I tremble with an uneasy feeling, and thankfully he is soon back. Placing his hand upon my shoulder, he angles me around to meet him.

"What's the matter, Helena? You're very, very pale."

"I'm just exhausted." I respond. "Worn out... I think from all the recent travelling."

"It's something more that tiredness." He kindly says, "I can tell."

"I... I..."

"You what?" he softly asks while snaking his arms around my waist and pulling me close. "You can tell me."

I withdraw the envelope from my pocket and hand it over to him.

"I found this with the... the lilies. It's... it's addressed to only... only..."

"Only?" he cocks an eyebrow.

"Only... only me."

A brief look of concern, of confusion crosses his face, and he takes my hand in his. "Come sit with me."

We sit on the sofa.

Taking the envelope from me, he dismisses, "Maybe the sender forgot to add my name."

"Why? It seems a peculiar thing to miss – writing the groom's name along with the brides, don't you think?"

"I do." He quiets and then answers, "Would you like me to dispose of this as well as the flowers too?"

"I'm not sure," I honestly say. "I'm curious as to who sent them."

"Well, unless you have the card dusted for fingerprints, I guess we shall never know."

He's right. I sigh and he twiddles the envelope in between his thumb and forefinger.

"What bothers you about that particular type of lily?"

I divulge. "Those lilies are called stargazer lilies, and are most often associated with funerals."

Ghostly silence surrounds us.

"Stargazer..." I take a breath... "Stargazer lilies also symbolize that the soul of the departed has received restored innocence after death – Who, Darius... Who would send such a flower as a wedding congratulation?"

His face ashen in colour, and without hesitation he opens it and removes the card from its host. After a few seconds, his face unreadable, he holds the card up and flips it back and front.

"It's blank." I sigh with relief. "I was half expecting...." I begin to sob. "I thought it might be from... from..."

"Baby, baby." He flings himself at me. "Try not to think of the past... No one... nothing can hurt you now. I won't let anything traumatic happen to you."

Nuzzling into his bare chest, I curl up onto his lap and sniffle.

"Promise, Darius."

"Promise, Helena."

"Firstly, let's agree to bin the card along with the flowers that are already in the disposal unit. Secondly after I have done just that, let me take you back to bed." He yawns. "Because I'm absolutely bushed and you are to."

I have to agree that sleep is in order because, after the last few days, I really need to switch off and relax, so after we toss the card into the waste bin, I let him lead me back to bed. Coiled around each other as he lulls me to sleep with romantic words, I drift off into a dream... A state which I never wish to visit ever again.

With a crown of white, stargazer lilies adorning her blonde hair, she, Alice looks down upon me. Her green eyes are boring right through to my very soul and as she whispers, "He doesn't love you, Helena."

I run my hand over my swollen belly, maternally protecting our unborn twins. I look up to her and say, "Your empty words don't hurt me, Alice. You could never hurt me."

"If he loved you..." she jibes, "and those unborn children growing in your womb, he wouldn't have left you for me, would he?"

"He hasn't left me... Has he?"

"Then why has he been sleeping in my bed for the last month?"

On hearing the latter, I violently lash out into the air, or so I thought, and as my fist impacted on something solid, something as taut as could be, I heard Darius in the distance wail out in surprise, "Fuck it Helena... What on earth was that for? Why did you just wallop me?"

I can't get past, past Alice's words of lies, so I lash again and again – at her, but the third time I feel a hand halt me midair by holding both of my wrists rigid.

"Get off me, you bitch!" I chant over and over, while trying to kick a heavy weight off me. "Let fucking go of me!"

"Baby, baby calm down... you're in a nightmare." He tries to soothe... "It will pass soon."

"Get off me, Alice, or I won't be responsible for what I will do you if you don't stop hounding me, or Darius!" I threaten. "Leave me, Darius, and our unborn twins, Athos and Lucy, alone!"

Suddenly it's as if some unknown entity has dragged me from the nightmare I have been thrashing within, and I have returned to reality. I flick my lashes open to see Darius. He is semi naked and straddled over me. His face paler than pale and his eyes are brimming with what I can only describe as a mixture of concern and confusion.

"What... what?" I look to him and ask with fear shaking in my voice... "What just happened? Why are you sitting over me holding my wrists? And why... why am I drenched in cold sweat?"

His grip lessens on my wrists, and he gently lets me go until my arms flops to my sides. With a concerned tone he replies, "You were having a nightmare, sweetie."

"I... she... she... Alice... she... was..." I gasp for air.

"Shhh..." He presses his mouth to my salty lips... "No need for you to explain..."

"I want explain... I need to make it clear to you why I... I... lashed out at you."

"It doesn't matter, baby..." He kisses me again. "You described it once already when you were within your nightmare."

"I was talking?" I say with a sob of despair.

"Well, I'd say you were babbling but coherent enough for me to decipher what was frightening you."

I shiver.

Slipping his arms underneath my soaking wet back, he pulls me forward until I am flush with him. Holding me tenderly, he rocks us both back and forth while pacifying me with soft words of reassurance that he will never leave me, and that no one on this earth, especially – her – will ever be able to separate us. We remain in this stance for several minutes until my body beings to tremor with the chillness of my almost real dream.

"I'll run you a warm bath." He kisses the top of my head. "And bring you some tea. Would you like that?"

"I'd like it better if you joined me in the bath," I say against his chest. Placing both of his hands upon my shoulders, I rest back onto my haunches, and we face each other. I stare at the pink scar over his heart only to see that the skin around it is a tingly red. Abhorred at myself for hitting him, for hurting him especially over his heart, I whimper, "I'm so sorry for hitting you... especially there." "I point at his heart.

"It's all right," he crookedly smiles, "You didn't mean it, and anyway, baby, I'm pretty tough... nothing's broken."

"I do love you," I emphasise while trembling.

He pulls me back to him, wraps his arms around me and breathes, "I love you, with all of me."

I sag into him with relief at his love for me. He then carries me to the en suite bathroom and as I bathe on my own, he brings me a cup of tea and then joins me in the tub.

Tuesday 25th December 2018
Christmas morning
Eight-thirty a.m.

As I enter the kitchen, I see Darius casually half-dressed.

He looks up from the pile of half opened congratulations cards and with concern in his voice. He asks, "How are you feeling on this Christmas morning?"

"I'm better." I half smile.

"Did you enjoy morning sex?"

"Oh yes." I fully smile. "I enjoyed it very much indeed."

Shoving the mixture of unopened congratulation and Christmas cards to one side, he holds up the cafetiere, asking me if I would like a cup. I answer to him yes and he gestures for me to join him. I do, and while he pours and I take my place beside him at the breakfast bar. Taking a sip of the steaming, dark liquid it scalds my lips; I recoil and place the mug back down onto the work surface.

"Too hot for you, baby?" he grimaces.

"A tad..." I half smile again.

"Let it cool a little and while it does would you like me to make you some breakfast?"

"Yes," I quietly reply.

"What would you like? Pancakes? A soft boiled egg with marmite soldiers perhaps?"

"Oooh!" I say as my tummy rumbles loudly, "I'd really like an egg please... with lots and lots of marmite soldiers."

"How many eggs... One or two?"

"Two."

"Then two it is along with heaps of marmite soldiers or would you prefer asparagus tips instead?"

"Yuk!" I reply, "I don't like asparagus."

"Then marching soldiers it will be." He laughs.

So as he ambles off to the workstation, I fixate upon my husband's glorious toned back and I feel a bit embarrassed when I see the marks of my nails left trailing down his toned back

Earlier this morning, when I first awoke, he was nowhere in the vicinity of the bedroom level. I went on a mission to find him. When I did see him working out in his private gym, I was left feeling full of admiration. He was pummelling away at the dumb boxer, and as a pool of sweat began trailing down his back and seeping though his vest, I had to turn around and leave him in his own world, for if I didn't I probably, no, I would've approached him and asked him to make love to me right there and then! And this was his space – his thinking time – as well as a segment of his daily fitness workout routine.

Plopping two eggs into the pan of near boiling water, he looks over at me, and sympathetically asks, "Are you sure you're feeling all right, Helena?"

Taking a sip of the now cooled coffee, I nod to say that I am fine. He begins to whistle away like someone without a single care in the world, and while I watch him butter and spread marmite lavishly onto doorstep hunks of fresh white bread followed by placing the eggs into their respective, shiny spiral egg cups, it dawns on me how lucky I am to have a man who loves me with such... such... kindness, sweetness devotion.

"You're quite a catch, Mr Carter, Le Chef!" I laugh.

"I know." He responds while slicing off the tops of my eggs. "I'm not only a dab hand between the sheets, but I am also magnificent right here in the kitchen!"

I smile at his description of himself, and as he places my breakfast in front of me, I smile.

"Eat."

I do, and while I dunk a soldier full into egg number one, the yolk spills wilfully over the sides. Scooping the golden, yellow liquid up with the pad of my finger, as I go to place it to my mouth, he has beaten me to it, and I wilt when he sensually starts to suck on my finger! Winking at me, he rumbles, "Mmm, tastes delicious!"

Releasing me from his hold, I wither even further when he picks up a marmite doused soldier, dips it in egg number two and whispers,

"Open your mouth."

I do, and as he feeds me until there is nothing left to devour, he never takes his eyes off me once!

"Full up?"

"Very."

"Come." He extends his hand to me. "Come, I have something I wish to show you."

I stand and let him lead me to where he wishes to take me. On reaching our destination, I look to him and I am amazed at what I see. The blinds to the lounge have been shut and the room is lit with arrays of white fairy lights. All wedding flowers bar my bouquet of red roses have been removed. In effect, the lounge has what I can only describe has been turned into Santa's grotto. By the floor to ceiling window is a large Norwegian Spruce Tree that is sparsely but elegantly decorated in reds, greens and whites. Underneath the tree is parcel after parcel... Each one I note has been tied with luxurious silk ribbon.

"It's magical." I squeeze his bicep. "When... How did you do all this?"

"I hired an army of elves," he chuckles, "And while we were sleeping, they did all of this."

"What clever little elves they are." I giggle.

"So you approve?"

"Oh I do." I turn and rise onto my tiptoes. Draping my arms around his neck, I kiss him lightly and whisper, "Do you know what would be really perfect right now?"

"Illuminate me." He kisses me back.

Moving his hand onto my belly, I say softly, "If we could make a baby."

On seeing his reaction unfurl before my very eyes, I was left breathless, shivery and in no doubt at all that this man did love me whole and that there would never be another woman on this earth or man that could ever come between us, and as he lifted me into his arms he informed me that we were now going to take a shower together while practising baby-making. I just warmed.

We are now sitting on the floor of the wet room, and as the warm water cascades down over us, I inch down over his cock, and he rests his back against the marble wall of the shower. Groaning, he mumbles, "This is the most perfect honeymoon, the most perfect Christmas ever. Don't you think so, Helena?"

With his girth stretching me, I moan into his mouth that yes it is.

"It couldn't be any better... I wouldn't have it any other way..." And then I tease, "Among other things, it has been one hell of a fuck-a-thon so far!"

He smirks, "I do so love a good fuck-a-thon, Mrs Carter!"

"And me, Mr Carter." I giggle in-between his partly spaced lips.

"Fuck me really slow, Helena?" he gently asks. "Make my, make our Christmas perfect."

"It will be my pleasure, Mr Carter."

I do as he requested, and after some time, as I release my hands from his broad shoulders and move them to his stubbly face, I hold him firm in my between my thighs, and gently nip upon his upper lip. Arching my back, I clench him tight and as an orgasmic, shattering wail warbles from the back of his throat, he thrashes upwards so strongly into me, almost shoving me off his body. With his hands gripping onto my hips, he releases one hand and slithers it around the back of my neck. Sensually growling to me that I must be still instantly for he is going to orgasm again. Before I nibble along the side of his strong neck, I ask, "Why must I be still?"

"Why must I still?"

"Because... because..." He bites me back but harder than my nip. "Because by stilling I promise you that you will be able feel every single drop of me filling you... and I so, so, desperately want to flood you, to make you never forget what it feels like when I spurt inside you."

I grasp his hand, place it upon my belly and say, "Can you feel you still surging hard inside me?"

"Still..." he trails, and then bites me hard again.

"Ow..."

He bites again, a little harder, and demands that I really must obey his ask and keep still.

"Ow... Ow..." I cry as he squeezes my buttocks hard, and jerks powerfully into me. "Baby, you... you..." I wail... "You..."

"Shhh... or I will have to release you..." he threatens without menace while staring deep into my teary, glazed eyes.

I don't wish to be released from him at present, so I still, and he momentarily halts, presses his palms flush to my damp belly, and as he tells me that yes, he can feel him inside me. Next as he powers upright hard and rages that he is already at his second climax, I sink further into him and collapse against his heaving chest. While I bury my face in the crook of his neck, and I do indeed feel every single drop of his thick, opalescent cum fill me, I sink my teeth into his neck and draw on his flesh leaving an indelible love note bruised within the deepest layer of his scented tasting skin.

While moments pass, and our breathings begin to labour, I draw back from him a little and chew on my bottom lip while querying, "Do you think we just made a baby?"

He broadens into a smile, knots his fingers in my tangled hair, and angles me closer towards him. Tilting his head to one side, he looks adoringly at me.

"I hope we have because you will make the most kind, perfect and loving mother."

"And you, my darling Darius," I skim across his lips..."Will make a loving and doting father to our babies."

And then he warms the cockles of my heart by adding, "Yes, I hope I will. To all three of our children we will be the finest parents that we can be... That I am sure of."

How does he know for certain that we are going to have three children?

Chapter Nineteen

Monday, January 7 2019

Another new year and another fresh new start. Hopefully, now I have been contraceptive free for a short while, my body will soon adjust to its normal hormone level, and I will be with child.

Closing the door to our London home – Holland Park – behind me, I take my first steps without Darius by my side. On reaching my car – the Porsche Boxster Darius bought me for my twenty-first birthday, I warm at the memories of that special day!

Arriving outside my place of work, I step out of the car and I feel about ten feet tall. I mean, here I am, plain little me, a married woman and not only that – I am wedded to the sexy, screen god, Darius Carter, and to boot, I am driving my dream car! There is excitement flooding my veins at seeing Angelica and I am dying to hear her news of her life with Xavier. I head into my place of work, and on entering the building I am rooted to the spot at what I have just seen. My reason for braking rapidly was that perched on my work countertop is... is... a cellophane wrapped bouquet of stargazer lilies. Assuming that Angelica must have taken an order for a funeral, I try to shake the thoughts of the past nightmare of Alice and lilies away but my words to Darius on the eve before Christmas Eve past, when we were back from our wedding, haunt me as do the anonymous sender of aforementioned flowers:

'Stargazer...' I took a breath and said to him.... 'Stargazer lilies also symbolize that the soul of the departed has received restored innocence after death – Who, Darius? Who would send such a flower as a wedding congratulation?'

To which in time he replied, 'Try not to think of the past.... No one... nothing can hurt you now. I won't let anything traumatic happen to you.'

Nuzzling into his bare chest, I curled up onto his lap and sniffled

'Promise, Darius?'

'Promise, Helena.'

Looking up from the lilies, as I see Angelica, I smile.

"Helena!" Angelica bellows, "Hey, honey, it's so brilliant to see you."

I remove my beret, and fling it at her. She catches it, grins and I reply, "It's great to see you too."

She runs full pelt at me and flings her arms around me.

"Hell, I've missed you."

"It's only been a few weeks since the wedding!" I smile.

"Still, I've missed you."

"And I've missed you too, my bestie."

"How about a coffee before we open up and you can tell me how your wedding plans are progressing?"

"Coffee's good."

While Angelica brews us a drink, I pull out my phone and glance at the message that just came in.

"I'm feeling dead horny, Mrs Carter... Are you free to talk dirty to mc right now?"

"I'm very sorry, sir..." I quickly text back... "No can do... Girl talk pressing! Maybe I might at lunchtime?"

"Well then, I'll guess have to talk dirty to you right now!"

"No, Darius... Don't you dare... Please stop it right this very instant!"

"No."

"Please?"

"Only if you let me say one thing before I go?"

"Something like, 'I love you?'"

"Something like that!"

"Oh all right...But be quick for this is my girlfriend time and you're intruding!" (I tease.)

One second later...

"Helena, Imagine this... Close your eyes and visualise that you are shackled to the Crux Desuccata. You are facing forward and you are blindfolded. The air around your naked body is tepid but comfortable, and you can feel my breath heavy in your ear. As something firm... something leathery snaps against your clit, you let out a long extension of an ongoing moan... And while you experience something pinching, something squeezing both your nipples tight, you begin to feel the sticky, slick wetness forming between your legs. You are fast approaching euphoria. Your swelling nub burns again, you want more, and then as you implore with me to kiss you down there, to soothe your ache with my tongue... the pinching rushes through your entire body and...!"

"Damn you, damn, damn you, sir! You know you have me intrigued about the Crux Desuccata....stop this taunt right this very moment or... or..."

"Or what Mrs Carter... What will you do?"

"I will do nothing!"

"Shame... So will you reciprocate, and talk dirty with me now?"

"No, I won't! Now go away and prepare for your photo shoot! I have flowers for births, weddings and... And funerals to sort!"

"But are you a little wet? Tell me before I go," he implores.

I am

"Yes....A little."

"Good..."

"Why good..."

"I'll see you later. Mrs Carter."

"Darius, before you go..."

"What?"

"Can we stay at the condo tonight?"

"Why?"

"Because there's nowhere for us to play in Holland Park, is there?"

"Maybe there is."

"No way... You can't possibly have a playroom installed in there... I've searched every corner of the building and not come across a room!"

"I don't think you have searched hard enough..." he says in such a secretive tone, and then questions. "Anyway, why do you feel that you want to submit to me tonight?"

"Because..."

"Because..."

"Because... I wish to... to... to see. I wish to touch the cross thingy you mentioned....

"Ah, the Crux... "

"Yes, the Crux..."

"So, tell me, Darius, do we have a playroom hiding somewhere with the home in Holland Park or not?"

And as I read his final message, I was, well left informed, astounded and highly intrigued!

Putting my phone away, and reeling from Darius's last message, Angelica plonks a mug of steaming coffee down in front of me, and I ask her, "So what's on the work schedule for today, Angelica?"

She turns the page on the day to day diary in front of her and while tapping her pen on the desk, she replies, "Pretty quiet considering since it is the New Year." "But tomorrow we have a booking for a mid-summer wedding, and your services have been specifically requested."

With curiosity in my voice, I appeal, "Why me?" She shrugs her shoulders and I enquire, "Who is asking for me?"

"A lady called Ms Ava Porter-Michaels."

"That's a very grand name," I say, taking a sip of my drink.

"It is, isn't it?"

"So, what time is my appointment with our bride-to-be, Ms Ava Porter-Michaels and where?"

"Three-thirty p.m., with milady," she says in a very upper class accent. "Apparently she's temporarily residing in the Piccadilly Suite at The Ritz hotel."

"Wow, she must be worth a bob or two to be able to afford such a grand surrounding as a temporary dwelling!"

"Yes, she must, so what do you say? Shall we Google her and find out some gossip on her?" Angelica says in a mischievous, secret tone.

I laugh and reply, "You are so completely bonkers at times, Angelica!" I tease. "I think I'll pass on trying to find out who she is and what she's worth."

"It helps to be a little bit crackers in this maddening world that we have been born into, don't you agree?"

"I do," I sigh.

I breeze through the morning with happy ease, while Angelica spends most of the morning lost in a furious text conversation with Xavier. On closing for lunch, since trade is slow, we decide to head to the bistro around the corner. Now seated, and with our light lunch of salmon Caesar salads before us, we sit for a moment in silence. A few moments pass, and Angelica leans over the table, grasps both my hands in hers, and smiles.

"Guess what, Helena?"

I think I know what she's trying to convey, so I say, "You and Xavier have set a date, haven't you both?"

Her face lights up, and she beams, "Yes we have!"

"When?"

"Since Xavier loves the autumn, we've decided on the 15 October this year."

"Fabulous." I clap my hands with glee. "Well then, this, my dear friend, calls for a lunchtime drink celebration!"

I signal to Marco, the drop-dead gorgeous Italian waiter who Angelica and I used to spend hours drooling over before we met the loves of our lives, that we are in need of his attention. He gives me a cheeky wink and indicates he'll be us in a few moments.

"If, just if," Angelica hushes. "If Darius never entered your life, would you have made a play for Marco?"

I circle the rim of my glass, pause and then whisper back, "I don't know... maybe. If you'd never met Xavier, would you have tried to snare our sexy, hot and extremely well buffed Italian stallion?"

She giggles into her napkin, blushes and by the reddening of her cheeks I have found her answer.

"Ladies..." Marco grabs our attention. "What I can do for the two of my most favourite and extremely beautiful women in the world?"

We titter in unison and I explain that Angelica is soon to be wed to my brother in law, so to celebrate her forthcoming marriage could we please both have one of Marco's famous Limoncello cocktails. With delight in his voice, he congratulates her first, and then turns to me.

"You are married now, Helena?"

"Yes." I smile, twiddling the thin band of diamond encrusted, platinum around my finger. "I am married to the most doting and loving man."

Placing his hand over his heart, he amuses us by acting, "My heart has not only been broken once today by Angelica falling for another, but also by Helena who is so loved by another!"

Now giggling like a pair of silly schoolgirls, we both say in unison, "We will always love you, Marco."

He grins widely, gives both of us a sexy wink of his dark come-to-bed lashes, turns and then saunters off to see to our drinks. As he meanders through the small aisles, dodging seats and customers, neither Angelica nor I can take our vision off his pert backside!

"Whoever snares him," I whisper, "Is going to be one hell of a lucky woman!"

She breathes back, "I bet you he can go some distance in between the sheets!"

"Angelica," I startle, "that's no way to talk for a woman who is soon to be wed!"

"Isn't it?" she says with lightness in her voice.

I chuckle and say, "Well, maybe it is... after all I suppose it's alright for us to have a look but definitely not to touch!"

"Of course it is all right," she whoops! "We are red blooded women who appreciate the male form in all its divine glory, and we live," she adds, as Marco settles our drinks onto the table, "we live in modern society."

I agree with her, and as Marco again struts off, we both can't help but once again, home in on that tight butt of his. Then out of the blue, Angelica gobsmacks me when she asks, "Do you reckon our Italian stallion...? Do you think he bats for the other team?"

Spurting out my sip of iced, lemony liquid, I gasp, "Angelica... Good grief! What a suggestion!"

"Ask him!" she dares me. "Go on, ask him!"

"No, I will not!" I say with aghast. "I will not invade his privacy!"

"Well if you won't, I will!"

"Don't you dare... Please no!" I warn.

"Oh don't be such a killjoy!" she sniggers. "I was only teasing. I wouldn't do such a thing as to embarrass him."

"Thank God! I am relieved. I thought you were serious there for one minute."

"So," she pokes her fork at her pink fish, "do you reckon he likes playing with girls in the park or dancing with boys in bed?"

I laugh at her analogy, but before I can respond, my jaw gapes because entering the bistro is a male. He is a tall, bleach-blond specimen of an Adonis, and I feel dreadfully guilty because I just cannot, I just cannot take my eyes off from him. His stature is so very agile, and as he strides forth, I note that his eyes are obscured by a pair of dark, tinted sunglasses. Turning to his dress, I note that he is immaculately styled in a bespoke, charcoal grey suit, with darker grey oxford shoes. I also see that he is carrying a gift bag which displays the Tiffany & Co logo. Lucky recipient! I think to myself. While he ambles towards the bar, he slowly removes his ray bans and seats sideways. I fleet a daring second glance at him... And my heart misses a beat as it begins to sink in on me who this man actually is. It couldn't possibly be him, could it? I quickly avert my gaze away from him, hoping he hasn't noticed me, and I look to Angelica, who has a quizzical look smattered across her face,

"What's up, Helena? You've gone quite pale."

I stiffen, fiddle nervously with my napkin, and under my breath, I say that I don't feel very well and I'd like to leave right now.

"Are you up the duff?" she asks, with a teasing slight. "Has one of Darius's busy little spermy soldiers gone and cracked your baby egg on its head!"

Wanting to laugh at the way she's just described conception, I can't raise a smile, for I feel quite odd indeed.

"No." I rise. "I'm definitely not pregnant or at least... at least, I do think I am... I just want to go. I think I might have a threatening migraine coming on."

She doesn't question me further, she just extracts a couple of twenty pound notes from her purse, places them under the base of her drink, and we both gather our belongings. As we exit, as we try to exit, we are halted in our tracks by a female sauntering through the open door. We step aside because she is what I can only describe as my double. This woman flowing through the room, heading towards him, is about my height, my weight, and more unnervingly so, she has the identical hair colour and style as mine. Her attire is pristine formal from the top of her auburn tresses to the tip of her nude Christian

Louboutin shoes. As a hush descends around the bistro, I do a double take and my heart splinters when I admit to myself that I now have to stop denying to myself that the bleach-blond Adonis opening his arms to her is a blast from my past. I crumple inside when I witness him in a fleeting embrace with the woman who is precariously teetering on her sexy pair of shoes. Making it outside, I grasp for dear life onto Angelica's arm, and whimper, "That woman... It was like looking in a mirror... It was bizarre."

"It was peculiar, I agree... They say we all have a double somewhere on this planet, and I guess we've just seem yours."

"But it was really daunting," I gasp while gulping in a large breath of air.

"It was quite ruffling," she says with concern. "Are you sure you're feeling all right?"

I stop, turn and face her.

"I'm not really."

"Why ever are you not, sweetie? Are you sure you're not preggers? Are you sick, like terminally ill or something?"

"No... I sigh, "I'm not pregnant nor do I have an incurable illness... It just that man at the bar kissing my double... It... It was him, Angelica."

"Who was it? What do you mean?" she cajoles. "Tell me."

"That was... was... was my... that was Connor."

"You mean, Connor, Connor? Your divine, first love? The well-endowed, rampant beach bum who bonked his way through half of Australia! He's man who loved you, looked after you when you first split from Darius?

"Yes," I meekly reply. "That's him... Connor"

"Wow!" she exclaims, "He's pretty hot totty!"

"Yes." I quieten. "He is."

"Are you feeling jealousy rising within you? Perhaps you are feeling a splattering of green envy?"

"No!" I snap, and then soften,

She frowns, and then states, "So let's recap, you've just clapped eyes on the man you lost your virginity to in the apple orchard, and you're telling me that you don't feel a teeny-weeny bit jealous that he's now with someone who looks similar to you?"

"No... No, I'm not jealous..." I desperately try get across to her. "How could I be, I have my Darius... I'm just quite shocked at seeing Connor again... You know seeing him looking so mature... so smart... and so very un-Connor-like. It's just taken the wind out of my sails a little seeing him looking suited and booted... seeing him with someone who resembles me... All this... It's just so very peculiar."

"I know," she soothes, and then lightens my mood by betting me a ten pound note that Marco is most definitely gay!

Tossing my head back, my anxiety leaves me and I laugh out, saying to her that she is an awful assumer and terrible muck stirrer! She laughs too, and I try to push Connor and his new love to the back of my mind. After all he, his life isn't any of my business any more, is it? We walk on. So as Angelica and I make idle chatter all the way back to work about the two most prominent men in our lives – Darius and Xavier. I start to feel better – A little.

That evening...

"What's the matter, Helena? Are you not feeling very hungry?"

Stabbing the lone cube of feta cheese with my fork, I swirl it into the herbed dressing, and chase it around my plate, with no intention of snaring the morsel at any time in the present. I look at Darius and sadly say, "Not really..."

He frowns, pauses and then asks, "Do you want to see the crux?"

"Not today."

Stunned he asks, "Why?"

"I just don't!" I snap "Is that okay with you?"

"Blimey, Helena, rein it in... I was only asking."

"I'm sorry."

"Are you sickening for something?"

"No... I don't think so... I just don't have much of an appetite right now."

He nods."So tell me, how was your first day back at work?"

"Uneventful," I lie, "It was very quiet. And how was yours? How did the photo shoot for GQ magazine go? Was it fun?"

"No, it was rather laborious but I think the chosen proof for the cover in the end will be just right."

Taking an interest in his day, I start to lighten up, so I probe, "What did you have to wear?"

"Nothing at all..." he divulges, and then wafts his hand through the air. "I actually posed completely buff naked!"

"What!" I exclaim with horror. "You did a nude shoot for a magazine cover?"

He laughs mischievously. "Yup! The full Monty!"

I anger inside at thought of an entire studio seeing my husband's private parts, and I cry out, "You showed the crew, the photographers, your crown jewels!"

"Ah-ha!" he nods and winks. "I sure did, and they loved it!"

Now red-raged, and totally pissed off at this whole rotten day, I sarcastically ask, "And were... were... were there any cock hungry women present at your rather bold and insensitive showing of your body parts?"

A wicked grin spreads across his face, and he chuckles, "Oooh, about four... Or was it five? Or was it six? I can't quite remember!" he jests. "Well anyways," he continues, "I posed in an artistic fashion, and soon the whole world will get a glimpse of what you my darling, what Mrs Carter has most days for her breakfast, her lunch and her supper!"

With his words sinking into me, tearing me apart, I place my hands to my face, and burst out into an abundance of uncontrollable tears. "How could you do such a thing to me?" I woefully sob into my palms. "How could you let another woman, other women, other people see you naked? At least on set when you are filming, you are...You are..." I can't finish my sentence for he's looking pathetically at me. His facial features have crumpled into a look of total confusion. Standing up, he comes around to me, and gently touches my arm.

"Get off me!" I rile. "Bloody well don't touch me!"

He places his hand on me again, and this time he holds me firm within his grip. Tenderly angling me up from my chair, he cradles my face in his hands, and sympathetically says, "I'm actually teasing you, baby!"

"Well, I'm not laughing!" I say with damp eyes, and dreadful hurt aching around my heart.

Wiping away the tears from my eyes, he sighs, "I don't get you at the moment, baby. You usually have such a laid back sense of humour. So something must have gone wrong somewhere along the way today to make you feel this way?"

I quiet.

"You're beautiful." He smiles. "Even when you're cross at me, (And I haven't truly done anything to make you mad,) you're delightful."

"I am?"

"Yes," he sorrowfully replies. "You, my precious are lovely all the way inside and all the way out."

I sag but smile at his willy-nilly description of my inner and outer beauty. "I'm sorry for misunderstanding you, I just feel a bit vulnerable today."

Placing his palm flush on my forehead, he muses, "You feel a bit warm... Maybe you're sickening for something."

"Maybe... It's my hormones... my time of the month."

"I thought you'd just finished your period a week ago?"

"Yes, I had... Maybe it's my hormones adjusting to not being on the contraceptive pill that's making me feel this way."

"Do you want to go back on it? We don't have to try for a baby just yet. I don't mind when we create a baby. I love you and I just want you to feel well and be happy.

"It's fine," I dismiss.

"Sure?"

"Sure."

Hugging me tight, he whispers that he is sorry for upsetting, for teasing me, and I tell him that is all right, and that I am feeling better from his cuddle.

"So," I mumble into his chest, "tell me, what did you actually wear for the shoot?"

"It was casual... You know white t-shirt, black leather jacket... jeans... that sort of fashion."

"I love you in casual...."

"I love you naked." He nuzzles into my hair.

"I love you naked too."

"Shall we get naked and do it really slow?" he breathes with hope.

"Yes... I think we should. It might make me feel heaps better..."

"It will," he sweetly assures. "Making love with me always will."

After the slow love-making had ebbed and subsided, I must admit that did indeed feel a whole lot better than previously.

Chapter 20
The Following Tuesday

I approach reception and wait to be attended to.

"How may I help you?"

"Hi!" I smile, "My name is Helena Carter, and I'm from 'Heavenly Baby's Breath', the florists. I have a three-thirty appointment with Ms Ava Porter-Michaels."

After she checks the hotel bookings, she replies, "Yes, of course, Mrs Carter, she is residing in the Piccadilly suite."

"Thank you."

While in the lift, I wonder as to what Ms Ava Porter-Michaels looks like. Is she a young woman or a more mature lady? Feeling quite excited at being able to arrange the flowers for my first wedding of the year, as the doors to the lift open and I step out, my phone buzzes. I look to it – Darius.

"Good luck, baby... Go spread flower power everywhere."

I laugh at his words, quickly text him back something sexual, – how could I not – and quickly shove my phone back into my jacket pocket. After I am shown into the suite by a member of the concierge, I am asked if I would like to take to afternoon tea. I do. As I take a bite of the coronation chicken canapé, I survey my surroundings. The room is very art deco – what is it about the style of art deco that interests people? I notice and there is the twee scent of lilies perfumed somewhere within the dwelling. As a soft, feminine voice interrupts my eating of my rare roast beef and horseradish canapé, as her soft tones float through the air, they immediately captivate my attention. I dab the corners of my mouth with my napkin and look up to the source of the voice, and rise from my seat.

"Mrs Carter," Ms Ava Porter-Michaels greets me, "Please let me say how very nice it is to finally meet you in person. You look equally as stunning as you do in the newspapers and various, glossy magazines. Our Mr Carter is a very, very lucky man indeed to have such an attractive wife by his side."

Our Mr Carter? What a peculiar phrase.

I am stunned at the woman before me – for she is the woman who I saw yesterday in the bistro. With my mouth dry and my heart thumping vividly in my chest, I rapidly deduce that she and Connor must be an item – This is *my* Connor's choice of bride? Why would he choose an image so very similar to me? And just who is she?

"Mrs Carter?" she questions and shakes me from my nightmare. "Are you all right? ...You seen to be somewhere else at this moment."

Oh Ms Ava Porter-Michaels, If only you knew who I am in relation to Connor you would know why I am somewhere lost.

Wishing the ground would open up and swallow me whole, I am rooted to the spot, when she seats opposite me, and again repeats how attractive I am. Although her words are highly complementary, by her choice of description of me, I begin to silently wonder whether if she's actually one hundred percent straight or if she's bi-sexual and is enjoying hitting on me!

Out of the blue, she offers bluntly, "I'm straight, Mrs Carter, so don't worry, your sexuality is completely safe in my presence."

Now feeling unnerved that's she's just read my mind, I ask her if I may use her bathroom. I need to escape from her, from this room, and gather my scattered thoughts. She provides me with the directions to the powder room, and I make haste. Staring into the mirror, I take a few moments and then I decide that I cannot do this. I cannot be part of Connor's life any more, so I choose to leave unannounced. On arriving back at work, I walk gingerly in to the shop, and come face to face with a very puzzled looking Angelica.

"What the hell's going on, Helena?" she demands.

I dump my file and bucket bag onto the countertop and heavily sigh, "You know our Ms Ava Porter-Michaels?"

"Yes."

"You remember that woman yesterday in the bistro?"

"Yes."

"Yes but what has all this got to do with our bride-to-be who I may add is rather perplexed that you left without a single word so she has cancelled her booking with us."

"She... She..." I close my eyelids, take a deep breath, and reveal, "She, our bride-to-be Ava, is the woman from the bistro."

As realisation dawns upon Angelica, silence briefly surrounds us, until she grabs hold of me, hugs me tight and while I weep into my best friend's arms, she soothes me with heartfelt words of everything eventually is going to be all right.

Would it? – Eventually all work out just fine?

Chapter Twenty-One

The weekend

Saturday

It's the beginning of the weekend and after experiencing one of the most bizarre weeks to date, I am so looking forward to just lazing around with Darius in our new London home. I have almost finished brushing my teeth, and as I fleet my look into the bathroom mirror, I see Darius stepping out of the shower. Clocking eyes upon him, I warm inside when I see him ruffling his hair with a towel. Winking at me, he proceeds to enlighten me that, that was one hot, mighty fucking session previously we endured, and that he really, really enjoyed me riding him until the moment I weakened, and he had to intervene by flipping me onto my back and giving it to me slow. Looking at me in the mirror, I roll my eyes, spit out the toothpaste into the washbasin, and he struts over to me. Aligning his damp, fragrant body over mine, he places his palms flush to the countertop and sexily breathes into my ear, "You look so gorgeous standing here naked with your hair coiffured up into a towel, so much so that I could easily fuck you all weekend long."

Rinsing my toothbrush under the tap, I place it back on the charger, turn around and rise on to my tippy toes. Nuzzling noses with him, I challenge, "Then, Mr Carter, why don't you do just that?"

His cock twitches against my belly, and outwardly I groan for it's been less than half an hour since he devoured me and I'm seriously beginning to wonder if I can keep up with this man of mine. Before I can contemplate, he has hoisted me up and my buttocks are flush with the white marble vanity unit. I balance myself and the room falls away because he has just sunk to his knees, parted my legs with his strong hands, and held me open. Looking at my freshly bathed centre, he takes a breath and kisses against the dip of my inner left thigh,

"You have such a beautiful, fragrant pussy, Helena and I am so lucky that you are all mine."

So very descriptive of you to say so, Darius!

"Yes, you are very fortunate that I am all yours." I moan with delight as he takes the first taste of me.

Blowing a light puff of air over my still prominent clitoris, as I whimper no, no, I can't possibly take any more of him... just yet anyway, he tells me that yes I can, and that this next act of sexual lust will be for my pleasure first and his second. So while he buries his head between my thighs and I swirl my fingers through his scented, wet locks, as he feasts upon me, his morning stubble chaffing my thighs, and my ever so tender folds, I lose control of my body, and I easily come to climax with such power. My back hits the back of the vanity unit, and while I flow, and contract wave after wave punishes my lower body, I yank at his hair hard, screaming for him to stop.

"I can't," I manage to pant into the heavily sex-drenched air of the en suite, "I can't take any more... please, Darius..."

"You can, and you will." He nips me on my clit.

I wail with ecstatic pain.

"You can and you will take more for I promise you, the next orgasm that is already threatening within you, will not only tear you to shreds, it will leave your thighs quivering and your heart wanting more... So much more of me."

"Please, baby, stop!" I plead trying to push him away with my heels digging into his shoulders. "Pleeeease... I... I... can't... Everything feels so tender... I feel as if I am going to faint."

He pauses, looks up at me from between my trembling thighs, and as he slides two fingers into me, pressing down to the back wall of my vagina, I bear down upon him. Within seconds, I spiralled into the most body racking orgasm and as my climax ripped through me and over him, he took a glance at me, raised his eyebrows, and I nearly slid off the unit when he began slowly lapping at my quaking centre, while grinning, "There, see, Helena, I told you could take more."

"Come here." I breathed with exhaustion. "Come up to meet me."

Slithering up to me, he cupped my face in his hands, and pressed his mouth to mine. Scrolling his tongue around mine as I tasted me on him, he parted my thighs with his knee, and rubbed the crown of his throbbing cock against my folds.

"Oh please no..." I groaned into his mouth as the first inch of him stretched me. "No more..."

"Oh yes, more..." he moaned into my mouth, and as he thrust so whole into me, I slammed hard into the wall mirror behind my back.

"I love you, you horny rascal." I bit deep into his shoulder.

"I love you, you enticing beauty." He sucked into my neck.

"Fuck me hard, sir?"

301

"Oh, I'm going to fuck you harder than hard because by the time I am finished with you Mrs Carter, you won't even be able to walk let alone remember your name!"

When he did finish with me, with us, we were nothing but a pair of love bite ridden, sweat sheened covered, tangled lovers who were left laying gasping for air on the floor of our lavish en suite bathroom.

A safe, sane and consensual Sunday

This safe, sane and consensual Sunday began with me reading what Darius had once verbally conveyed to me. After he was satisfied that I understood every single word and I was completely sure that I wished to participate in a session, I signed and he introduced me to the room in the attic...

'Helena, remember the common dictionary states that safe is to be "secure from liability to harm, injury, danger or risk". In this context, Dominants and submissives see safe BDSM as taking care of their partner so that no matter how intense the scene may be, no unwanted injury, transfer of danger or disease will occur. All precautions must be taken to minimise any potential dangers. This means doing research and being knowledgeable about the chosen kink activities we desire to embark upon. In order to be safe, you must know the risks of BDSM and which activities add spice without causing permanent or lasting damage to the emotional, mental or physical state of either me the dominant (top) or you the submissive (bottom)

Through the BDSM lens, dominants and submissives must act responsibly and exercise good judgement at all times. The ability to engage in an appropriate self control is a big part of the 'sane' portion of this philosophy. If you cannot control yourself, you should not, and I repeat not, enter into a situation where power exchange is a key respect. BDSM should not be used as a solution for serious psychological conditions or mental health concerns; playing with a partner where one person has some deep rooted concerns can trigger emotional releases that neither person is able to handle within the boundaries of the BDSM scene in play.

Consensual – giving informed consent. The importance of it being consensual is paramount the keep within the BDSM ethics and ensure that this relationship of ours is a healthy one where both partners are supported by each other. If consent is not obtained by either of us prior to play, then it is not only is it damaging to our relationship but it can point to an abusive dynamic. It is important that consent is obtained prior to every single session we choose to embark upon and most certainly never and not during or after play has ended and after care is about to be brought into the scene. This is particularly important because when endorphins are running hot from play, neither you nor I will be able to make sound decisions and by this, we will fail to think through the situation with sensibility. So before I introduce you to the Crux Desscuta, do you understand all, and I mean everything that has been inked here, Helena?'

"I do...."

"Please sign..."

I ink my signature directly below his...

Chapter Twenty-Two

The Attic Room -take one

"You can open your eyes now, Helena," Darius whispers into my ear.

I do, and as the attic room comes into focus, I do my utmost to drink in every object that is present within. These are the contents that Darius has chosen to grace our attic playroom in this house in Holland Park: In my own mind, I have categorised them as follows to make it easier for me to remember what each item is and for it/their particular use(s)

Firstly, Stimulatory Items: A glass fronted cabinet which was adorned with various flogging implements. To name a few: Floggers, nipple clamps and spanking paddles. All were neatly hanging from their respective, numbered pegs.

Secondly, Sensory Deprivation Items: Blindfolds. Various textures i.e. leather, velvet and latex to mention but a few.

Thirdly, Restraining Items: Laid out upon a highly polished cherry wood table, was a cache of eye popping items! Some were obvious to me in their creation while others were positively mind boggling! Passing the ones I recognised, as I fleeted my fingertips along various rolls of different widths of duct tape, numerous designs of wrist restraints/bondage cuffs, and lastly a spreader bar, I turned my attention to noting the furniture.

Lastly, Bondage Furniture: A Crux Decussata – Which I have been deadly curious to experience. A table with a padded top and multiple fixing points strategically placed around it, and finally a rather enticing massage table. Of course there was a footstool which aids the submissive when she/me is in suspension.

"What do you think of our new personal room of pleasure/pain, Helena?"

"It's very stark..." I truthfully reply, "I think it could do with some photos on the wall to liven it up!"

Nibbling my earlobe, he whispers, "What kind of photos would you suggest, Mrs Carter? Landscapes?"

"No... I think we should have a selection of snaps of you and me..."

His tone surprised, he asks, "You want romantic photos of us, up in here?"

"No... I want photos of us in... You know... In the act..."

"What!" he exclaims. "You want black and white photographs of you submitting to me? Of me dominating you?"

"Yes, I do. I think it would be rather stimulating to see photographs of us like that especially when we are actually in D/s mode in this room."

"And there was me," he chuckles, "thinking all along that I was the real bona fide kinky one in this relationship!"

Turning, I swat him lightly upon the chest, tell him that it is his fault that I am the way that I am because over time he has converted me from just a plain vanilla, sex freak into the kind of woman who loves – neopoliation, a varied harlequin of different flavoured sex! He guffaws with laughter at my description.

I ask, "When will you introduce me to the Crux Decussata?"

His face shows concern, and he replies, "Soon"

"How soon?"

"When I am totally confident that you will be able to endure the entire length of the lesson..."

"Why do you have to be confident?"

"Because..." he runs his fingers through his mass of curls, "before I introduce you to the Crux, I need to be one hundred percent sure that you understand the all the practical safety aspects that come with being restrained upon the cross."

"Well, why don't you explain them to me over a light brunch?"

"Sure?"

"Sure."

Brunch it was.

The conversation that followed between Darius and me over our delights of buttery croissants and Strawberry Bon Maman jam turned out to be more of an informative one than a to and fro of discussion. It was very businesslike and matter of fact. Darius led the way and I occasionally chipped in with an inquisitive ask.

"Helena, you already know that in general, BDSM play is usually structured such that it is possible for the consenting partner to withdraw his or her consent during a scene for example, by the subject in play using their safe word."

"Yes, I do, Darius."

"Well, when you find yourself shackled to the Crux Decussata, you will not be able to speak to me."

"Why will I not?"

"For you will be gagged."

Astounded, I halt taking another bite of my French pastry, and ask, "Explain, gagged."

"The restriction of your speech which will heighten your other senses and at the same time your lack of voice will elevate my senses too."

"Explain further?"

"You will just be able to make intelligible speech, and even though you will still be able to permit loud, inarticulate sounds that may indicate you need assistance, you..."

"So if I can't speak," I interrupt, "and I can't honour my safe word, then how do I inform you that things may be about to progress beyond my limits?"

"There are two set choices that are commonly used in BDSM."

"Enlighten me as to what they are?"

"You can either choose to hold a small rubber ball or a tiny bell in your hand. If and when you reach your limit, depending on which object you have chosen as your safe word, you will either drop the ball, or ring the bell. This is your withdrawal of consent from play, and I will halt whatever I am doing to you, for you, for us immediately."

"You would stop instantly, wouldn't you?"

"Good grief! How could you ask such a thing of me?"

"I needed to ask..."

He nods in understanding.

"Helena, if I failed to honour your safe word, it would be considered a serious misconduct on my part, and it could, just might even change the sexual content of our situation into a crime, depending on the relevant law with our country."

"I understand."

"You do, fully?"

"Yes, I do, completely."

"There is one more thing that I wish to explain to you before I am confident that you are absolutely certain that you wish for us to step forward."

"Go ahead."

"Helena, the erotic pain that you will feel during your time on the cross, will be more arousing and more intense than you have ever experienced during play before. Also, the longer you remain in play, opiates, natural painkillers will be released into your bloodstream and they will create a feeling of euphoria within you. In a sense, after play has ended, and you are in my arms and aftercare is in situ, I can assure you will never forget your time upon the cross, and when you pass those memories through your mind, I guarantee you from this act, you will have not only pleasured me, your dominant, your husband, but you will have also strengthened from within."

"Darius...?"

"Yes?"

"I'm absolutely certain."

"Sure?"

"Sure."

"So now we have established that we are both comfortable with taking our D/s relationship to the next level, these are the four things that I require you to do before entering the room;

Firstly you will take a shower and use only unscented, glycerine soap to cleanse your body with. Secondly, you must under no circumstances apply deodorant or perfume to your skin. Thirdly, you must remove all jewellery from your person. Finally, you must secure you hair into a pony tail. Do you understand, Helena?"

"I do, but why must I do these things that you ask."

"By being pure, without any artificial scents upon your person there will be nothing that can interfere with your senses, and secondly jewellery, if worn and caught, snagged so to speak, can cause injury during play.

"Okay."

"And," he adds, "these are the three things I wish for you to do after entering the room."

One: Choose either the rubber ball or the bell.

Two: Choose the implement or implements that you wish for me to stimulate you with.

Three: Kneel before the Crux and take time to offer it your respect. If you respect the chosen bondage furniture, it will in turn respect you."

"Understand, Helena?"

"Yes, sir, I do."

"Perfect"

The Attic Room – take two.

The temperature within this room is slightly cooler than one would've expected – I wonder as to why. Kneeling before the Crux Decussata, I place the crop, a set of nipple clamps, and my safe word, the bell, on the wooden step before it, and while I wait for my dominant to enter the room, I turn my respect to the cross. Time passes so very slowly, and while I focus on the four restraining points of the bondage furniture looming before me, a strange calm envelopes over me.

Will I have to ring the bell, I wonder.

Darius has arrived and before we began, he told me that this lesson in my art of submission would be something that I would never forget. He of course, was correct in his assumption.

"Rise"

I rise.

Darius rests his hand upon my shoulder, and asks, "Which hand are you holding your safe word in?"

I indicate my left.

"Show me."

I uncurl my hand to show him the little bell in my palm.

"Good... Now take a step up."

I step up.

"Turn around."

I turn.

"Step back."

I step back.

"Drop your head forward, take a moment and breathe."

I do just that, and while he secures the ball gag around the back of my head, I don't take my vision off his bare feet.

"Now rest your head back."

I do, and as I feel something choker-like support my neck, a small whine escapes from my throat, and the bell does a slight tremble in my clenched fist.

"Spread your arms."

I do, and he restrains my wrists with the soft downy leather straps.

"Now do the same with your legs."

I do, and he restrains my ankles with the soft downy leather straps. He steps back and looks admiringly at me, and then he walks to the table and picks up his Canon camera... Well, I did ask for photographs for this room, didn't I! Focusing upon me, he then quite simply takes a series of snaps!

"You look the perfect picture."

Do I? I can't wait to see it!

This experience had to be, to date, the most animated I had ever encountered. During play, I was barraged with numerous emotions, a cache of new feelings and at certain times I was enraptured, and at others I felt as if I had been intoxicated on the finest champagne. Firstly I entered the excitement phase: Physical or mental erotic stimuli. As my erogenous zones were heightened, my body began preparing itself for sexual intercourse – Will we have vanilla sex after this scenario completes?

With each caress of the crop, as Darius trailed it slowly up and down the insides of my thighs, I felt my heart rate and my breathing increasing... And his past words floated gaily through my *drunken* mind...

'Helena, the erotic pain that you will feel during your time on the cross, will be more arousing and more intense than you have ever experienced during play before. Also, the longer you remain in play, opiates, natural painkillers will be released into your bloodstream and they will create a feeling of euphoria within you. In a sense, after play has ended, and you are in my arms and aftercare is in situ, I can assure you will never forget your time upon the cross, and when you fleet those memories through your mind, I guarantee you from this act, you will have not only pleasured me, your dominant, your husband, but you will have also strengthened from within.'

He was correct regarding the feeling of euphoria – Can one actually become drunk on the offshoots of love? I think so. He halted his tease, stood tall before me, and while he looked into my eyes, he whispered to me that my nipples are erecting and it's highly possible that they could stiffen further. Clamping them between his thumb and forefinger, he pinched them tight and I felt my thighs begin to quake. Again I felt another pinch, but not by the warmth of his fingers but instead by the coolness of the metal nipple clamps that I chose earlier to use as a stimulatory item. I mewled against the ball in my mouth and as saliva formed, I clenched the bell, my fist firm. My nipples were tugged again, and as endorphins began to seep, and the elation of being *set free* enraptured me, I found myself being transported onto cloud nine. While Darius spoke of dark, erotic scenarios, I visited each and every one. It was as if he had physically held my hand and taken me up the stairs to the seventh heaven! The only way I can describe this play, was as if I had entered paradise but not through the normal channels!

While I breathed steadily, each assault upon my nipples and each snap of the crop against my swollen nub, I whimpered out. He kept eye contact with me throughout, searching out my soul, while taking me into a non-symphonic rhapsody until the second I rang my bell. Within an instance, all restraints were unleashed and the ball gag removed from my mouth. As I slumped into his arms and he cradled me, rocking me back and forth. I looked up at this man who had by his dominance taken me somewhere that only I will ever know.

His mouth closed softly upon mine and he murmured, "Are you okay, Helena?"

With the natural happy hormones soaring high through my body, and the heat of his scented flesh letting me know that he is physically with me, I kissed him back. He beamed me the most magnificent smile because I replied with softness, "I'm very, very okay. When do you think can we do this again?"

He quite simply smiled and carried me to our en suite and the aftercare he bestowed upon me was so sensual, so magical and mystical to say the least that it will always be somewhere that only he and I would ever know.

Chapter Twenty-Three

Five-thirty a.m.

"Wake up, Helena." I hear little whispers into my ear.

"Why?" I roll over and sleepily mumble against Darius' warm lips.

"I want you to."

"I don't want to wake up." I grumble, "So no, go away, Darius. I need more sleep." I say as I begin to turn away from him.

Gently pulling me back, he grabs my attention when he sexily breathes, "I'll only let you go back to sleep if you open your eyes and look at me."

I flutter my lashes open to see him crouching over me, and I liquefy inside because he's giving me that knowing look.

"It's to... toooooo early," I yawn, "for sex, vanilla or otherwise."

"It's never too early for any type of sex especially with you."

"Mmmm." I kiss against his mouth... "Maybe..."

Next, as him and his cock wish me the brightest of very early mornings, I shiver at the warmth of his manhood pressing against my belly.

"You like?"

"Of course I like!"

"You want me?"

I sigh, "I want you but I really do need to go and take a pee first!"

As he smiled, and it was a slow, sexy, seductive curl of his lips, I was drawn into his beautiful aura. Pressing his mouth to mine, he wilted me even further by suggesting, "Later, baby... You can pee later."

"But... But..." I go to complain, but am silenced by his tongue darting into my mouth.

"You can pee after I have had my breakfast, baby."

"Breakfast?" I arch my back into the mattress, "What do you mean breakfast?"

With his morning glory now pulsating against my belly, he dreamily says, "My fill of you..."

"You mean the filling of me," I lazily retort.

"Whatever I mean, you are soon going to be flooded with the fluid that's been pent up inside me all night long, very, very soon."

"Oh am I?" I say with a tired but interested longing in my voice.

Dipping his tongue again into my mouth again, he retreats slightly, and then as he rubs the crown of his cock up and down my moist folds, I truly give in to my fuss about needing the bathroom. Stilling, he lingers above me, and with the cheekiest grin imaginable he winks and replies, "Yes, Mrs Carter, you most certainly are."

With my bladder starting to spasm for its release, I pray that I am not going to wet the mattress, for as he took me fast, deep and so very hard, I had to hold on with all my might! I had to clench my muscles tighter and tighter in the hope of making it to the end of *early breakfast* without letting go!

Within moments he had released into me, and as he flopped back onto the bed, air whooshed from the depths of his lungs, and he declared with gusto, "Jeez, Helena, you were so fucking tight... I'm so sorry, I just couldn't stop myself from orgasming."

"Was I?" I say, hopping up from the bed, now achingly desperate to flee to the bathroom.

"Yes, you were and you felt fucking amazing."

"Why, thank you kind sir!" I whimper while trying to cross my legs running!

"I think you'd better go and pee before you wet yourself." He chuckles while stroking his deflating cock.

On making it to the bathroom, I look into the mirror and to be truthful, I don't look very bright this morning – Maybe I just need more sleep, or maybe... Climbing back into bed, Darius was already in slumber, and snoring lightly, so I spooned my body into his and we slept in that position until the alarm pierced shrill through the air.

Seven-thirty a.m.

Post showering.

Ruffling his damp hair with a towel, Darius asks, "So my angel, since it's your day off from arranging flowers and the like, what you are going to do with your free day while I am working hard pretending to be someone that I am not?"

Taking a sip of orange juice, I revel in its freshly squeezed taste, swallow and then reply, "I thought I might go and hunt down a wedding gift for Angelica and Xavier."

He raises an eyebrow, rubs his chin and then frowns.

"What's the matter? Don't you think I should go present hunting?"

"No, of course not... I think that's a lovely idea. Would you do me a favour?"

"Name it!"

"Would you please take the Porsche and not your somewhat faltering Mini?"

"Why?"

"Because the Porsche..." he sighs deeply, "...It's more reliable than your old Mini."

"I love my Mini. She may be ancient but she's never let me down in the past," I say with defence in her honour!

"I know, sweetheart, but just do me one simple favour without arguing or protesting for once."

"Name it."

"Just please take the Porsche today okay?"

"Okay." I give in. "The Porsche it is but I want you to know that I still love my Mini much more than the Porsche."

With a glint in his eyes, he chuckles, "I know you do... And that's good that you do – loyalty and all that!"

"Thanks."

"I'm glad you have agreed to take the Porsche."

"Why?"

"Well, for one moment I thought I'd only birthday gifted it to you, so it was going to be solely used as a fuck vessel!"

"Well you have to admit, Darius that it was one hell of a good birthday fuck!"

He grins broadly and I amuse when he pretends to scribble in the air, "Note to Self: Suggest a repeat of said fuck, soon!"

I laugh at his silliness, and he steps into his underwear, and sexily shimmies them up over his lean hips, I instruct,

"Don't pull them up!"

Both his eyebrows shoot up and he quizzes, "Why on earth not?"

I walk over to him and kneel between his legs. Starting to stroke his cock, I answer, "Because you are so beautiful, and I want to suck you before I let you go off to the studio."

Looking down on me, he smiles and I giggle when he grasps his cock in his hand and squeezes it, and replies, "Be my guest! This adorable big fella is forever at your beck and call!"... And then he adds, "And Helena?"

I look up at him, and with a sexy tone in my voice, I can't help but salute, "Yes, sir!"

He groans at my action and then tickles me when he so seriously responds, "Please maintain eye contact with me at all times because having you look up at me while I am in your mouth just drives me fucking crazy!"

Widening my eyes, magnetically drawing him into my chocolate-caramel, coloured irises, I sweetly say, "As you wish, sir."

In no time he had knotted both his fists in my tresses, and he has angled my face towards his freshly perfumed, lower midriff. The scent of Chanel Bleu makes me feel lightheaded and so very attracted to him. I look lovingly up to him.

"Suck me now, baby," he says with such sensuality dripping from every pore of his stunningly, beautiful being. "Suck me until I can't hold back any longer and I have to... I just have to release into your pretty mouth while I scream out your name to the heavens!"

This will be my pleasure for your pleasure, Darius.

So as he leans back and rests his buttocks upon the lower rail of the bed, I begin by holding him in my left hand, and as I start seductively swirling my tongue around the soft, spongy head of his circumference, trailing it along the sensitive fraenulum of his cock, I start pumping him with my fist, gently at first. With my other hand, I lovingly massage his perfectly

317

smooth balls, while intermittently trailing my nails along the inner of his thighs.

"Jeezzzz... Hel... en... a" he drawls..."You're killing me here."

Pausing with my mouth, I still massage his girth, his length with my hand, but as I do, I tongue-lap him gently over the perfectly formed ridges of his testicles – each one in turn, and then in turn again. His eyes are closed and I wonder if I've transported him to a place that only he will ever know. Next, I take him again between my lips, and I arouse him further by murmuring "Mmmm" with him in my mouth, and as the vibrations of my erotic sound travels over and through his cock, he groans that my technique, my mouth, my tongue and my lips are all very delightful... He rasps that this is almost too much for him to bear any longer but then again on another note could I please never, ever stop desiring to perform oral sex on him.

As if I could! As if I would ever wish to stop pleasuring my husband in this way? – Never – He looks too delightful at the mercy of my mouth!

While I continue my sexual onslaught onto him by giving him seven shallow sucks, followed a single deeper draw, his thighs tremble and his grip on my hair intensifies. Next, I perform six shallow sucks and two deeper ones, until the moment that I see his chest has begun to flush with the tell-tale redness. His thighs jolt hard against my shoulders. This man of mine is about ready to burst and I for one with my aching jaw, are most definitely ready to receive what he has to give. Almost coiling his body down full, as I see his mop of curls fall foreword and drop over his forehead, he warns, "Baby, baby, I'm so close... Please... Please..."

"Mmmm..." I say with another teasing vibration against his throbbing cock, followed by a firmish cup and ply of his tightening balls.

"I'm about..." his body racks... "I'm... I... H... e... l... e... n... a..."

And as he hisses out my name between his clenched teeth, I stare hard at him, and his eyes pierce right through to my very soul. I jerk him into the final moment and as I clamp my mouth around him, I don't pause, I just quickly bring him off into my mouth and take each hot, generous swallow after swallow! On releasing him, he slowly unwinds my hair from his tense fingers, and slumps to his knees. Grasping out for me, he cradles my face in his hands, while hungrily crashing his mouth to mine, while so emotionally bleeding from his heart,

"Don't ever stop loving me, Helena."

"I won't... I promise." I say with teary eyes. "Don't ever stop loving me, Darius."

"I won't... I promise... I can't. You perform fellatio so amazingly beautiful..."

"Do I?" I reply, knowing full well that that was my best performance to date.

"Yes, you do, so promise me you will never stop loving me, pleasuring in that way."

"I promise..."

Eight-thirty a.m.

Sauntering out of the kitchen, while shimmying into his leather jacket, he shouts to me, "Helena, don't forget tonight we are dining out with Xavier and Angelica! They want to divulge their wedding plans."

Eager for him to leave, for I have something very pressing that I need to attend to alone, I holler, "Don't worry, I haven't forgotten!" then add, "You had better hurry up, Darius, or you're going to be dreadfully be late for work."

On seeing him rush back through the door, I amaze when he comes over to me, cradles my face in his hands and breezes against my lips, "Thanks for the blow!"

"My pleasure to serve..." I giggle into his mouth while scrolling my tongue around his.

"I love you, Helena." He kisses me deep.

"I love you too, baby." I kiss him back.

"I wish I didn't have to go into the studio today."

"I wish you didn't either." I half-heartedly fib...

For some strange reason unbeknown to me, he looks a tad worried, so I dutifully ask, "Is there anything bothering you that I should know about?"

"No." He kisses me again. "There's not anything perplexing me at all."

"Sure?" I quiz with uncertainty in my voice. "You seem to almost be somewhere else.

"I'm sure," he replies with not much conviction, and then tells me he will most definitely be late if he doesn't get a move on this instant.

"Okay, baby." I smile and press my lips to his. "I'll see you around sixish?"

"Sixish it is."

"Oh and by the way I've left you a little something on your pillow."

Before I can ask what is it that he has gifted me, the door to the penthouse shuts behind him, and I am left alone to my own devices. I decide that I will seek out gift that he has left me later on for I truly need to get this pressing task of mine over first, so I sit down at the breakfast bar, and pull out the oblong package from my nightgown pocket. Twisting and turning it over, running my fingers over the cellophane wrapper, I rise and proceed towards the bathroom...

On exiting the bathroom, holding the used object in my trembling hand, as I stare at it hard; that was the moment when I realised that mine and Darius's lives were about to change forever. There is now another new chapter in the making and the following is the reason as to why:

Opening my eyes, I looked to the stick that I was holding between my thumb and forefinger. Doing a double take, my heart swelled when I saw that it has indicated to me that I was pregnant. Darius will be elated. Now here are the perplexing questions I asked myself; do I tell Darius before our dinner with Xavier and Angelica? Do I announce it over dinner? Or do I... do I take the bull by the horns, and surprise him at work and share the wonderful news in this way? After hardly any deliberation, I decided that the latter option seemed like a most wonderful idea.

As it turned out, with hindsight, I wished I'd never set foot in the studio, let alone pushed open the door to his dressing room.

Chapter Twenty-Four

Twelve-thirty p.m.

Since I am not actually going out gift hunting for Angelica and Xavier, I do not see why I need to honour Darius's earlier ask, and so as today turned out not to be a red Porsche day, and instead had evolved into becoming 'I'm pregnant!' day, I decided to drive my green Mini to see Darius. So after locking my car, I patted her on the roof and thanked her for once again not conking out on me. She's been with me for many a years now – Connor, my dear sweet first love Connor chose her with me... we'd had lots of fun escapades in this car! And even though I adore the Porsche, I still have chosen to make my Mini my number one car. Turning around, I look up at the vast studio building – It's quite simply called 'The Studio' – This is my first ever visit here. Darius never forbade me to come here, we just came to a common agreement that there was no need for me to see him, see him on set creating romantic, and sometimes quite sexual scenes with the current leading lady of the day! I brush the thoughts of him acting out screen kisses and bedroom and along with sometimes non bedroom antics (Not the D/s kind I may add... that's purely our domain.) and head towards the door. Inside this vast building of creativity, somewhere is my Darius, and I for one can't wait to see him and tell him my, our very important news. Running my hand over my belly, I whisper, "Shall we go inside, Impy and tell your daddy the exciting news?"

Of course, Impy – as I have temporarily named our unborn child, doesn't respond.

"Good morning, Mrs Carter," a broad shouldered doorman greets.

"Good morning," I chirp back.

On entering the reception area, I approach the marble topped, curved counter and ask the well groomed, thirty-something receptionist where I might find Mr Darius Carter.

"And who are you may I ask?" she politely asks.

Surprised at thinking she doesn't recognise me, I reply "I'm Helena, Darius's wife."

"Ahh," she reveals, "I actually thought that you were." She smiles.

"Why did you think so?"

She then taps with her red, perfectly manicured fingernail on the cover of a glossy, gossip magazine that is displayed on the top of the desk, and replies, "You and Darius are in there somewhere."

"Oh," I say with not much curiosity, "another article on our past?"

She doesn't respond to my question and I don't really have the patience to probe her, so as I listen to her informing me that as luck would have it, Darius is currently off set, on a break, and she believes that he is in his dressing room which is situated on level three.

"Would you like me to call him up and say that you are on your way up to see him, Mrs Carter?"

"No, no... Thank you." I decline and then swipe the magazine off the surface, stuff it into my tote bag and kindly say, "I want to surprise him."

She warmly smiles, points me in the direction of the lift, and wishes me a lovely day. I too wish her a pleasant rest of the day.

The lift doors open and I step out into the foyer of level three. As the scent of freesia's fill the air, enveloping my senses, I again run my hand over my belly and tell Impy that we are nearly with his daddy. Finally on reaching my destination, I look to the door. The gold plaque simply reads – Darius Carter. I smile – for my gorgeous husband and the soon -father-to-be of our first child is just moment's way from becoming the happiest man on the planet! Taking a deep breath, I choose not to knock and instead I place my hand over the door handle. Depressing the handle, as the door swings open and the room comes into my view, the world around me falls away, and I stand rigid with shellshock! Darius is not alone as one would've, as I would've expected. Time moves slowly. Perched on his desk, with her back facing me is... is... a female – Her presence has blocked out my view of Darius, who I know is in here because I can smell his timeless, freshly laundered fragrance. I assume he must be sitting in the chair opposite her. With the fleeting glance I have of her, I note that her hair style and colour are practically identical to mine, and with this unnerving vision before me, hiding the man that I am aching to see, I begin to feel extremely uneasy. While I try to open my mouth as to announce my presence, this is the conversation between them that followed:

"Have you missed me, Darius?"

"No, I am afraid I have not missed you in the slightest."

In a sickly, baby girlish tone, I hear her breathe, "Not even a tiny, teensy little bit, my sexy sir?"

My sexy sir? How very dare she!

A brief pause between them occurs, and then as my Darius responded to her, the bombshell dropped, promptly landed and exploded right in front of my very eyes!

"Maybe I have a little..." His voice turns lower than low, and I see stars dancing before me as I hear him add, "Alice..."

This is no wonderland I have been thrust into yet again – This is a pure pit of horror!

As I hail into the air, "Oh God, please no, Darius." Alice turns and I crumple inside for... she, Alice is... is... is... Ava Porter-Michaels... Or is Ava in fact, Alice?

And as Darius comes into my view, I see that his hair his damp and I fail inside when it is perfectly obvious to me that he is top naked. All I can focus on is the scar over his heart and those dreadful memories of the past come flooding back. I waver and hold on to the back of a chair. His taut torso is covered with tiny beads of post-workout moisture, there is a wet cooling towel that has been spiralled and draped around his neck. My vision halts when I see the top two fasteners of his jeans are undone revealing the band of his white boxers – The underwear that I pulled up over his trembling thighs this morning after I had relished; after I had savoured in the taste of his morning glory climax.

Has he been working out after acting? I know he has a private fitness gym here at the studio and that he finds exercise is an excellent stress reliever for him – Or has he been working out on her? – Ava – I mean with Alice right here on the desk in his dressing room? – Has he just flogged her, whipped her sorry, lying arse with his wet towel? Has he fucked her hard while she, his ex-submissive is engaged to my first love, Connor? Has he? Have they? Did they?

With all these cracked up thoughts soaring through my mind, I scream an abundance of murderous words at them both and finish aiming my hurt firstly at Darius, then without a blink... at her!

"You,... you cheating, disloyal two-timing bastard, stay the fuck away from me and you, you, you..." I point my finger at her. "You... you conniving bitch, Alice or Ava, whoever you are, break it off with Connor. He deserves better than a slut, better than a whore of a husband stealer, and way better than a marriage wrecker for you than a wife!"

Darius puffs out his chest and rises, but the wrath within me has now been unleashed and as he catches my warning glare for him to back off, he is rooted to the spot, albeit briefly.

"Helena, please," he soulfully breathes, and I soften a little at his voice. As he then takes a tentative step towards me, while pitifully imploring, "Please why won't you let me explain?"

Before I can answer, Alice then intervenes, slipping off the edge of the desk, she smoothes her too short of a mini skirt down, and begins to secure the fourth, the third and then second button of her white silk blouse, while hissing, "What will you do if I don't break up with Connor?"

She's had her blouse unbuttoned? Had Darius been undressing her? Or was she stripping off for him?

"I'll tell him who you really are!" I howl. "I'll tell him what you are."

"And what am I?"

"You're nothing but a common whore who fucks for money," I scream. "A jealous bitch who Darius never, ever wanted to commit to... He didn't want you as a future wife, as the possible mother of his children."

Turning to see Darius whose torso is now shaking with rage, my stomach churns at the tone of her sickly, syrupy voice as she sweetly asks, "And do you think I am a whore Darius?" I wait anxiously for his response.

His fists knotted by his sides, he with definition in his voice, replies, "Even though you came from a high end escort agency, yes I do, Alice. I do think that you are a whore, so get the fuck out of my dressing room, this building, and mine and Helena's life before I have you escorted out by security."

"Don't fret, I'm going... and before I do I want you to know that it was you that made me into a whore, sir. You fucked the whore into me with your big, thick, film star cock, and as you broke me in, the whore loved your filthy words and your precious dick so much, that the whore within me decided never to leave!"

As the bile rises in my throat at the sheer vulgarity of her declaration, Darius grasps his t-shirt off the back of the chair and roughly shrugs into it. Shoving her out of the way and as he reaches me I lash out and slap him hard on the side of his face.

"I hate you!" I shriek, while watching his head jar to the right. "I hate... hate... hate you!"

She cackles with triumph, and I hit him hard again. Darius's eyes are now blazing with hurt, confusion and shock, and as he tries to reach out for me I dart backwards successfully dodging him.

"Fuck off, Darius!" I snap through the air "Fuck you, you twisted bastard!"

"Helena! Stop this now!" he cries with desperation in his voice, "There is a perfectly reasonable explanation why she, Alice is unfortunately here."

"A reasonable explanation you say? She shouldn't have even been here in the first place... alone with you ... my husband and the... the..."

"The what?" he asks.

I quake. I quiver. I feel like I'm literally dying inside.

Before I can tell him that I am with child, Alice intervenes and adds more fuel to this fire by spurting, "Connor won't believe you if you tell him who I am, for he's fallen in way too deep, and he needs me to keep him afloat."

A nervous glance at Darius, whose face is full of anger, and with my voice shaking, I waver. "What do you mean, he's in too deep?"

And as I hear her say that he's shaping up to be the most excellent dominant she could ever wish for, a much more disciplined and a more controlled dominant than Darius, my heart feels as if it has been gripped in the hand of the devil and that is being squeezed until it beats it last pulse.

Alice is training Connor to be her dominant?

"Fuck you, Alice!" Darius growls through clenched teeth.

"No, fuck you, Darius!" she viciously retorts.

Suddenly I feel as if I am a spectator at the grand finale of Wimbledon, and as I watch their tennis rally of hate, of pure spite for each other unfold. I flinch as his fist comes down hard and impacts upon the surface of his desk. While his phone leaps off the desk, and plonks onto the floor, he grates, "What the fuck have you been up to...? What the fuck are you playing at, you immoral bitch?"

"Chess!" she viciously rasps back, and then laughs wildly while grabbing her handbag. "Since my old king – you, ditched me for that cow over there you call a wife," she waggles her perfectly manicured finger at me, "I've been training my new, sexy, hot blond, king how to adore his queen."

Suddenly out of all this madness thankfully my epiphany, my enlightenment arrives – as that was the moment when I suddenly felt that I could no longer dwell with Darius in this living nightmare so I quite simply, within that split second of time, decided to leave him forever and never to return, and while I was doing so, I pledged to myself to eradicate all memories of him, Alice and Connor from my mind and more importantly my life. I spin on my heel, and slam the door behind me shut encasing them in their torrid world of hatred for one another. Fleeing, with my head in the most tumultuous of whirls, I don't have the tolerance nor do I have the extra time to wait for the lift to take me back down, so I locate the stairwell and bolt as fast as I can until I reach the reception.

Someone for my entire flight has been thundering close behind me – Darius? With the ground beneath my feet passing rapidly by, and the sickness of hurt cursing through my venous system, I pelt at full speed, expertly dodging the masses of people milling around until I reach the exit. Holding the door open for me, as I fly through, the doorman tips his hat and wishes me a good day.

A good day? How on earth could this be a good day? How could it possibly get any worse? My husband has been entertaining his ex-submissive in his dressing room! He's... he's missed her a little... That's a little too much for my liking! And Connor? Connor's dabbling in D/s?... D/s isn't a *game* to be delved into lightly... I for one know that for sure... And to boot! I'm secretly pregnant!

"Helena, stop!" I hear Darius's voice boom through the reception that is now buzzing with people on their lunch hour. On seeing a sea of people instantly hush and focus upon my dishevelled looking film star husband, I grasp onto the doorman's arm, and while I cling on to him for dear life, I plead, "Don't let Mr Carter anywhere near me... Please?"

Stiffening into his full height, he looks stern and then affirms, "Yes, Mrs Carter."

"Thank you." I sink inside. "Just promise me you won't let him near me."

"Of course I won't let him near you," he reassures me.

And as he stands in front of the door blocking any one's entrance or exit, he folds his arms across his wide chest. "Go, Mrs Carter," he firmly orders. "Go now."

Before I did go, I turned to see Darius staring at me through the window frontage. His stance is terribly unnerving for a man of his normally graceful stature, for a man of his aura, and as I see that he is barefoot, I had no choice but to temporarily pause my hate for him. Quickly coming back to this disastrous reality, I hear his voice, desperate, and as he spoke through the barrier of glass between us, I lip read, "Helena, please stop... I am begging for you to listen to me."

I shake my head – no.

"Helena! Helena! Please... please wait!"

Time momentarily stands still for us both. Placing his palms flush to the window, he mouths to me, "Please?"

I want so desperately to press my palms to his, to *feel* him, but I can't bring myself to do so, so I curtly signal another no by shaking my head. He inches forward and rests his forehead to the glass, rhythmically thumping upon it. I crumple inside at seeing him in such turmoil. He looks up and before I see his mouth move, I home in on his left hand. While he strokes his wedding ring, I too touch mine. Seconds abate and I then look directly at him. He removes his t-shirt, crumples it in his fist, and he shocks me and most probably everyone around who is listening to the very core by the following words and actions:

Tapping the pink scar over his heart, with tears openly streaming down his cheeks, he cries, "I love you so much... I need you, Helena... Please stay for if you go, I know my heart won't ever be able to timely beat again... I know that will never be able to breathe organically without you... I will suffocate and die and I don't want to die again... I want to have long and fruitful life with you... I want to grow old and grey with you... I want to have children and grandchildren with you... I want to sleep with you in the green, green grass when our hearts have failed at the exact same moment... We've been through so much together in the last couple of years... We need each other... Please, baby I'm begging for you to stay with me... Let me explain... I love you... I love you...I love you... Please come to me and make us whole again?"

I almost falter...

Almost but not quite.

How on this earth could I ever go back to him? Trust between us has been broken... severed into two irreparable halves by Alice's quest to hurt Darius, hurt me and use Connor for her gain. I never for one moment in my wildest dreams thought that I would, on my first visit to Darius's studio, find him with his ex-submissive perched suggestively upon his desk and in the throes of undress. Nor did I ever imagine that my beautiful, husband would be semi-naked, and sitting opposite her. A thousand unanswered questions rage through my mind: Did he call her up and request her services? Was I not enough for him? Was he about to unbutton his jeans, and command her to service him with her slutty mouth? Was she waiting for him to chastise her with his damp, spiralled towel before she finally knelt before him, went down on him, and gave them both what they craved? Whatever they were up to I guess I shall never know – I don't wish to know. So as I move back from the window, and he steps back too, I whisper, "Goodbye" to him, and say that a part of me will always care for him. A wave of blind panic crosses over his face, and within a heartbeat he's flown from his spot, and is heading full pelt towards the doorman, my protector, whilst shouting my name out in vain to the stunned colleagues now babbling among themselves. I regretfully flee with the heaviest of weights dragging in my chest. Halfway down the street, I turn, seeking him out. He's nowhere in my sight. So as I continue scarpering like a thief who's almost been discovered pilfering precious possessions in the night. On making it to the safety of my car, I slump back against her, run my hand over my belly and express to Impy that I'm very sorry we didn't get to share our news with his daddy... I then tell Impy that daddy was distracted so it wasn't the right moment to say hello. – It will never be the right time to say hello.

I'm sure at that precise moment I felt a little butterfly flutter deep inside me."

"Impy," I hush, "I have just named you, Athos. You will be your mummy's brave little musketeer and we will stay strong together on the uncharted journey that lies ahead for us – I will keep you safe from harm... I promise."

And after my pledge to our unborn child, I settled into my car, and sat staring bleakly at my phone. As expected there were numerous messages from Darius, trying to explain to me what I had witnessed. I read every single one in turn before coming to the conclusion that our love... Well, that our love that I believed could never have been tainted, had once again in fact been soured by the untimely presence of Alice, and that for me, this time, I felt pretty adamant that there was no way back. So I switched off my phone and as I drove through one of the loneliest nights I had ever encountered, with the full intention of never turning back, my journey was interrupted by the need to vomit. I performed an emergency stop onto the verge, and literally flew out of the car. As I crashed onto all fours, and began retching hard onto the ground, a flash of headlights enveloped me. Wiping the spittle from my chin on the back of my jacket cuff, I glanced to the left towards the beams of stark, white light, and as I blinked the world around me descended into an eerie darkness and I promptly fainted. On waking, it became apparent to me that the cause of me needing to expel the contents of my stomach was brought forth by shock from witnessing the Alice and Darius scenario and not from the child who was silently growing inside me. I shifted against damp grass beneath my back and as my eyelids flicked open, I began to openly sob at the sight of who was looming over me. While I muttered, Athos's name, followed by Darius's I asked myself this question, "Are you dreaming all this, Helena?"

A muffled voice then asked me, "Who is Athos?"

I couldn't declare who Athos is, for I was now mute with exhaustion. Bound by a sinking fear in the pit of my stomach, as I felt an unfamiliar, warm wetness began to pool between my upper thighs, I tried to whimper out Athos's name, but my vocal cords were strictured with panic. So as I found myself looking directly up into a blurry set of red, rimmed eyes, the irises of this stranger dulled with a soft compassion. On feeling a pair of strong arms snake under my back and angle me up into a sitting position, I was then cradled like a forlorn child, and a light kiss was projected onto my forehead. An all too familiar scent somewhere from my past then began rapidly to invade my senses, I weakly murmured to my saviour, who was rocking me back and forth, "Darius... Is that you?"

Or is it you Connor?

Who are you?

I vaguely heard a response but I couldn't, I just couldn't fathom out the stranger's name.

Who is this man that is holding me like a precious cargo in his arms? Who is this man telling me over and over that he loves me and he will never ever let me go out of his sight again? And more to the point, who is this man declaring that he has always loved me, and that he always will, while I lay here, unbeknown to him, presently in the throes of losing my unborn child?

Who is he?

'A Cosmic Dance'

The final book, which completes the *Gentle Dominant* series, is now in the making.

Follow the author online for updates:

https://twitter.com/jl_author